"An action-packed nail-biter from beginning to end, filled with enough twists and turns to put *24* and Jack Bauer to shame! I couldn't put it down. Many thanks to Andrew for hours of entertainment and frantic page turning."

LYNETTE EASON, best-selling, award-winning author of the Blue Justice series

"A fast-paced novel that drew me into the adventure from the opening pages. The characters wrestle with faith, forgiveness, and redemption in a gripping plotline packed with suspense, action, and danger."

GLENN KREIDER, author of *God with Us*

"What a ride! *A Cross to Kill* explodes with action (right from the beginning!) and has an even better story to tell. Andrew brings each scene alive with amazing detail."

ROB THOMAS, founder and CEO of Igniter Media

"Let's hope we all now get to follow John Cross from book to book and movie to movie. What a thrill to imagine carrying Christ into every kind of job and seeing the impact it has in this page-turning story. Get to know Cross. Get to know Huff. I think we're going to be spending a lot of time with them both."

RANDY HAHN, senior pastor of The Heights Baptist Church, Virginia

D0913273

A CROSS TO KILL

A SHEPHERD SUSPENSE NOVEL • #1

A CROSS TO KILL

ANDREW HUFF

Kregel
Publications

A Cross to Kill
© 2019 by Andrew Huff

Published by Kregel Publications, a division of Kregel Inc., 2450 Oak Industrial Dr. NE, Grand Rapids, MI 49505.

The persons and events portrayed in this work are the creations of the author, and any resemblance to persons living or dead is purely coincidental.

ISBN 978-0-8254-2274-4, print
ISBN 978-0-8254-7618-1, epub

Printed in the United States of America
19 20 21 22 23 24 25 26 27 28 / 5 4 3 2 1

CHAPTER ONE

MILLIONS OF PEOPLE would witness the murder of Christine Lewis, and not one of them could do anything to stop it.

Greasy hands forced her into a chair. An orange jumpsuit pulled tight against her body. The fabric hid months of abuse at the hands of her captors. She choked back tears as slick hands tugged her blond hair behind her ears and lifted her chin. Thin fingers slid a trail of grime down her neck.

"Head up. Straight ahead."

She obeyed without argument and stared into the dead black eye of the camera a few feet in front of her. Weary and broken, Christine's former existence as a courageous, perhaps brazen, reporter standing in the middle of Jordanian rioters only a few months ago hung as a mere shadow in her mind. Life before her kidnapping seemed a dream. Now she only submitted to her captors' commands, resistance no longer a choice.

She was going to die.

With her peripheral vision, Christine examined the half dozen or so masked terrorists gathered to witness the event, each nearly identical to the others: nameless soldiers clad in faded military attire and cradling an assault weapon. The *shemaghs* wound around each head disguised any features, save eye color. At the beginning of her captivity, Christine had studied each passing face for a sympathetic glance, but as the inevitable approached, she'd lost all hope of salvation.

Months had passed—she still wasn't sure of the exact length of time—since they'd grabbed her from the streets of Amman. The riots she'd covered for the North American Broadcasting Channel turned out to be a smoke screen to the more illicit practices of the Alliance of Islamic Military, or AIM. While the public protested the government in the streets, AIM picked off key policymakers in the shadows. She sat in the front row of the real conflict, prison bars gagging her words of warning to the world.

Replaying faint memories, Christine scoffed at her ineptness. She'd been preoccupied with crafting a headline to drive the political conversation back home: "Demonstrators in Jordan Support Current US Policy" or some such nonsense. She could understand, even affirm, her kidnapping if there'd been a real scoop in her hands. Instead, she was just another sideshow attraction in AIM's shell game.

The executioner barked orders in Arabic, and the hooded figure behind the camera pressed a button. A red light pulsed above the lens. More orders were given, and a thumb jutted upward, signaling the start of the show. The favorite new trend of militant radicals across the globe? Beheading journalists on live camera. And the stream of her execution just went active to anyone with an Internet connection.

The executioner pressed the cold blade of his knife against the small of her back and produced a ripple of goose bumps down both arms. He raised his free hand and pointed a finger toward the camera with vigor. The *shemagh* wrapped around his chin muffled his speech, but in clear English he forced his words through the cloth.

"Mr. President, we are outraged by your insolence toward the Islamic Alliance and your refusal to cooperate with the leaders of our military. We warned you about your unity with our enemies and your support of the continued bombing of our communities. As a result of your actions, we have no choice but to retaliate with the life of another American citizen. If you insist on holding a blade to the neck of our country, we must hold a blade to the neck of your people."

The executioner slipped the knife from behind Christine and waved it near her neck. A soft gasp escaped her lips as the tip brushed against her skin.

"And now, I send my warning out to any country wishing to take the side of the American president and go to war against our people. This is what we will do to any who brings harm against us."

One of the men watching from behind the camera took a step forward and thrust a sheet of paper into Christine's hand. He grunted in Arabic and prodded the paper with his index finger.

Christine gripped the sheet with both hands, her chipped and stained fingernails pressing through the paper and pinching her palms. Emotion beaten from her over the past month bubbled deep in her heart like a spring discovered in the desert. A script would be her last words. Fitting, given her chosen profession.

"My name is Christine Elisabeth Lewis," she said, staring more into the camera than at the print. "I am thirty-one years old and a reporter with NABC. I am guilty of crimes against the Islamic Alliance and of allegiance with the war criminal Jefferson Gray, the president of the United States. Mr. President, it is because of your actions against the people of the Islamic Alliance that I must pay for my crimes. To all those who would support you and your illegal activities against this people, I say this . . ."

Christine's voice trailed, her eyes locked on the camera. The men behind the camera tensed at her unplanned pause. She released her grip on the paper, and it fluttered to the ground at her feet. "Mom, Dad," Christine said. "I love you. I'm sorry. I'm so sorry." Tears stung the corners of her mouth as she spoke.

The executioner slapped her cheek. Christine shrieked, life returning to her abused spirit. She raised a hand on instinct to defend her cheek from a second blow. Her murderer knocked the hand away, grabbed a clump of her hair, and pulled her head back to expose her neck.

"President Gray, we demand justice!" the executioner yelled. He placed the knife on Christine's neck. She closed her eyes and considered crying out to God.

It'd been too long. There wouldn't be a reply.

A loud pop startled her, then a swarm of bees buzzed in her ear. She opened her eyes. Her heart pounded against her chest as her adrenaline refused to wane. The knife gone, her executioner stood next to her, shaking his limbs as if trying to fling them from his body. A black disc with glowing tentacles of electricity clawed at his chest. Christine watched in horror, expecting his body to explode any second.

It didn't explode. The black disc released its victim, and he slumped to the ground, unconscious. Christine turned to find the armed soldiers behind the camera just as confused. But then she spotted him: one of the guards in the back of the room held a black alien-looking handgun. A faint wisp of smoke snaked its way out of the barrel.

Along with Christine, the other men realized the presence of the intruder, and it took only seconds for chaos to erupt in the tiny room. Her mouth agape, Christine watched the gunman aim the pistol at the nearest soldier to his right and pull the trigger. A second disc exploded from the gun and latched itself to the man's shoulder. He screamed in agony and fell to the ground, wrapped in the powerful embrace of an electric shock.

Soldiers raised their automatic weapons. With the pistol in his hand, the gunman whipped one of the militants, stunning him. In a blur of movement, the attacker shoved two men together. A rifle discharged, the noise ricocheting off every wall in the room.

Christine cupped her ears and ducked. Her brain screamed *run*, but her muscles refused to cooperate. She sat frozen in the chair, watching the melee. Fists connected with chins and boots with kneecaps.

She counted three men on the floor. A fourth raised his rifle. The black barrel pointed at the attacker's head. Christine caught her breath. A valiant effort to stay her execution, but now it was over. Her savior would be shot, then her in turn. A sob worked its way up her throat as the terrorist pulled the trigger.

A rapid succession of clicking sounds announced the ammo clip was empty. An Arabic oath preceded a frantic attempt to reload. The attacker leapt over an unconscious body, grabbed the rifle, and shoved it into the man's nose.

Movement caught her attention. The executioner clutched at his chest. He pulled the black disc away as it protested with a blast of sparks. He tossed it aside, then crawled across the floor to the knife. He jumped to his feet. Fire blazed from his dark eyes. He drew the knife back, ready to plunge it into her.

Christine screamed. The knife plummeted toward the bulging arteries in her neck. The distinct pop of a weapon discharge reverberated around the room. She felt the weight of the chair give way beneath her. A burst of debris from one of its legs showered her foot. The chair fell forward, taking Christine with it. She slammed face first into the concrete floor. Blood erupted from her nostrils.

A rush of wind from above ruffled her jumpsuit. The mysterious gunman collided with the executioner, and they crashed into a stack of barrels and wood scraps. Christine twisted her head on the floor to watch, but the dizziness from the impact clouded her eyes. The two distorted figures grappled until one gave the final blow and stood victorious over the other.

Christine's vision returned, and she pushed off the bloodstained floor. Hands grabbed her shoulders from behind and pulled her to a sitting position. The masked gunman knelt and cradled her head in his strong hands. He pulled the *shemagh* from his face, and Christine gasped at the sympathetic hazel eyes of an American man staring back at her.

He unwrapped the *shemagh* from around his short-cropped hair and used it to wipe the blood from her mouth. "Sorry about the nose," he said. "My name's John. We've got to go."

Questions beat against her forehead, but she could only think to respond, "Go?"

"Yeah," he said. "Home."

Christine couldn't stop herself from laughing and crying at the same time. She died. No, she was supposed to be dead. Why was this strange man with a firm chin talking about home? And yet she believed him; somehow, she knew he would get her home.

"Christine," he said.

"You know my name," she replied. Why wouldn't her mouth close all the way?

John repeated the command, this time with vigor. "We have to go."

The power in his voice brought Christine's mind back into focus. She stood and took one last look about the room before John grabbed her by the hand and led her to the exit. Bodies were strewn about the place, subtle groans the only clues her captors lay unconscious and not lifeless.

John led her through the door and down a dark hallway. He put his hand to his ear and started talking. "Control, this is Shepherd. I have the asset in hand, and we are en route."

Christine imagined the mechanical voice inside John's ear responding with operational vocabulary in kind.

"Copy," he responded and pulled his finger from his ear. He glanced over his shoulder at Christine. "Don't worry. Our ride will be here any second."

A set of wooden stairs greeted them at the end of the hallway. Warm rays of sunlight peeked through boards nailed against the windows of the staircase, and dust swirled in a violent dance within the light. They made it halfway up when a door near the top of the staircase swung open and the largest creature of a man Christine had ever seen stepped through. She gasped. Muscle wrapped around muscle, and between tattoos were scars and abrasions. One of his eyes appeared hazier than the other, which only added to the terror of his visage. He opened his mouth and roared his disapproval.

John made an immediate reversal in direction, pulling Christine close behind. "Not that way," he said.

They picked up speed as the drum of heavy boots marching downstairs chased behind. Christine looked back long enough to catch a glimpse of the big, hazy-eyed man reaching the bottom of the stairs, a handful of his friends on his heels. He roared again, but to Christine's ears it sounded like a bell being rung.

They ran through door after door. John never broke stride as he used an elbow to bully them open. Her legs felt like soft noodles, but newfound determination encouraged her to try to match his speed. He kept a tight grip on Christine's hand, and energy seemed to flow from his hand to hers, giving her a boost despite months of incarceration.

They descended another flight of stairs and burst through one last door into an abyss of blinding white light. Christine choked at the blast of hot air. A sour smell invaded her nose, and the chaotic noise of street vendors and playful children bombarded her from all directions. They were on the street and still running.

Christine's vision returned, to little avail. Their pace disoriented her. She focused on John and noticed his hand digging into his ear canal. She tuned her own ears to sift through the street noise and find his voice.

". . . compromised. Moving north on Al Nasira." He pulled her in tighter behind him as they squeezed through a crowd of tourists. "Copy that. We're on our way."

John's pace slowed, and Christine finally gained her bearings. Vendors surrounded them as they walked through a small roadside market. None of the merchants hawking their wares paid mind to her disheveled appearance as they presented scarf after purse and promised the finest quality in exchange for the lowest charge.

Christine winced as she pulled air through her broken nostrils. She rubbed her sleeve against the caked blood on her upper lip. Still wet. As she inhaled with her mouth, the beat of her heart normalized. She felt a strange sense of security in the bustle of the market. She imagined if they were to be attacked now, the peddlers would come to their rescue, determined to protect the prospect of a good sale. A comforting fantasy.

They passed with relative ease through the crowd packed into the small market. Christine's feeling of safety waned, and she looked over her shoulder, longing to return to the shelter of the chaos.

She shouldn't have looked.

The horrible man with a hazy eye stood a full head above a couple bargaining with a trader near the back of the market. His good eye locked on to her. Christine cried out and collided with John's back. He stood motionless at an intersection as blurred streaks of buses and cars sped by.

"John!" She grabbed his forearm and spun him around.

His eyes widened as he made eye contact with their pursuer. The hectic activity of the market faded away, and Christine believed she could hear nothing but their breathing.

The commotion of the street corner came booming back into her ears. A horn blared as a car zoomed by. The hazy-eyed man made wild gestures in their direction, and a wave of brawny, menacing thugs exploded from behind him, running through the market, shoving tourists into vendors, and turning up carts of merchandise.

John squeezed Christine's hand tighter and pulled her into the street. A moped came close to shaving his chest, but he didn't lose a step. They crossed the intersection, dodging car after truck after motorcycle. The prospect of being taken a second time only heightened Christine's doubt of surviving this real-life game of *Frogger*.

Just when she thought they would be smeared across the roadway, John's boots landed on the sidewalk. He kept running. She glanced over her shoulder to see the men trying to follow their path through traffic. One of the men misjudged the speed of a car, and it struck him. He rolled across the car's hood and cracked the windshield before sliding to the ground. His compatriots ignored his mishap and maintained pursuit.

John ducked into an alley and led Christine up a flight of narrow stairs. They emerged from between the buildings on a street resembling the one they'd just left. Their hands were still locked, and Christine matched John's speed down the road. She welcomed the adrenaline, thankful for the active lifestyle she'd enjoyed before her imprisonment. If she knew where they were headed, she even felt like she could take the lead and beat him to the tape. Freedom proved to be a better energy boost than three shots of espresso.

They approached another intersection, and John slowed.

"Where are we going?" Christine asked.

"Our extraction point," he replied.

"Where is that?"

John shouted over the backfiring of a passing truck. "About three klicks northwest."

"Really? They couldn't get any closer?"

"Yeah, well, nothing seems to be going my way today." He didn't sound happy.

Their route through the intersection cleared, and they started across. Christine took another look over her shoulder and couldn't spot any of the men in pursuit. She turned back in time to spy an approaching vehicle out of her peripheral vision. A black mass of metal and rubber tore down the road, intent on flattening them to the pavement.

Christine took the only second available to react. She pulled free from John's hand and shoved him in the back. He stumbled forward. She jumped backward and tumbled to the road. The SUV braked and its tires squealed. It came to a stop, separating Christine and her liberator.

As she pushed herself off the ground, Christine searched for any sign the car had missed John, but a pair of dusty khaki pants leaping from the open passenger door of the SUV blocked her view. Someone grabbed her under both armpits and lifted her off her feet.

"Let go of me!" She wriggled against the vice grip and dug her heels into the pavement. Pulling an arm free, she threw her elbow behind her head, hoping to connect with a vital organ.

He didn't yield, and rough hands forced her into the back seat of the SUV. She lashed out once more with her hands and feet, but the door slammed shut. The smell of burning tires flooded the interior as the driver pressed down on the gas pedal.

Christine yanked at the handle, but her door wouldn't budge. She turned to try the opposite door and screamed. The man with the hazy eye sat next to her. He stared out the back window and growled in Arabic to the other men in the car. She didn't speak Arabic but knew a few phrases and slang words thanks to cheerful guides during her reports. And the horrible man used an unpleasant word she knew.

More than once.

Christine turned in her seat and looked out the back window. In the distance, a motorist yelled at another man who appeared to be in the process of stealing the motorist's motorcycle. The theft couldn't be prevented, and the new owner of the motorcycle sped off in pursuit of the SUV.

The SUV took a sharp turn and threw Christine against the man beside her. He shoved her away and continued yelling at his companions. The driver mashed his fingers against the armrest of his door. All the windows slid downward, and wind whipped the interior. The torrent caught Christine's hair in a furious dance. The man in the passenger seat climbed halfway out his window, brandishing a semiautomatic weapon.

Instinct told Christine to cover her ears and close her eyes. The force of the weapon vibrated through the speeding vehicle. Ignoring her instincts, she opened her eyes and peeked over the back seat to witness John's demise.

The motorcycle weaved through traffic as bullets ricocheted off the street. The high speed of the SUV threw the gunman's aim. Familiar streets faded in the background as the driver took them on a route away from where John had led her—away from their rendezvous point.

John needed her help. Christine searched the car frantically. Leather seats, headrests, a sunroof. Nothing useful. She glanced outside and spotted the barrel of the gun sitting right outside her window. Within reach.

She took a deep breath, let the tilting of the vehicle shift her sideways, and kicked her foot out of the window as hard as she could. Her shoe connected with the barrel just as the man pulled the trigger again.

He managed to hold on to the gun, but it carried him in an arc away from his bead on John. The gun still fired, strafing parked cars and building windows. A bullet bounced off the pavement and back into the car, tearing through the gunman's shoulder before exiting through the roof. Blood stained the upholstery, and he cried out in shock.

The man with the hazy eye barked more obscenities at his men and lunged at Christine.

It was her destiny to die today.

CHAPTER TWO

CURRENT EVENTS DIDN'T line up with how John Cross had planned his morning to go. He tightened his fist around the handgrips of the motorcycle. The rubber pads popped under the pressure. Bullets zipped through the air around him, but foremost on his mind was what he would tell Al when he got home.

"That's it," he would say. "I'm not doing this anymore."

His imagination took him no further as his focus turned back to the SUV dead ahead. The man hanging out of the passenger window left evidence of his poor marksmanship on parked cars and street signs along the sidewalk. With perfect conditions, the chances of him hitting the motorcycle were still low. Cross didn't have to maneuver much to evade a fatal wound and closed the gap between himself and the car.

A shoed foot popped out of the open window of the SUV and kicked the barrel of the gun. Cross snorted. "Nice." He leaned into the gas pedal. The motorcycle took off with a burst of energy.

He veered to the left of the vehicle and saw a struggle in the back seat. The gunman in the front grabbed at his shoulder. Fresh blood splatter covered the interior. An opening for Cross to make his move.

He pulled the motorcycle alongside the back driver's-side window. He slowed to match the SUV's speed. In the back seat, Christine clawed at the big man's hands clutching her neck. With the motorcycle as close to the car as he dared, Cross planted on the footrests, squeezed his thighs against the chassis, and thrust his upper body through the window.

He wrapped his arms around the big man's head. A spit-fueled exclamation soaked Cross's forearms. He pulled as hard as he could and leaned backward. The man's body obliged and his upper torso followed Cross out the window. Fleshy knuckles filled Cross's vision. He ducked as the big man swiped. With his other hand, the man grabbed a seat belt, and they both jerked to a stop.

Cross used his body weight to keep the motorcycle under him and parallel to the car while squeezing tighter around the big man's head. The man clawed at Cross's arms but couldn't wrench himself free.

Advantage: Cross.

Now what to do with it?

Cross yanked harder, but the man proved to be too big to follow him completely through the window. A barrage of car horns alerted Cross to a busy intersection ahead. He needed another option, fast.

"Christine!" he yelled.

She stilled the coughing from the attempted strangulation and made eye contact with him.

"Jump!" He didn't have to explain further. She made for the open window on her side of the car, but the driver turned and grabbed at her jumpsuit. He jerked the steering wheel, and the SUV banked into the motorcycle. Cross used his free hand to match and prevent his leg from being crushed.

The big man took hold of Cross's arm and dug his fingers through to the bone. Cross gritted his teeth and tightened his muscles around the man's throat. Nails threatened to break skin. Sweat beaded on Cross's forehead. His arm burned, and he wondered if the man was strong enough to crush it with just his fist.

The driver reached between the seats. Releasing his choke hold on the big man, Cross dropped free from the car, slammed his foot on the brake, and slid behind the SUV. The driver leaned out the window and fired a handgun in a random pattern at the spot the motorcycle had previously occupied.

The SUV and motorcycle drove through the intersection in tandem. The SUV clipped a sedan crossing its path, spraying sharp metal bits into the air. Cross gassed the motorcycle to avoid a collision with a food truck. Brakes screeched and steel crunched. The flow of traffic came to a disastrous halt.

The SUV picked up its pace, and the gap between the two vehicles grew. Cross clenched his jaw. The chariot reserved for Christine waited in the opposite direction, and it wouldn't wait for long. He didn't have to look at his watch to know their window was rapidly closing.

More gunfire popped, from behind. He glanced over his shoulder to see another black SUV bearing down on him.

Great. Could anything else go wrong today?

More bullets missed. What was with the amateur marksmen? Still, he couldn't push his luck. Cross pushed the motorcycle harder and leaned in close to the chassis to make himself a smaller target.

He recognized a landmark in the distance and felt fortunate he had visited the city before. They were moving southeast. That meant Al Urdon, a major Amman highway, was coming up. New plan: secure Christine before they reached the intersection and use the road to his advantage. The pit trying to gnaw at his stomach gave up. He let himself believe it would be enough to reach the extraction in time.

Crowded streets made evasive maneuvers tricky. The SUV behind him gained ground and seemed to inspire the gunman's aim. A bullet ricocheted off a nearby car and sliced a few hairs off Cross's ear.

His hands ached from gripping the handlebars. With each passing moment, the options narrowed. Even if he could intercept the vehicle, getting Christine out would be impossible. He imagined making the rendezvous and organizing a second attempt. No. She'd be dead by then. God in heaven, help.

Focusing ahead, Cross noticed a tow truck on the side of the road just beyond the lead SUV. The truck's flatbed trailer tilted backward, scraping the ground, its owner taking a break from prepping a van for loading to wipe his brow. A stranded motorist watched with arms folded.

There was no way it would work, but Cross added one more prayer and pressed the gas. The motorcycle groaned as it mustered more speed. He shot past the lead SUV and veered toward the trailer.

The front wheel bounced as it cleared the bottom of the trailer. He pushed his body lower to balance the motorcycle. At the last second, he turned the grips and directed the motorcycle back toward the road.

Both wheels lifted off the flatbed, and the motorcycle flew into the air. The black roof of the SUV passed underneath. Cross let go and let himself slip off the seat. He slammed into the roof with so much force it buckled beneath his weight. The rear wheel of the motorcycle just missed his head and skimmed off the side of the SUV.

The motorcycle rotated in midair and smashed into the pavement beside them. Its parts littered the street corner. The second SUV swerved to dodge the shrapnel.

Cross made a grab at the roof to find a handhold as the vehicle rocked back and forth. His hand slipped across the glass of the sunroof, and on instinct he snatched it back. A geyser of glass exploded upward as a parade of bullets tore through.

He rolled too far and slipped off the side of the car. His fingers found a lip of the roof and clamped down, stopping his fatal drop, and Cross found himself staring through the open window at the wounded thug in the passenger seat.

The thug's mouth fell open, and his eyes bulged. He blinked and yelled something indiscernible at the driver. Cross recognized the flash of a black muzzle and let go of the lip of the roof as the driver fired.

His fingers found the window frame on his way to the road, and he grabbed tight. Searing pain shot through his knees as his boots slammed down and were dragged against the rushing pavement. Sweat coated his palms. His grip on the window slipped.

A woman screamed. Christine? His ears ached, and his eyes blurred. That was it. He was going to be roadkill.

Not the finale he preferred. At a break in the gunfire, Cross forced air through his mouth, and his adrenaline surged. He pulled himself up from the side of the door and into view in the window.

Cross grabbed the wounded man's better arm and pulled him through the window, blocking the driver's aim. Arabic oaths filled the air around them. Cross used the man's upper body as leverage for his own and hoisted himself off the unforgiving roadway.

In one motion, he grabbed the lip of the roof, stepped on the man's chest, and somersaulted back onto the roof of the vehicle. He let out a yelp as he came crashing down through the hole in the damaged sunroof and landed on the center console.

The shouting stopped. Cross and the driver met each other's eyes. Cross offered an aloof grin, then crushed the man's nose with his fist. The car swerved across the road as the driver threw both his hands into the air in a failed attempt to block the punch.

Cross shoved his elbow into the face of the wounded man. He twisted his feet off the seatback and kicked the driver's knee. The wounded man recovered and wrapped his bleeding arm around Cross's neck.

His lungs were denied air, and his brain felt like it would pop. He caught a flash in the rearview mirror and watched Christine kick against the big man next to her as she grabbed at the wounded man's face. He shrieked as she used her fingernails on his eyes.

The fleshy noose relaxed, freeing Cross's larynx. "The door!" he yelled.

Christine lunged for the handle to the passenger-side door just as Cross kicked against the driver and pushed his own body against his seatmate.

The door popped open, and the wounded man tumbled out of the car and slammed into the ground. Cross fell out of the car right behind him, but Christine grabbed his shirt and stopped his momentum. He flinched as the man's body rolled to a stop in the middle of the street.

He turned back to Christine to express his gratitude just as the big man sitting next to her in the back grabbed for her hair. "Look out!" Cross yelled.

Too late. Her head snapped back, and she let go of Cross's shirt. Cross snatched the loose seat belt and pulled himself back into the car. The driver corrected the car's drift and leveled the black eye of his handgun between Cross's eyes.

Before the driver could fire, Cross grabbed his wrist and twisted the barrel away. The man's finger squeezed the trigger. The bullet ricocheted off the frame of the car into the back seat. Cross heard a scream through the ringing in his ears.

Oh no.

His grip relaxed as he turned to the back seat, fearing the worst. Christine showed no signs of injury. The big man, on the other hand, grabbed at his ear. Blood seeped through his fingers and down the back of his hand.

A flash of movement caught Cross's eye, and he turned back to the driver in time to see the flat side of the gun about to connect with the soft side of his face. The barrel gouged Cross on the lip, and in retaliation he squeezed the man's wrist tighter and slammed the gun back into the man's own forehead.

Stunned, the driver took his foot off the gas pedal, and the car slowed. Cross leaned forward and pressed the driver's body between his own and the door. He grabbed for the handle and pulled. The door flew open, and the driver shrieked as he tumbled out and slammed into the rushing pavement. Cross slid into the driver's seat. Using the door to correct his momentum, he pulled it shut, grabbed the steering wheel, and hit the gas.

The big man in the back seat opened his own door and jumped free of the SUV. Cross checked his side mirror to see the big man roll to a stop on the shoulder of the road.

"Where did he go?" Christine yelled over the burst of wind through the open door.

"I guess he didn't like his odds without his friends," Cross replied.

Christine stretched across the seat and shut the door. Cross slowed the vehicle to a cruising speed and gained his bearings. He spotted the exit for Al Urdon whisking by. They missed it. "Hold on!" he shouted. He slammed on the brakes and turned the wheel at the same time. The car drifted one hundred and eighty degrees, its tires smoked, and it hopped a median as it sped back in the opposite direction.

They passed the big man standing on the side of the road, still holding his ear, then the driver grabbing at his ribs in agony. Just ahead, the other SUV barreled toward them.

Cross reached into the back and pushed Christine to the floorboard. "Get down!" He ducked behind the dash just as the other SUV passed and unleashed a barrage of gunfire. Bullets decimated the windshield.

The gunfire ceased, and Cross popped back up in time to see the exit for the Al Urdon highway. He banked the SUV hard, missed an oncoming bus, and took the exit at top speed.

Christine jumped from the back into the passenger seat. "Are we going to make it?"

"I don't know." They were already minutes behind schedule, and there was no telling how much traffic they would find on Al Urdon.

They pulled onto Al Urdon to find it busy but moving. Cross guided the SUV around taxis, mopeds, and delivery trucks. He refrained from braking as much as possible, but a van switched lanes and caused him to back off his speed.

"Your lip," Christine said, leaning in to inspect.

He could still do it. After a year (or was it more?), his mind still pressed through pain signals during an operation to remain focused and clear. He let the throbbing rage and tasted blood on his tongue.

He sensed a finger waving near his lip.

"Looks like you're leaving with a little memento," Christine said.

It must be quite the gash. He took his eyes off the road to check out the injury in the rearview mirror. He didn't see the bloody lip, only the other black SUV driving straight into them.

On instinct, he hit the brakes, and the two cars collided. The impact threw him and Christine forward, then jerked them back into their seats.

Cross shook his head to clear the dizziness in his eyes and glanced back. The big man with the hazy eye glared back at him from the driver's seat, his passengers armed to the teeth.

The surprise of the rear-ender bought them only a moment, but Cross didn't need more. He gunned the engine, and they took off as automatic weapons appeared out the windows of the SUV.

Gunfire rained down on them from behind. Christine covered her head with her hands. Cross stayed as low as he could and still see over the dash. A hailstorm. That was what it sounded like. A loud, deadly hailstorm.

Traffic ahead parted like the Red Sea. Cross increased his speed. The men increased their barrage. A sharp turn in the road granted them a reprieve from the bullet storm. Cross fought with the steering wheel to keep the car upright.

The road straightened, and he glanced back. The other SUV slowed for the curve, and the firing ceased, the gunmen reserving their ammunition.

"Those guys are really starting to annoy me," he admitted aloud.

"Annoy you," Christine said. Cross sensed sarcasm in her tone. "That's all?"

"Open the glove box."

Christine obliged and snorted when a gun fell out of the glove box into her lap.

"I need you to check and see if it's loaded."

Before Cross could offer instruction, Christine ejected the magazine and counted the rounds. She snapped it back in, then grabbed the slide and examined the chamber.

"You've got a full mag with one racked." She handed the butt of the gun to him.

Cross looked at her, dumbfounded. "All right. You've impressed me."

"I'm just ready to get out of here."

Cross hesitated, then took the gun from her. It felt familiar and foreign in his hand at the same time. He sensed the tremble of emotion building in his limbs. His fingers ached as he forced them to hold steady. He took three deep breaths and tightened his grip on the handle.

If he wasn't careful, what he would do next would change everything.

CHAPTER THREE

CROSS LET UP on the accelerator. Their pursuers gained speed.

Christine braced herself on the dash. "What are you doing?"

"Trust me." Cross focused on the road ahead, taking only the occasional glance at a mirror to track the approach of the other vehicle. The nine-millimeter grip felt damp in his hand. This would be the first time he would pull a trigger. First time since . . .

The reverberation of a hemi engine shook the frame of the car and the distant memory from his head. No mirror check needed. He knew they'd been caught. That meant only seconds before they'd be treated to a bullet shower.

Christine rotated in the passenger chair and peeked around her seat. "Behind us!"

Right on cue. Cross stepped onto the gas pedal. His hungry engine growled in response. The SUV behind stuck like glue. The breeze against his neck felt like the hot breath of the hazy-eyed man.

"They're going to shoot!"

Cross ignored her, his eyes locked ahead.

Christine smacked her seatback, cursed, and shouted, "Don't just hold the gun—use it!"

He heard the first pop from an automatic rifle, shifted his foot off the gas, and jerked the steering wheel hard left. The back end of the SUV took a few bullets but evaded the full brunt of the assault. The car behind them raced by, the big man slow on his reflexes.

Cross hopped the median and crossed an oncoming lane of traffic, to the chagrin of several irate motorists. He sped the SUV up the exit lane for Al Istiklal, another major Amman highway.

"John!" Christine's hoarse voice barely registered over the wind whipping through the open windows and bullet holes. "I think you're going the wrong way!"

Yeah, on purpose, but he didn't have time to explain. Instead, he shouted back, "When I tell you, hit the floorboard."

Christine nodded and braced herself against the doorframe.

A merging sedan appeared ahead of them. Cross swerved around it. Sparks flew through his window as the SUV scraped the side of the concrete barrier. He corrected back on course and took deep breaths to calm his racing heart. The near-death experience with another vehicle or the instrument of death in his hand? He couldn't determine the cause of his beating chest.

The exit from the highway, now their entrance, lay beyond the next curve. What were the odds they would meet another car in a head-on collision at a fatal speed? Cross couldn't recall studying Amman traffic patterns at this particular time of day. He maintained his speed and said a quick prayer. "God help us."

"What?"

They both leaned into the curve. Christine grabbed at Cross's arm to steady herself as the SUV skidded off the ramp and across two lanes heading the wrong way down Al Istiklal.

"Down! Now!"

Christine fell onto the floorboard and covered her head with her arms.

Cars sped by them, horns blaring. A farm truck slammed into the guardrail. Just ahead, blocking their path down the highway, was the other SUV. Right where he wanted it.

Men cradling automatic weapons occupied every open window. The big, hazy-eyed man crushed the steering wheel with his rage-charged hands. This one wasn't about to back down. His scowl betrayed his simple, probable plan: drive straight through the path his men would carve into Cross and Christine's car.

The distance between them ticked by faster than the seconds. Cross slowed his breathing, counted to two, then shifted into second gear. He rotated the steering wheel against its will, and the car skidded sideways to the right.

As they turned, Cross stuck his arm out his window. With a firm grip on the nine millimeter, he locked eyes with the big man.

Uncompelled, his finger pulled the trigger.

One shot.

The big man disappeared from view as they turned 180 degrees to join the proper flow of traffic. Cross spotted the other SUV in his mirror. Its engine spewed black smoke from the fatal wound he'd inflicted with his precise shot.

He slammed on the brakes and brought the car to a near stop. The sputtering SUV plowed into them from the rear. The sturdy frame of their own SUV refused to crumple. Cross peeled away, leaving only a section of the bumper in his wake. Weapons fire chased after them, but engine smoke obscured their escape.

Christine pulled herself back into her seat. She massaged her temple.

"You OK?" Cross asked.

"I'll be all right. That was . . ."

"Impressive?"

Christine rubbed her eyes. "I was going to say nauseating."

"I'll take it."

Cross kept his foot on the gas. "Hold on. We're not out of the woods yet." He took the next exit off Al Istiklal, followed by two roundabouts.

"Wait a minute," Christine said, her head halfway out the window. "I know where we are. This is the Al Hussein Youth City."

The Youth City was the center of the sports culture in Amman. They passed several well-groomed fields and a handful of athletic facilities. They rounded a corner, and the Amman National Stadium appeared over the treetops.

Cross maintained his speed as they tore through the parking lot of the stadium. He tapped at his wireless earpiece. "Control, this is Shepherd. We are at the rendezvous. Sorry we're late."

Static pricked his eardrum, and he heard a metallic female voice. "Copy, Shepherd. Rendezvous secure."

He destroyed a guardrail to get into the stadium tunnel. The car jumped out of the tunnel as they tore onto the stadium grounds.

Christine gasped. A Black Hawk helicopter sat yards ahead of them in the middle of the field. Its spinning blades beat the grass into a perfect circle.

The SUV left mud tracks in the turf as it slid to a stop. Cross tossed the handgun onto the floorboard and jumped out the door before Christine could grab her handle. He ran around the car and met her exiting. Putting an arm around her shoulder, he kept her low and guided her to the Black Hawk.

A man decked in sandy camouflage jumped from the helicopter and ran to them. Cross motioned back to the SUV and yelled over the thump of the copter blades, "Torch it!"

The man nodded and ran past them. A pair of additional soldiers stood ready to receive Christine into the helicopter. After helping her up and into their waiting arms, Cross turned back in time to see the SUV in flames and the first soldier coming up behind him.

Cross allowed himself to be pulled into the Black Hawk, and he squatted next to Christine. A female Ranger with pleasant eyes strapped her in as he grinned and shouted above the whir of the engine, "I told you we were going home."

Christine's eyes fluttered. "She says I've lost some blood."

For the first time, Cross noticed the bruises and cuts covering Christine's neck and hands. The brutality of what she must have faced at the hands of the men who'd kidnapped her infuriated him. Giving her a second chance at life made the last half hour of mayhem seem like a small price to pay.

"I bet they can take care of that." Cross glanced over at the Ranger and watched her administer a sedative to Christine with a syringe.

"You'll be all right, ma'am. This will help you during the ride back to base." The Ranger stowed her medical supplies and strapped in to the adjacent seat.

Christine propped her head against the Ranger's shoulder.

Cross turned to strap himself in, but Christine caught him by the elbow. He turned back to her and smiled as her eyes strained to stay open. "Hey," she slurred. "Shepherd. What's your real name?"

"I told you. It's John."

"No, your real name. What is it?" And with that, Christine slipped into a deep sleep.

Cross smiled. He took his seat next to the chopper pilot. The Black Hawk lifted off the ground as he fixed his belt and slipped a radio over his ears. "Make it quick, Commander," he said to the pilot. "I've got to be in church in the morning."

CHAPTER FOUR

SHE WAS DEAD. Or so Christine thought as the haze lifted from her subconscious and she became aware of a bright white light flooding her vision. The light flowed in a liquid form before her, varying shades of eggshell cascading through clouds of light dust.

A dull noise surrounded her. It sounded like the purr of an auto-tuned kitten. Christine's mind pushed its way through the fog. She searched for a memory, a feeling, anything that might give her a clue as to what had happened.

A face.

She pictured the faint outline of a face, the last thing she remembered seeing as she faded into an unconscious state on the helicopter. The face of the man who rescued her from death.

That's right, she thought. *I'm not dead.*

The cobwebs cleared, and the strange apparition standing before her took shape. She lay on her back staring at the ceiling of a well-lit room. Several bright hanging lights shone back at her, making it difficult to judge the size or make of the room. It was made entirely of metal, or so she thought because of the glow emanating from the walls.

The purring sound grew louder and less soothing. Christine shifted her head on the soft pillow and spotted the IV drip stationed close to her bedside. Her eyes followed the plastic tubing connected to the machine all the way to the needle taped into her forearm.

Out of the corner of her eye, she spotted movement, and her gaze

ANDREW HUFF

darted up to catch a woman entering through a door across the room
from her bed. A patch with the familiar caduceus symbol of a medical
professional was sewn into the bicep of her uniform. This particular
nurse or doctor had her sleeves rolled to her elbows. A stethoscope
rested around her neck, and she studied a clipboard.

The woman lifted her head from the clipboard and made eye contact with Christine. She flashed a smile and said, "You're awake. My
name is Beth. I'm your nurse."

"No kidding," Christine responded, then bit her lip. Awake and in
full control of her tongue. Not always a pleasant combination. "I'm
sorry," she added. "I just woke up before you walked in."

Beth laughed. "No problem, Ms. Lewis. You've been through a lot.
And I've seen a lot worse."

Christine smiled, then took a cursory glance around the room as
the focus in her eyes improved. Standard medical equipment, cabinets,
and a couple of small chairs. Other than that, a rather bare room.
"Where am I?" she asked.

"Aviano Air Base in Italy."

"Italy?"

"That's right."

"How did I get here?"

Beth laughed again. "A couple of Ranger hunks escorted your lifeless body on board a C-17 from Turkey oh three hundred hours ago."

"What did they look like?"

"The hunks?" The nurse paused, confused. "Hunks, I guess. Honestly, I wasn't even paying that close attention."

"Did one of them have dark hair? Dressed like a terrorist?"

Beth slid into a chair near the bed and laid the clipboard in her lap.
"Honey, I don't know what you're talking about. You've been through
a lot, so some things might be a little fuzzy at the moment."

Christine shook her head and sat up. She did her best to ignore the
sharp pricks of pain shooting everywhere in her body. "No, you don't
understand." She took a breath, then added, "I need to know."

"Know what?"

"A man rescued me. A man named John. Did he come too? Is he here somewhere?"

"Ms. Lewis." Beth placed a hand on Christine's shoulder and leaned close. "A Ranger unit out of Saudi Arabia rescued you. One of them may have been named John, but I don't know. They dropped you here, then left just as fast as they got here."

"I know." A wave of nausea rose from her stomach. "But there was also a man. One of the men who pulled me out that wasn't a Ranger. He must have been a spy or something."

Beth chuckled and cocked her head to one side. "A spy? Well, now I know you're still a bit fuzzy. Maybe you should rest."

Christine wanted to argue, but the nausea forced her to sink back into the mattress. She closed her eyes, and as sleep overtook her, she mumbled, "They called him . . . Shepherd."

CHAPTER FIVE

NOT MANY PEOPLE would find flying at just under Mach 2 relaxing, but the hard passenger cockpit seat of the F-16 jet might as well have been a thick mattress at a deluxe hotel for John Cross. It would be the best sleep he'd experience in months. After delivering Christine to the C-17 waiting to transport her to Italy, Cross hopped from Incirlik Air Base in Turkey to Morón Air Base in Spain in less than two hours, thanks to the F-16's remarkable speed.

It was a longer flight back to the States, with a midair refuel thrown in the middle, but no sightseeing. Nothing but blue ocean. The bumps and shifts of the aircraft only served to send him that much quicker to dreamland.

It wasn't until the jolt of wheels touching down in Washington that Cross's eyes fluttered open. Through the visor in his helmet, he made out the familiar landscape of Andrews Field. The jet taxied down the runway to a small hangar.

He sensed the stench of a CIA escort before a conspicuous black SUV appeared in his field of view. Cross checked his watch as the F-16 came to a stop. Still afternoon, thanks to the time zone difference. He was still on the clock. For now. It would be a forty-minute drive to Langley, then God only knew how many more hours for debriefing before he would be allowed to leave.

He calculated a two-hour drive home in favorable traffic conditions, but it was wishful thinking. The twenty-one-mile stretch of I-95 between Old Keene Mill Road and Quantico would be hard to beat for the top spot as the busiest section of highway in the country. And it was Saturday. In the spring. Tourists, weekend warriors, and workaholics united.

Cross groaned at the thought of bumper-to-bumper traffic extending his travel time well into the evening. He took solace in the power nap the F-16 had blessed him with. It was shaping up to be another sleepless night.

He slipped off his flight helmet and climbed out of the cockpit, a small backpack slung around his shoulder. He stripped his G suit off, and an airman promptly gathered it and carried it away.

Cross walked toward the SUV. The driver's-side door opened, and a man hiding behind a dark pair of sunglasses stepped out. The man's broad shoulders threatened to rip through his black suit. Cross noted the bulge of a service weapon just below his armpit.

"Officer Cross," the man said. The close crop on his head failed to hide the dirty-blond curls. "If you'll accompany me please."

"What?" Cross replied, feigning the disappointment in his voice. "No flowers?"

The driver cocked an eyebrow.

"Doesn't matter. I didn't bring you anything either." Cross patted the man's shoulder on his way to the back seat.

The SUV accelerated off the runway and into the midday hustle and bustle of the nation's capital. The one request he'd made greeted him in the back seat. He picked up the large white paper cup from the cup holder and closed his eyes as he took a sip. The thick black coffee scorched his tongue and slid down the back of his throat.

When he'd left the Central Intelligence Agency, he couldn't stand the stuff without copious amounts of milk and sugar. But he'd embarked on what he thought of as a "cleanse." The months passed, and he found the taste of black coffee growing on him. Now he couldn't even imagine soiling the liquid with syrups, creams, or sweeteners.

He shifted from sips to gulps as the beverage cooled, and he watched the countryside flash by his window as his driver ignored the speed limit. Soothing, sure, but not as hypnotic as the F-16 ride. The tree line ended abruptly, and the view opened to a panoramic of the sun falling to the horizon over the Potomac River. His chauffeur chose the Beltway to get them from Andrews to CIA headquarters in Langley. Not the most direct route, but they bypassed downtown DC.

The car slowed as traffic merged ahead. Cross checked his watch. Rush hour was waning, but it did nothing to assure him he would be home at a reasonable hour. He needed proper time to prepare for Sunday service. He took another gulp of coffee and breathed deeply.

No time like the present, I guess.

He set the coffee cup back in the cup holder and opened his backpack. A notebook and brown leather Bible went in his lap, the backpack into the seat beside him. He flipped through the notebook to his notes, then thumbed through the tattered pages of the Bible to the book of Philippians. Tomorrow morning he'd be preaching on chapter 2, or at least beginning a series of sermons on chapter 2. He imagined he wouldn't get very far, as thorough as he tended to be.

The hair on the back of his neck alerted him to the discreet stare of a pair of eyes. He caught a glimpse of his driver in the rearview mirror before the man could avert his gaze back to the road. *Here we go.* The same conversation as always.

"What's your name, big guy?" Cross lifted the coffee cup back to his lips as he waited for the driver to respond.

"Officer Paulson, sir."

"Well, Officer Paulson, I appreciate the lift."

"My pleasure, sir." The cabin fell silent for a moment as the SUV passed a large tanker. Paulson relaxed his grip on the wheel and turned back to the mirror. "I've heard a lot about you, Officer Cross."

"You can call me John. I'm not an officer anymore."

"Sorry, Mr. Cross."

Cross rolled his eyes. Protocol always got in the way of a friendly conversation.

"So it's true then."

Cross cocked an eyebrow. "Excuse me?"

"You're not on Company payroll anymore. At least, not officially."

Cross sat back in his seat. How long had it been? Eighteen months? Twenty? If not more. And yet his sudden exodus was still only rumor. Granted, he'd spent little time at Langley, preferring office hours in exotic locales. He made a mental note to ask Al if they were still denying the story of his resignation. Although it didn't help he still took occasional jobs, his name popping up on reports once or twice a month.

"I do a little contract work from time to time," he admitted. "But I'm thinking I might not be available for even that anymore."

"And they let you walk?" Cross imagined Paulson's eyes were bulging behind the dark sunglasses. "Just like that?"

Cross chuckled. "I wasn't the kind of guy running around with national secrets, Officer Paulson. I couldn't tell you how to get to Pennsylvania Avenue, much less nuclear launch codes or how to infiltrate PEOC." Truth be told, Cross wasn't even sure they used the president's Emergency Operations Center under the East Wing of the White House. He guessed it wasn't nearly as dramatic of a location as Hollywood made it seem.

Paulson gulped. "I'm sorry, sir. It's just, from what I've heard . . ."

"What have you heard about me, Officer Paulson?"

"Your unmatched valor and intelligence in the army resulted in an offer to join an elite, covert Central Intelligence unit. You were involved in almost all the nation's top intelligence operations over the last decade. And for who knows what reason, you walked in one day last year and quit."

Cross nodded, a broad smile across his face. "That's an excellent summary." He swallowed the last dregs of coffee and asked, "What reason have you heard for my abrupt departure from the CIA?"

Paulson hesitated. He clicked the car's blinker and performed a slow lane shift. Probably stalling. "Well," he said, finally. "The rumor around Langley is that you got religious."

There it was. Cross loved it when the topic came up. It was an easy way to share his story with those least likely to want to have the conversation. "It's not rumor. It's true. I got religious."

Paulson didn't respond, and Cross didn't blame him. The admission was often a conversation killer, but Cross didn't care. "I had an experience that changed my life. And meant I couldn't do my job the way I had been doing it. Unfortunately, that meant leaving the CIA altogether. Although they've obviously been trying to draw me back in however they can."

"With the exfil ops." A statement of fact, not really a question.

"Yes."

"But how do you—"

"How do I pull it off with my newfound perspective on life? Well, up until now there's never been an op that required engagement." Cross decided Paulson didn't need any more details. He knew the officer's brain filled with memories of his own military service and any combat he might have participated in. Deployment was an instant connection between anyone across the services. If you'd discharged a weapon against another combatant or watched an IED detonate from across the street, you knew what it was like on the field. The emotions, the adrenaline, the doubt. "Tell me, Paulson. Are you religious?"

"Anglican, sir, though not as observant as my parents would like."

An opportunity. If the first admission of religious conversion didn't kill the conversation, that question was the death blow. Paulson even mentioned family, a rare topic for someone in the intelligence community. Cross wasn't about to let this opening go to waste.

"I'd probably agree with your parents. It's good to know you don't shy away from the Anglican label, at least."

Paulson cracked a smile for the first time. "The church was good to me, sir." He weaved through another knot of traffic before nodding his head at the notebook. "I noticed you studying. If you don't mind me asking, I heard another rumor around the CIA. About what you've been up to."

"That's funny," Cross interjected. "I don't remember making a formal announcement about my new career path."

"You and I both know you can't escape the microscope."

"I tell you what, Paulson. I'll make a deal with you. You promise me you'll find an Anglican church to try in the morning, and I'll let you in on my little secret."

"Well, sir, I would, except I'm on duty in the morning. Next Sunday?"

"That'll do." Cross looked down at his notes. It wasn't really a secret, and he was proud to say it. "The rumors are true. I left the CIA to become a Baptist minister."

The remainder of the drive proved to be a more pleasant conversation than Cross expected with the officers ferrying him from the airfield to Langley. Paulson asked questions about Cross's church, the sermon he was working on for the morning service, and even for advice concerning a romantic relationship. Before they pulled off onto the private access road that would take them to headquarters, Cross performed an online search for an Anglican church near Paulson's home address.

They put the vigorous exchange on hold as they produced the proper credentials to pass through a guarded entrance gate, and Cross gathered his study materials into his backpack while Paulson silently navigated the SUV into a restricted subterranean parking garage.

Cross jotted his number on a piece of notebook paper and handed it to Paulson. "Give me a call sometime and let me know how that church works out."

Paulson agreed and shook Cross's hand. Cross exited the SUV and headed to the service elevator beyond a thick glass door. The SUV pulled away, and Cross prayed a quick prayer for the hope of a future phone call. The chance to mentor someone from his old life would be a nice change from pretending that life never existed.

A quick swipe of his keycard granted Cross a green confirmation light for the elevator, and he took a deep breath as he entered the car and demanded his floor with the press of a finger. The ride, though short, gave Cross time to rehearse his speech. His lips curved into a smile as he recalled rehearsing a similar speech in the same elevator thirteen months ago.

His second speech would contain fewer choice words.

Unlike the first confrontation with Al, this one wouldn't involve any dirty laundry. All that had been aired. Now it was just going to be disappointment. A half sigh, half laugh slipped from Cross's mouth. *Or maybe relief.* He hoped Al was already reconsidering their arrangement as well. That would make the debrief go smooth.

Still, he knew Al Simpson. And there would be bargaining. There was always bargaining.

The elevator doors opened, and Cross stepped through into an Apple Store. At least, that was what it looked like. Computers and glass, then more glass and computers. The Central Intelligence Agency had been built on subterfuge within shadows, but the shadows in the modern world were all online. Field officers played second banana to the young, tech-savvy information foragers in the new order. Cross was efficient on a computer, but his particular set of skills was not useful inside a cubicle.

No one looked his way as he strode down the middle of the glass desks and bright display monitors. Even on a Saturday afternoon, the office buzzed with activity. National security was a 24/7 business with ample supply and crushing demand. A handful of analysts were likely working on the cleanup of the Christine Lewis rescue mission, but that was only one of a dozen or more high-priority operations demanding full attention.

Guinevere Sullivan, a tall brunette with cream-colored skin and wide eyes set inside square black frames, marched toward him. Both arms guarded a leather portfolio against her blouse. Without missing a step, she met him in the center of the room, spun on a heel, and matched his stride.

"Welcome home, Officer Cross."

Cross looked away, unable to stop himself from smiling. "It's not 'Officer' anymore, remember, Guin?" She remembered. This was their game.

"It's Officer Sullivan to civilians, mind you."

Few ever called her Guin. And using Guinevere guaranteed the threat of bodily injury.

Cross snorted. "I didn't think civilians were allowed to talk to the assistant executive director."

"Assistant *to the* executive director, and while you may insist on informality, I can assure you our relationship has resided, and will continue to reside, on a level somewhere above professional."

"Come on. We both know you could do Al's job one handed. This whole 'assistant to' thing is demeaning and unjust."

"What's demeaning is your lack of respect."

Cross's smile widened. He believed she enjoyed the back-and-forth even more since he retired.

She dipped her chin and peeked over her glasses. "Good flight?"

"Got a full five."

Guin's confident steps ceased, and she stared at him. Cross stopped as well, his smile fading and his eyebrows creasing. "What is it?"

"Incredible."

Busted.

Guin shook her head. "You're going to do it again, aren't you?"

Cross took a deep breath and adjusted the backpack on his shoulder. "I'm sorry, Guin. It got complicated."

One of her fingers tapped on the leather portfolio as if it were the only part of her allowed to show emotion. "Of course it got complicated, John." First name. That was really trouble. "Did you think it would never get complicated? You're better than that."

Cross kept his eyes fixed on hers. "Actually I thought I was good enough to keep it that way. Now we know."

"He's not going to like it."

Despite the expression of disappointment across Guin's face, Cross shot her a smile. "Did Al start liking things while I was gone? I thought you were better than that."

Guin narrowed her eyes and breathed through her thin nostrils. "And I was just getting used to having you around again." She started walking again.

Cross fell into step by her side. "Yeah. Me too."

They were silent the rest of the way to the smoky glass door of the conference room. Guin placed her hand on the knob, then paused. Her smile returned, and she said, "I'm glad it didn't get too complicated."

"You and me both."

She opened the door, and Cross stepped in. Guin didn't follow. She closed the door behind him and no doubt left to find a corner to hide in until the cease-fire.

"Hey, Al."

"Hey, Al?" came the response, a little louder than probably intended. "That's all you got, is 'Hey, Al'?" Or maybe the uncomfortable volume was intended after all.

Cross stepped to the nearest black chair behind a classy glass board-room table in the center of the space. He sat and placed his backpack on the chair beside him.

Al Simpson, executive director of the Central Intelligence Agency, stood on the opposite side of the table, his hands buried into the pockets of his suit pants. His thinning gray hair stuck up in front, probably from pushing his fingers through it, and he scowled. All in all, pretty much as expected.

Cross stretched across the table and snatched a glass cup and matching water pitcher from the center. He filled the glass, replaced the water pitcher, and took a nonchalant drink. He sighed, then said, "Well, I'm not going to kiss you."

"Ha! I think I deserve a kiss after saving your sorry behind in Amman."

"Saving my behind? I'm pretty sure I saved your public relations backside when this sorry excuse for an op fell apart before I put my pants on this morning."

Both men laughed aloud. Simpson slid into a seat and grabbed his own glass, but instead of water, he opted for a flask hidden in his inside jacket pocket. "I'd offer," he said as he poured.

"But you know what I'll say."

Simpson tipped the flask at Cross, then tucked it away. "More power to you, son."

Simpson called every male officer "son," but Cross felt it meant something with him. Memories of success and failure on the field flashed through his mind. Beside him at every turn was Simpson offering support. Cross shifted his eyes to the table. He didn't want to look. The disappointment would be crushing. A son betraying a father. For a second time. Wounds would reopen. Deep wounds.

Simpson took a sip from his glass and cradled it in both hands. "Listen, I know the op went bad, but you did good work out there. The fact that you and Ms. Lewis made it out alive means it was a win in my book."

"It did get bad. Honestly, I don't know why we're still alive."

"I thought a man of your convictions saw miracles all the time."

"I almost took a life today, Al." The smiles faded. "There are about a million other ways this could have gone where I would've had to kill."

He put the word out on the table just as he had a year ago.

Simpson set his drink on the table and folded his hands. "OK, I get it. The op went bad. You made choices. That doesn't mean it was like before. Even if you'd had to, this is a completely different scenario. We're talking self-defense, John. Even someone like you should be able to see that."

After his first resignation, it took nine months before the two men reestablished contact, another three before Cross agreed to work pro bono. Simpson hadn't gotten over it, that much was certain. "Someone like you" was the way he put it. As if Cross sprouted wings and grew a tail.

"Justifying it is not the point," Cross replied. "It's about balance. If I have to take a life, it's just adding to the scale on the other side."

Simpson spread his hands and leaned back in the chair. "Look, this was a hot one. The intel was bad, and you stepped into the middle of an execution. How many has it been? Five? Six? So we found a bump. That's all it is, John. A bump. We can move past this. I can guarantee that the next six will be smash and grab." Simpson grinned and let a curse slip. "We can even talk about some black-bag jobs where you don't have to talk to anyone."

Cross put a hand on his backpack and downed the last bit of water in his glass. "Al, I'm sorry, but—"

"Think about what you're about to do," Simpson interrupted.

Cross sighed. "I got a new job," he said after a brief pause.

"Don't tell me it's the bureau. It'd break my heart."

Cross forced a smile and shook his head. "Actually, it's at a church."

Simpson didn't respond. His eyes narrowed a bit. An audible exhale exited his nose.

"I'm a pastor now. I preach every Sunday. I'm preaching in the morning, in fact. It's a small country church. They're just happy to have someone, and I'm taking classes. Online stuff." Cross knew he was rambling, but this might be the last time they spoke. "It's just going to make it harder. And we both know what this was."

Simpson leaned forward and stared into the clear liquid in his glass. Without a word, Cross stood from the chair, slung the backpack over his shoulder, and moved to the exit.

"If you walk out that door . . ."

Simpson's voice paused Cross's hand against the door handle. Here came the speech. Cross turned to face him, but Simpson kept staring into the glass.

"You're going to leave a big"—Simpson caught the expletive he was surely about to use—"hole in the only thing keeping this country together. Everybody on the Hill is only trying to pour gasoline on the fire. Without us, the whole thing goes up in flames. They need us to contain the fire, John. Maintain the order."

"Al, you don't need me. You've got a lot of good officers." Cross turned the doorknob. "Come by sometime. We'll get a cup of coffee."

Simpson looked up from his drink. He turned a corner of his mouth up and relaxed his thin eyebrows. "I will."

Cross left the conference room knowing it was a lie.

CHAPTER SIX

He stood in the open doorway of his new home, staring at the black silhouette of the Rural Grove Baptist Church across the street. His heart swelled, and he recalled how different his life had been only six months ago as he'd searched for a church to call home. Megachurches provided the blessing of anonymity, but that meant sacrificing his quest for isolation. So he opted for something small. And now here he was, the pastor of a church. Less isolated now than he'd ever been in his life.

RGBC wasn't a large building, but picturesque even at night, thanks to the traditional steeple rising from its sloping roof. The skeleton of an unfinished expansion framed the silhouette, a behemoth of debt saddled to the church, serving as a monument to the nearsighted vision of the previous shepherd.

Cross would never admit it to anyone attending the church, but he liked the blemish of the unfinished building. They paid a loan for it and couldn't use it, but it reminded him of the grave responsibility of leading the small group of Christ followers.

With a deep breath, he finally released his gaze and stepped into the house, closing the front door in his wake. He preferred the house dark. Tonight, however, he needed light to work by, so he flipped on a table-side lamp and tossed his backpack into the arms of a lonely armchair.

He took a detour into the kitchen and opened the refrigerator. Bare, as he'd left it. His doors were never locked, and the little old ladies of his congregation were too generous. He'd expected a surprise casserole or baked pie.

No covered dish sat next to the half-full jug of skim milk. And yet he smiled. Just the picture of Mrs. Templeton or Ms. Johnson doting on him always brought a smile to his face. His smile grew as he grabbed the jug of milk and closed the door.

He filled a bowl with bran flakes and added the milk. He returned the milk to its home, grabbed a spoon, and headed back to the armchair. Cradling the bowl in one hand, he pulled his notebook and Bible from the backpack and balanced them on his knees. He shoved a spoonful of bran into his mouth, then slid the bowl onto the side table. Flipping the Bible and notebook open, he said a quick prayer and buried his thoughts into his sermon.

The hours drifted by until daybreak softened the blackness of night.

Rays of sunlight kissed the rich stained-glass windows adorning the walls on either side of the small sanctuary. Cross knelt at the altar, his head hanging low and his hands clasped. Sleepless nights meant more time for him to be alone in the building before the service, a time Cross spent in deep contemplative prayer. It kept him sane.

Refusing to let the sun disturb him, he prayed until Gary Osborne, the head deacon and song leader, arrived in his bright-red pickup. Like a game of reverse dominos, the arrival of one would prompt the arrival of another. Gary first, followed by the pianist, Kim Young, then various choir members in sequential order. Though small and often stubborn, the congregation proved to be faithful.

Cross, aware of his antisocial tendencies, forced himself to speak to members as they arrived. "Good morning, Gary," he said first, his hand outstretched. "Any new adventures in homeowners insurance this week?" He struggled initiating social interaction, but found sustaining a conversation easy. The one skill from his days in the CIA he discovered useful to his new role as a pastor was his uncanny ability to absorb information.

"Every week is an adventure when it comes to insuring one's property," Gary replied. His dry delivery hid a playful spirit hard to detect until you knew him. "I can at least guarantee it's more exciting than the world of small town ministry."

"That's what you think. I've had my share of adventure." Cross grinned. "Prayers of blessing over pregnant cattle can be harrowing." Though he'd never admit to Jerry Walter his true feelings on the effectiveness of laying hands directly on the cow.

Gary flashed a squinty smile, a rare demonstration of glee, and proceeded to busy himself in preparation for the morning. Kim entered the sanctuary, next in line for greeting. Cross recalled an earlier conversation about her annoyance with a certain boisterous student and used the details to greet her in warm dialogue. He studied her eyes to see if she detected any hint of the makeup cocktail he'd mixed and used to cover the nicks and bruises on his face and hands. Yet another handy skill.

As each person arrived, Cross accessed his mental database of details and worked through fresh facts on Mrs. Templeton's medical scare and Shea's new job opportunity. He stored all the new information and asked for more. His other ministry skills were young, but listening to and remembering every detail of each individual's personal life bought him the most credibility with the church.

At least, that was what Gary had said over and over again at the business meeting late one Sunday night when Cross found his name listed as the committee's recommendation for the job. Despite his limited ministry education, they hadn't let him refuse.

The faith those people had shown in that short meeting weighed heavily on Cross as he'd begun his new journey into church ministry. He took the position seriously and wanted to prove his worth every week.

As Gary and the choir began the first song for that morning's service, Cross felt a lump form in his throat. Images of places he'd been and things he'd done in his former life flashed across his mind and reminded him why he'd said yes.

Redemption.

For Cross, being the pastor of a church had less to do with a calling and more to do with proving he wasn't that man anymore. The images faded as they sang hymns and read Scripture aloud. Gary left the stage sooner than Cross liked. He always did. If they could only keep singing and reading into eternity.

Cross stepped up to the pulpit and spread his notebook and Bible open. He allowed himself to be nervous. Confidence tended to dull the senses. Another skill that survived his conversion.

"Open your Bibles to the book of Philippians," he instructed the congregation. "We'll be reading this morning from chapter two." He paused as pages rustled. When it became quiet again, he started to read, his consistent and proven method of surviving a half hour of public speaking: read, then regurgitate what smarter men had said about what he'd just read. And it worked. He rarely made eye contact, as heads hung low over notebooks and wide-margin Bibles, pens scribbling furiously.

At least the first few rows. The heads in the back probably hung low for a different reason.

His sermon lasted twenty-eight minutes on the dot, just as he'd rehearsed it. The useful skill sets he'd perfected in the field were piling up. He closed in prayer and released the church for the day. He breathed for the first time since opening his Bible, and he stepped to the floor to take his customary position at the front of the room.

Gary shook his hand and nodded in affirmation before mingling with a group of older men huddled near the piano. A beaming young couple brought their newborn baby by to show off. Right behind the couple waddled Barbara Templeton, her puffy white hair refusing to move despite the sway in her step.

"Wonderful sermon, Pastor Cross," she said as she planted a kiss on Cross's check.

"Please, Mrs. Templeton, it's John." He grinned wide.

"Oh dear, you're our pastor now, so you'd better just get used to the respect." Mrs. Templeton pulled John close and lowered her voice. "I had a whole dish of green bean casserole left over from the ladies' knitting group last night. I took the liberty of sticking it in your fridge before service. I hope you don't mind."

"I hope you don't mind if I eat it all in one sitting."

Mrs. Templeton chuckled. "Just let me know if you do, dear, and I'll whip another one up for you tomorrow."

"If we were Catholic, I'd nominate you for sainthood."

"Oh, I don't think being Catholic matters none about that. Besides, I'm pretty sure I have to be dead first." She chuckled again and squeezed his bicep before walking back down the center aisle.

Lori Johnson took Mrs. Templeton's spot in line, her hands balled firmly against her hips. If Mrs. Templeton was a saint, Lori was the Virgin Mary. Cross wouldn't say no if Lori ever offered to officially adopt him. He stepped forward and wrapped a firm arm around her shoulders.

"How are you, Ms. Johnson? We missed you last week. I hope the sinus infection is long gone."

"It'll take something more serious than an infection to keep me away for more than a week," she replied as she returned the embrace.

At her age, an infection was nothing to be flippant about. Her health occupied the top spot of Cross's prayer list.

"I'd be lying if I said I would've preferred you stay home and rest."

"Lying wouldn't be too becoming of our new young pastor, now would it?"

"No, ma'am."

"You look rested, son"—he liked it when she called him that—"and that makes me feel even better."

His smile broadened. "I should add miracle worker to my résumé."

"I know what else you need to add to that résumé of yours." Here it came. A glint brighter than the sunlight through the stained glass appeared in her eye. "Married with two kids."

Cross laughed, as he always did when they had "the talk."

"I'm serious, John. You've got to go find Mrs. Cross and get her in here with you. Then this place will be perfect."

"I tell you what, Lori. If you see Mrs. Cross, you give her my number."

"Actually . . ."

Cross's smile faded. Usually "the talk" was fun and flighty and ended with Lori vowing to hunt down the right woman even if she had to travel all the way to the capital. Today the conversation took a different turn.

"Now that you mention it, I was talking to Kathleen down at the parlor. She has a niece who just graduated from college and is in the running for an internship at a big company in Richmond. Gorgeous girl. Kathleen had pictures."

"Lori, you didn't give Kathleen my number, did you?"

"John Cross, would I do that without consulting you first?"

Cross caught the sigh of relief before it could leave his lips.

"I promised Kathleen I would talk to you first. But I really think you should call this girl when she moves in. You need a nice girl, and Kathleen spoke very highly of her."

"Well, I'm glad I know now."

Lori's brow wrinkled even more than it already was. "Know now what?"

"That when you say you're going to do something, you really mean you're going to do it!"

Lori feigned offense and adjusted the strap of her purse. "Don't ever say I didn't help you, John Cross."

Cross laughed and squeezed her shoulder again. "You're the best, Ms. Lori Johnson. Don't ever change."

"I don't have enough time left for that—don't worry. I'm going to run by the pharmacy for my refill and then go read in bed. If I feel up to it later this week, I'll drop some fresh apple pie by."

"I would love it. Thank you."

Lori patted Cross on the back, flashed him a smile, and walked out with the last remaining congregants. Cross stood alone in the center of the sanctuary, the hard pews and wooden columns basking in vibrant hues of blue, purple, and green.

And then, for some reason, he thought of Christine.

CHAPTER SEVEN

CHRISTINE RODE THE elevator to the fifty-seventh floor of the American Electric Building in New York City and marveled at the fact a week had already passed since that morning in Amman. The more time passed, the more her experience seemed like nothing more than a bad dream. The military emergency care had been top notch, and she was well enough to reunite with her family within days. Even Philip, her transient stepbrother, called from whatever new place he called home. She let them cry over her, yes even Philip, for an appropriate amount of time before she hopped the train back to NYC.

"Always moving," her mother said about her, true even in her infancy. Christine couldn't sit still, and she argued the network was anxious to send her on a circuit of interviews and appearances. "NABC Reporter Rescued in Jordan." Not the most dramatic headline, but the story already reeked of drama. They'd use the term "hero," self-indulgent as always. She'd bet money on it.

Whenever she thought of Jordan, she also thought of John. The real hero of the story. She planned to use her triumphant return to the newsroom and the subsequent media circus as a smoke screen to gain access. Access to network resources. Access to inside sources. The biggest story of her career wasn't going to be the firsthand account of a kidnapped reporter. She'd get the scoop on the man who single-handedly pulled her from the depths of hell and delivered her back into the land of the living.

As she pictured his face, the man called "Shepherd," she tried to imagine him in his environment. He sounded American, so maybe a penthouse in Georgetown or Arlington. But he could be anywhere, which made the hunt even more enticing. She'd track him down. But she wouldn't tell his story, not at first. First, she'd do what she couldn't do in Amman: thank him.

If she survived the party, that was. Steven Jacobs, her assignment editor, confirmed the worst over the phone. On the other side of the elevator doors would be more attention than anyone would wish upon herself. He said there would be champagne, hadn't he? Ridiculous.

It really wasn't a celebration for her return, but for the ratings boost the network was sure to experience in the wake of the countless interviews and special reports. She grew weary thinking about how she would tell her story, then retell it, then elaborate, then expound, then speculate, then just flat out start making up something new. She would be interviewed about Amman, about AIM, about being taken, about the military operation, about public perception of the terror response, about her feelings, more about her feelings, and even more about her feelings. Every new angle the network could take, they would, not all of them 100 percent accurate.

Jacobs didn't tell her any of that, of course, but he didn't have to. Christine lived and breathed the fifty-seventh floor of the AE building and would demand the same if she were the news director. Welcome to the reality of modern news programming, ladies and gentlemen. Higher ratings meant more cash, so the more sensational, the better. It didn't always have to be true.

Christine sighed. Except this one was true. Somehow, she was in the middle of the most true-to-life sensational story she had ever worked on. But the worst part was, she couldn't tell the story in its entirety. At least, not yet.

Every single time she'd asked about John on her way home, she got the same response. "A United States Army Ranger unit out of Saudi Arabia conducted the operation in conjunction with information provided by America's finest information-gathering agencies. We cannot comment to the identities of the men and women who risked their lives to bring you home. It's a question of national security. I'm sure you understand."

Oh, she understood all right. Shepherd was a covert operative, and his existence was going to be denied at all but the deepest levels. That was where she needed to go. And before she found him, her story would be missing major details.

There were only three people she would tell the truth to. Her parents and—

The elevator doors slid open, and a loud shriek of joy invaded the cramped space. She groaned. When she'd used her keycard downstairs, it had alerted the party planners to her arrival. Her chance to slip in discreetly slipped by without her.

"Christine!" She heard Janeen's voice over the cheering. Not a surprise considering Janeen's voice was the loudest sound in the known universe. As Christine stepped out of the elevator, she spotted Janeen's head towering over other colleagues gathered in a semicircle to greet Christine. Janeen's red hair flowed in perfect formation around her face and down to her shoulders. It refused to move from place as she elbowed her way through the mass.

"Thank you," Christine shouted over the applause. Janeen tripped over her own feet but caught herself and stopped short of taking out a pimpled copywriter. Her jaw dropped open, not to speak but in concern over the fate of the tall paper cup in her hand. Satisfied nothing had spilled, the dazzling white smile returned and Janeen bounced into Christine's personal space.

"Here!" she said too loud as the applause died down. "Your first latte since you left!"

Christine took the cup and laughed. "Girl, we already went over this: they called my order in before the plane even landed." Besides her mom and stepfather, Janeen was the only other phone call Christine had elected to make on her arrival.

"But this is your first *real* latte, not that airport junk." Janeen pretended to preen as a reception line formed, and the two of them started the slow procession into the newsroom.

Christine couldn't think of anything else to say other than "thank you" to all the employees of NABC shaking her hand, hugging her, and patting her back. She didn't know half their names and wasn't on speaking terms with half of the other half. Those she didn't know picked spots at the front of the line, a good way to show company loyalty, then escape back to the appearance of work. Deeper into the newsroom, closer to her desk and Jacobs's office, stood the coworkers she labeled "friends and acquaintances."

Janeen beamed the entire way down the line like a mother showing off a newborn. In between hugs and handshakes, she offered her own commentary on the proceedings. "See why I work in sales? Less likely to get kidnapped."

Christine snorted. "Think it's a little too soon for wisecracks?"

"If you're still dealing with your emotions, you can come with me to see Kendra next Thursday."

"I still say not to trust a therapist named Kendra." The banter did its job stalling the tears of joy at seeing her friend. She expected a cry fest to break out in the middle of the newsroom at any moment.

As they passed, the receiving line dwindled. Janeen leaned in close and spoke in a soft tone. "Thank God you're back. I was dying without you. 'Cra-neen' together at last, just like it should be."

Christine cringed at the celebrity-couple nickname the other staff had bestowed on their friendship. She preferred the alternative "Jan-tine." Slipping an arm around Janeen's waist, she smiled and replied, "I promise as soon as we're done here, the two of us will play hooky and grab a greasy street hot dog."

"Ew, gross." Janeen pantomimed a bout of nausea, and they shared a laugh.

Steven Jacobs stood at the end of the line, holding his arms open wide. On instinct Christine fell into his embrace and immediately regretted it. She made it a point not to make physical contact with any members of the opposite sex, a residual habit of her upbringing, and especially with Jacobs. He made no secret of his affection toward her.

He pressed his scruffy cheek against her ear and said, "Welcome home, Chris."

No one called her Chris.

"Thank you," she said as she pulled herself away.

Jacobs kept a hand on her shoulder as she shook hands with writers and assistants gathered around them. Janeen, her guardian angel, brushed Jacobs's fingers away and wrapped an arm around Christine's waist.

"Steve wanted to give your desk away." She sneered. "But I fought him off."

"She knows I wouldn't never do that, Jan."

Why did he always have to shorten a name?

"I'm glad you didn't," Christine said. It felt like too sweet of a sentiment, so she added, "Otherwise I would've had to sue."

"Maybe we still should," Janeen added with a flick of her tongue toward Jacobs.

Christine scanned the rest of the newsroom and flashed a frown. "Where's Mike?" Mike Murray, her cameraman in Jordan, was on her short list of people she wanted to hug. He hadn't been taken with her, and it proved difficult to find out what had happened to him since.

"It's OK," Janeen assured her. "Mike's fine. He got out after you were taken. He wanted to be here today, but he's on assignment in Spain."

Christine sighed with relief. As soon as Mike got back, she would treat him to a steak dinner. And she would get Jacobs to pay for it.

"Listen, Christine." Jacobs was suddenly all business. "There is no expectation for you to jump right back in. I've already talked it over with Pat. You take as much time as you need to get back into the swing of things. You'll always have a desk at NABC."

It would be the millionth time, but she said "thank you" anyway. "I'm good," she continued. "I know what's ahead. And I'm ready for it."

Janeen's smile grew wider. "That's my girl," she said with a squeeze at Christine's waist. "We've already been fielding other networks, newspapers, magazines, even movie producers. Of course, you get the final say. If I were you, I'd accept nothing less than Rosamund Pike playing myself in the movie."

"Wait. You mean playing me or actually playing you? She doesn't have the hips for you."

Janeen cocked an eyebrow and let her arms fall to her sides. "Looks like somebody's sense of humor survived too."

The glint in Janeen's eye made Christine feel more at home than any of the computer monitors or cubicle walls ever could.

Jacobs waved his hand in a rude manner. "Janeen, if you would excuse us, I'd like to go over some things with Christine. Then when we've got a game plan, I promise you can take off and spend the rest of the afternoon reminding her why this is the greatest city in the world."

"You heard the man. It's a promise." Janeen smacked her palm against Christine's backside and trotted off.

"I know I don't have to tell you this, Chris, but Pat and the others are expecting you to be all anyone is talking about for the next few weeks."

Christine guzzled the lukewarm latte as Jacobs reclined in his over-sized leather desk chair. Though small, the office boasted a window overlooking Forty-Ninth Street that added a touch of luxury despite the mirrored glass of an adjacent building obscuring 90 percent of the view.

"We're all willing to work with your schedule when you feel ready for it, but I've got to tell you, the *Evening Report* is busting down the door to get you on tonight at the latest. They wanted you live on the plane, and I had to give up my Christmas bonus to keep them from showing up at your house." Jacobs interrupted his spiel with a handful of pecans from a dish on his desk.

"I get it, Steven, and I'm good. I really am."

Jacobs snorted and lobbed a curse in her direction. "Come on. You can't be serious. Insurgents held you for months under extreme conditions. You dropped like a dress size and a half. Don't get me wrong. You needed the help, but it couldn't have been a trip to the spa."

Christine lifted the cup to her lips and rolled her eyes as Jacobs tossed another handful of pecans down his throat. Classic. He knew how to be charming when he needed to be, but the misogyny was strong with this one.

In between audible chewing, he asked, "How was it?"

"I'm sorry?"

"Where you were being held. What was it like?"

Christine paused. She'd given her parents the story in its entirety, but now she needed to edit. How she'd been treated for months in captivity, the really scintillating details, would be perfect fodder for the newshounds. The specifics of the attempted execution needed editorial care.

"It was the worst thing I've ever been through." For the next fifteen minutes, she gave him everything he wanted. Well, maybe not everything. But she added all the best notes in her summary of the kidnapping and her subsequent detention. The dark, windowless room she had been held in. Being chained to a chair for hours on end. The lack of proper food or hydration. Her bout with dysentery.

Jacobs salivated at the guaranteed boost from the publicity.

"Then," she continued after another mouthful of the cold coffee, "last Saturday something changed. I could hear the men arguing. I was given new clothes to wear and then dragged into a larger room. They put me in a chair and pointed a video camera at me."

Jacobs's eyes widened, and the corners of his mouth drooped. "Hold on," he said as he held up a hand. "They were really going to execute you?"

"How did you know?"

Jacobs bolted from his chair and sifted through paper stacked in neat piles atop filing cabinets. It looked like a mess, but Jacobs searched with calculated hands and within half a minute he found what he was looking for. He sat on his desk and held a photo in front of her face.

Christine gasped. She snatched the photo from his hands and studied it closer. A man stood in a black robe holding a knife while another sat on his knees, his hands behind him, dressed in an orange jumpsuit. They appeared to be in the desert. "What is this?"

Jacobs tapped the photo with his finger on the body of the man in orange. "Jared Downey, BBC. Those Islamic Alliance dopes have been putting execution videos on the Internet. They seem to find the irony of beheading newspeople to make the news."

"Alliance of Islamic Military," Christine murmured, her eyes still locked on the eyes of the man wrapped in the black robe. The memories intensified. Details came into focus. Her heart beat against her rib cage. Could it be the same man? "When did this happen?"

"Last month. It was the last one in a string of them. I guess you were going to be their next statement."

Christine felt the flood of emotion forcing its way to her tear ducts. She broke her stare and thrust the photo back at Jacobs. He took it and placed it facedown on his desk. His eyebrows squeezed in, and he leaned forward. "I'm sorry. I didn't mean to remind you."

Christine took a deep breath and pressed a finger against her eyelid. Dry, but no doubt red. "It's fine. It's just sometimes hard to believe I came that close . . ."

"Tell me what happened. Just like you will in tonight's interview." Jacobs leaned back and folded his arms. His eyes narrowed, and he cocked his head to one side, his ready-to-offer-critique pose.

His rudeness helped her regain composure, and she finished off the latte before continuing. "They made me read a statement into the camera, but before anything else could happen, the rescue team took out the terrorists."

One lie.

"It all happened so fast, I don't really remember how it all went down."

Now two.

"Somehow I got smacked in the face, and the next thing I knew the men were all lying on the floor."

That one didn't really count as a lie.

Christine paused to rewrite her next statement, and Jacobs interjected, "Were they dead?"

"Yes."

An unnecessary third lie. Christine caught herself before she said another word. *It doesn't have to be dramatic. Just vague.*

Jacobs held his breath.

"I mean, no," she added. "I don't know. It was all so unreal, like a dream. There was blood." True, her own. "But there was also a stun gun involved. After the men were down, the team pulled me out of the room and I was taken to a helicopter that flew us all out of the city."

Jacobs shook his head. "Wow." He repeated the word, then stepped around the desk and dropped back into his chair. "This is going to be great." He held up a hand. "I mean, no offense. I'm sorry for what you experienced and glad you're alive, but I don't know if any of us realize how big this is going to be."

"And that's not even the real story."

Jacobs's expression blanked. He held back any words.

"You asked me to tell you what I'm going to say tonight, and that's what I did. I told you the story I'm going to tell everyone. But it's not the real story." Christine leaned forward and poked her finger into his desk. "The real story is even bigger. And as soon as I can prove it, it's going to launch this whole thing into space."

Jacobs cursed and grabbed the can of pecans with enough force to launch a couple of them onto the floor. "What are you talking about?"

"It wasn't a team who got me out of Jordan. It was one man. One man on his own. He stopped the execution, fought off the terrorists, and delivered me to the unit that flew me out. I never saw him again, never knew his name. He had to have been a covert intelligence officer. CIA, I don't know. No one will own this, but I'm going to track him down and prove it."

Jacobs didn't jump out of his chair, let out a war cry, and start dancing, as she imagined he would. Instead, he sat in his chair crunching a pecan between his teeth and rubbing his temple with an index finger. "You mean to tell me," he finally said, "a spy rescued you?"

"Yes. That's exactly what I'm telling you."

"Was he British?"

"What?"

"You know. Did he have an accent?"

Was this a dream? Christine shook her head, hoping a different, more caring Steven Jacobs would magically appear. It didn't work. "No, he was American. I'm telling you the truth, Steven. A man named John rescued me from the execution, and kidnappers chased us through Amman."

"I thought you said you didn't know his name."

"Well, he said his name was John, but that's obviously not it."

"You don't know that. Maybe it is his name. I don't think James Bond ever used an alias on his missions."

"He wasn't British." Jacobs chuckled but averted his eyes as Christine gritted her teeth and folded her arms. "I'm being serious," she said. "I'm not going to tell the whole story yet because the government will just deny it. Let me find him and prove to you it happened. Think about the legs this story will have if I can prove I'm right."

"Oh, you don't have to tell me." Jacobs dug his fingers into the can of pecans only to pull them out empty. He frowned and wiped the fingers against his pant leg under the table. "A story about an American spy rescuing a beautiful journalist prints its own money. Hollywood would make the film whether you wanted them to or not."

"So let me do it."

"What, prove your story?"

Christine nodded.

Jacobs rolled his eyes. He sat silent for a moment, staring into Christine's face. She thanked God he couldn't read her thoughts. Suddenly, he bolted upright in his chair, grabbed a legal pad, and began writing. "I tell you what," he said as he wrote. "I want you to call this number. A guy named Kevin is going to pick up. Works for an RBS affiliate in Washington." Jacobs handed the paper to Christine. "He's going to want to set you up in an interview. Let him. In return, he'll get you connected with some sources out of the intelligence community. If your guy John exists, this would be the best place to start in tracking him down."

Christine held her new possession in a firm grip and expressed her joy with bright eyes and a smile. "Steven, thank you for this. I promise, it's going to be big."

"Just do me one favor."

Her smile faded, positive he would ask for a date.

"When you find the guy, thank him for me."

Confused, Christine stammered, "Why?"

"For bringing you home."

The hints of charm were a sly trick. Still, the sentiment felt genuine, so she smiled and blushed. Rising to leave, she replied, "Don't worry. That's the first thing I'm going to do."

CHAPTER EIGHT

CROSS ENTERED THE house after sunset for the third day in a row. He ignored the light switch and headed for the kitchen for his customary dinner of bran. The memory of eating Mrs. Templeton's green bean casserole the previous Monday presented itself in his mind, as did the temptation to order out. It took a deep plunge into his reservoir of inner strength to quench the flame of selfish desire.

His self-imposed dietary purgatory served as a contemporary update to mortification of the flesh—pious Christians of the past paying penance for sins with self-inflicted abuse. He made exception for the casserole after the weight of guilt he carried from the first time she'd brought him one and he'd thrown it away. Same with the endless occurrence of church potlucks. He only ever ate enough to be kind to the aspirant cooks of the congregation.

Cross's version of mortification of the flesh extended beyond his humble diet. The guilt hiding in the corners of his heart demanded extreme reparation. Nothing pleasant to eat or drink, only enough sleep to survive, no entertainment whatsoever. If he wasn't caring for members of his congregation, meeting new people in the community, studying to preach, or working on class assignments, he read and prayed.

Thanks to years of honing the art of discipline, Cross buried the temptation of a hot, appetizing meal and dug into the bran flakes and milk. Instead of carrying the bowl into the living room to study while he ate, Cross granted himself the luxury of leaning against the counter.

In the moment of stillness, he thought of Christine. An odd habit had formed since his return. Amman wasn't his first rescue mission, and though he could recall every face and name, the others rarely interrupted his thoughts. Christine did. What was it? Why did she stick?

He replayed the operation in his mind, focusing on her. She'd thrown out the script they'd handed her and defiantly offered her own last words. She'd rebounded from her injury and matched his pace during the escape. She'd pushed him out of the way of the SUV. And knew a thing or two about handguns.

More than anything, he remembered his own feelings when they'd finally reached the awaiting Black Hawk. The relief he felt knowing she was safe. He wanted her to be safe. Wanted her to be home.

He wanted to know how she was.

I could call her. The thought came so suddenly, he dropped the spoon. He watched it fall and clatter on the floor. Call her? Out of the question. He didn't have her number. He bent his knees and retrieved the spoon.

I could get it.

Calling her risked blowing his cover. He assumed she was good at her job. The wrong move and she could expose his name, location, maybe more. And who knew what might be brought down on the little community he called home.

She wouldn't do that.

Even if Christine kept his secret, she'd be vulnerable. All someone would need was the hint of a connection. The old John Cross had enough enemies.

Just one call.

The urge grew in strength. He balanced the spoon on the bowl, dug his hand into his pocket, and pulled out the phone. With his thumb, he flipped the burner phone open, and the twelve simple buttons glowed back at him in envy green. He stood still, the bowl cupped in one hand, the phone in the other, and stared at the buttons. She could be his second call. It would take approximately six minutes before he would hear her voice.

The display flashed brighter, and the ringer shrieked. The bowl slipped from his palm, but he squeezed his fingers tight and prevented a cereal catastrophe. He examined the incoming number. Area code 202.

DC.

But it wasn't Simpson or a CIA number. He didn't recognize it off-hand, though something about it did feel familiar. Curious, he pressed the Confirmation button and held the phone to his ear.

"Hello?"

Multiple scenarios played through his mind. Depending on the response he received, there were no less than seven available escape plans, two of which involved an accidental fire to the parsonage.

Stop it, he told himself. *You're not going to set fire to the house.*

"Officer . . . sorry, *Mr.* Cross? It's Eric Paulson. From Langley. I was your driver last weekend. Do you remember me?"

The house survived another night. Cross slid the cereal bowl onto the counter and shifted his cautious tone to a cheerful pastoral register. "Yes, Officer Paulson, I remember you. Thank you for calling me."

"Is now a bad time? I understand if you don't feel comfortable with this, since, well, you know."

"Since I made my retirement status official?" Cross laughed into the receiver. "I think that makes it OK, Eric. You're only talking to a pastor now."

Paulson breathed a sigh of relief. "Thank you, sir, um, I mean Mr. Cross."

"You can call me John."

"That's going to take some getting used to, if you don't mind . . . John." His name felt like a foreign object fighting its way out of Paulson's tight lips.

"I also accept Reverend Cross, Brother John, and Preacher."

He got a laugh out of Paulson with that one.

"I'm sure your new life has taken some getting used to."

"You have no idea." Cross liked talking to the younger man. He didn't feel the need to hide feelings and details about his choice to leave his previous occupation. "Did you get a chance to try out that church we found?"

"That's part of why I'm calling. I know you wanted to know how it went."

"I'm only a little surprised you actually went through with it."

"I almost didn't. I had made up my mind not to the night before, but honestly I was afraid you might call me right after."

Cross mentally kicked himself for not thinking to call after church the previous morning. A careless, uncharacteristic neglect. Come to think of it, there'd been multiple occasions over the previous week where he failed to remember important details. After the call, he'd diagnose whatever brain disease afflicted him. "Well, I'm glad you did."

"I am too. It was refreshing. What I needed."

"Anything stand out to you?"

"Well, you're not going to believe this, but the sermon was out of the book of Philippians."

"Uh-oh," Cross replied. "Now you know how bad I am at my job."

Paulson laughed again. "It was interesting to hear someone else preach after we'd just had that conversation. It was a lot more similar than you think."

"I'm glad I'm keeping up with the experts. Do you think you'll go back?"

Paulson paused. Cross imagined the younger man trying to determine the most delicate way to say no. But the pause lasted longer than it should have. "Eric? You can say no."

"Sorry, sir, I was distracted." The "sir" was back, and his voice was softer.

Cross stood straighter. "Are you on duty?"

"Yes, I'm sorry. It's just a routine security detail. I'm alone in a car."

"What's wrong?"

"Nothing. I just thought I saw something."

"Describe it," Cross said in a stern, commanding voice. All other thoughts disappeared from the front of his mind to make room for the incoming information.

Paulson responded as he would to any superior. "White male approaching secure area. He is wearing a large jacket but does not appear to be armed."

"What kind of jacket, Officer Paulson?"

"Ankle-length pea coat, sir. I just radioed it in, and we're standing down. Nothing to be alarmed about."

Nothing to be alarmed about? Who was running this operation? "Are you wearing a jacket?"

Another pause, then a confused "Yes?"

"What kind?"

"My suit jacket, sir."

"But you don't really need it. It's seventy-one degrees outside."

The line went silent again. "Sir," Paulson said at last. "I'm afraid I'm going to have to call you back."

"Please."

"Oh, and one last thing, John. I thought you might like to know Ms. Lewis is going to be interviewed on NABC's broadcast news tonight."

Cross felt his face soften into an involuntary smile. He shook his head to erase the accidental display of emotion and refocus on the conversation. "Thank you, Eric. And be careful."

"Copy that." He hung up.

Cross didn't move. He pictured Paulson in his mind, pictured the suspicious individual, and prayed the situation would be resolved without harm to either party. Once he finished, he snatched the bowl off the counter and marched to the living room. The NABC broadcast would already be in progress.

The unimpressive old TV had been furnished with the house, and Cross approached it with apprehension, certain it would refuse to cooperate. He grabbed the remote and pressed the Power button. Thankfully, it turned on.

He cycled through the local network affiliates and found NABC. The beautiful face of Christine Lewis appeared in crystal-clear quality, her interview live and in progress. The anchor, a man named Bill Lawrence, filled the left side of the split screen.

". . . knife to your throat?" Lawrence finished saying.

"It was certainly a traumatic experience, Bill," Christine responded. "All I could think about was how I would never get a chance to see my family again."

"And then what happened?"

"Right when the man was about to use the knife to decapitate me, a United States Army Ranger unit stormed the building and took out the men."

Cross's mouth stopped mid-chew, and bran squished between his teeth. So she'd accepted the official military story. Good. Unfortunate about the lie, but it had to be. The military PR machine disavowed his existence and role in the operation. Everything by the book.

"They shot and killed the men holding you hostage?"

"No, Bill. Fortunately, they used very sophisticated electroshock equipment to subdue the terrorists. No bloodshed."

"I'd like you to tell us more . . ."

"Except I did manage to get hit in the nose during the skirmish and left some of my own blood on the floor. I also had quite the headache." Christine scrunched her nose and rubbed a nostril with her index finger.

Cross exhaled a loud breath through his own nose. Not quite the thing he wanted her to remember him by.

Lawrence chuckled. "And we here at NABC are certainly glad that was the only injury you sustained that day."

Her healthy, jovial appearance warmed Cross's heart. He didn't have to call her after all.

A lie. He wouldn't sleep tonight unless he did.

CHAPTER NINE

CHRISTINE TOOK MEASURED sips of the steaming cup of frothed milk and espresso cradled between her palms. The extra two shots did little to ease the throbbing in her head after a late flight from New York to Washington and less than four hours of whatever it was she got in the hotel room. Certainly not sleep. More like mandatory unconsciousness.

Another glance at her smartwatch reminded Christine it was early. Earlier than the agreed upon time she and Kevin would meet. Kevin Hays, the owner of the phone number Jacobs supplied, suggested a rendezvous at Corner Cup Café on the corner of Ninth and M Streets, eight thirty in the morning. He assured her it would give them time to chat before the beginning of his hectic news producer schedule. Not an early bird, unlike her.

She groaned after swallowing another sip of the coffee. The regret of offering Hays an exclusive second interview didn't sit well with the hot liquid in her stomach. He worked for a Republic Broadcasting System affiliate serving a minor market in the area. Not the type of platform NABC would like her to maintain.

Eight thirty-one. Ranting about his tardiness in her mind proved a distraction from the pressure she felt from her own network. From the network, or from herself? She didn't want to weight the arguments either way. Christine dared a giant gulp of the latte to stall the mental anguish building in her brain.

The ring of a bell signaled her attention to Hays walking through the door. He ducked slightly to fit under the average doorframe, a few strands of longer brown hair falling across his eyes.

Tall and handsome. She'd forgive him for being late.

He nodded her direction, then ordered a cup of coffee from the counter. He took the seat across the table from her and offered his hand in greeting. "Nice to meet you in person, Christine. And I guess congratulations on being alive."

She shook the hand and replied, "Thank you. It's nice to meet you too. I'm glad we're going to be able to help each other."

"Yeah." Hays glanced over his shoulder at the entrance to the café. "About that. What exactly are you looking for?"

"Our mutual friend told me you could get me some information from inside the CIA."

Hays stopped studying the entrance and eyed Christine with a peaked eyebrow. "He said that?"

"I believe the phrase he used was 'intelligence community.' I figured we would start with the CIA and work our way out from there."

Hays chuckled as he took a drink from his coffee cup. "Yeah, sure. I can just ring up the CIA and get you whatever you want." The beverage did nothing to soften the bite of sarcasm in his tone.

Christine rolled her eyes. For once could a man not use her gender as an excuse to not treat her like a professional equal. "I know it's not that easy, but this isn't a hard question to answer."

"All answers are hard to come by with the CIA."

"I just want a name."

Hays narrowed his eyes. "I thought you said this would be easy."

"I've got something to help." Christine slid a note card across the table.

Hays studied the word written on the card. "Shepherd?"

"It's a code name. All I want is the real name it goes with."

Hays propped an elbow on the table and held the note card between two fingers in front of his face. He looked to the café entrance again and then out the window. "All right," he said finally. "I think I can help."

Christine smiled and downed a swig of her latte. "Good, because I brought my best interview outfit and was hoping to use it tonight."

Hays slid the note card back across the table. "There's a dry cleaner just down Ninth in this same block. Walk inside and ask to see Peter. He can help you."

Christine stared at Hays. "Excuse me?"

"You wanted my help, didn't you?"

"Yeah, but I thought you'd make a phone call and send me an email."

Hays finished off his coffee and flashed a sarcastic grin. "Looks like you're in for more excitement than you expected."

Christine narrowed her eyes. "I'm not really in the market for excitement."

"Trust me." Hays leaned forward, both elbows on the table. "Just do what I say and you'll get your answer." He winked, then stood up and cursed. "You might even get more than you thought you needed." He buttoned his suit jacket and stuck his hand in her face.

She shook it as he said, "I'll see you tonight, four o'clock. You know where the bureau is, right? Just a mile down the road on Desales."

Christine nodded and dug a hand into her shoulder bag for hand sanitizer as she watched Hays leave the café. She sat there trying to make sense of what just occurred. How had Hays been prepared to have her meet his contact so soon? At least she knew why he picked the café. Proximity to his source, not the coffee.

She slung her bag over her shoulder and walked out into the bitter morning air. Rays of sunshine promised a spring warmth later in the day. It took Christine less than a full minute to find the dry cleaner a mere three hundred feet from the corner café. She stared at the unassuming red facade trimmed in green with CLEANERS stenciled in white paint underneath a large three-pane window. A hint of steam snaked out the corner of the open entryway.

Christine took a deep breath, then walked inside. The scent of fresh laundry permeated the air. A comforting smell. A counter with a cheap laminate top dissected the sparse front room. Behind the counter, another open doorway. Just beyond, Christine spotted shirts, pants, and dresses hung on wire hangers, along with the occasional blurry movement of employees operating machinery.

On the countertop, next to a register, sat a small bell with a smaller sign taped to its front, reading SERVICE. Christine tapped the bell a few times and waited.

An older Asian man appeared in the doorway, nodded at her, and walked up to the register. "May I help you?" he asked, his accent thick.

"I'm here to see Peter."

"He's not here today."

Christine furrowed her brow. "Five minutes ago I was told to come here and ask for Peter. If he's not here today, where can I find him?"

The Asian man started to respond, then caught his words before they could escape. He looked past her to the open entrance, glanced back at Christine, then smiled and said, "I think he might be here. Let me check."

He disappeared into the back, leaving Christine alone in the front room. "Great," she mumbled. "This has got to be some kind of joke. I bet Steven's in on it."

A younger Asian man stepped through the back doorway and asked, "Can I help you?"

She took a quick breath. "Are you Peter?"

The man nodded.

"A mutual friend told me to come see you. His name is Kevin Hays. Do you know him?"

Peter nodded again, his eyes piercing her own as he studied her.

Christine swallowed. "He said you could help me."

"Help you with what?"

Christine opened her shoulder bag, pulled out the note card, and handed it to him. "I'm trying to find someone."

Peter read the card, handed it back, and shook his head. "That's not a name."

Christine took a deep breath to quell her rising temper. "I know that. It's a code name. For an operative. I'm guessing Central Intelligence. That's you, right? This place. It's a front."

"I don't know what you're talking about."

"Is that so? Then if I were you, I'd be concerned about all the surveillance equipment hidden in your business." Christine pointed to all the tiny cameras she'd identified when she first walked into the dry cleaner. One in a corner of the ceiling, one over the back doorway, one in the register. She threw a thumb behind her at the window and front entrance, lined with wire. "It looks like you could tell when a cold draft crosses that threshold."

Peter's eyes brightened, and one corner of his mouth inched upward in a hint of a smile. "Lots of burglaries on this street. Can't be too careful."

Christine crossed her arms and wrinkled her nose. "Are we going to play this game all morning? Kevin said you would help me. If you're not willing, I guess I could just start interviewing your neighbors about how it feels to have the government spying on them from next door."

Peter sighed, glanced over his shoulder at the doorway behind him, and turned back with his palm open. "Let me see the card."

Christine handed him the note card again, and he pulled a pen from his pocket and wrote on it. He slipped the pen back into his pocket and slid the note card across the counter. Christine picked it up and read what he had added—*625 Douglas Road, Mechanicsville, Virginia.*

"What's this?" Christine asked. "I thought you had a name."

Peter snorted. "You'll find what you're looking for there. But make sure you go on Sunday. Oh, and one more thing." His face tensed and his voice deepened. "Don't bother coming back here. There won't be anything left after today."

Peter, probably not his real name, stepped through the doorway into the back room. Christine pocketed the note card, breathed in the fresh scent of dry pressed clothing, then exited the building.

She didn't bother calling a cab. The sun offered her the right amount of heat for a walk back to her hotel. And according to Peter, she had time to kill.

Five days, to be precise.

CHAPTER TEN

CROSS MUST HAVE been ten or eleven the last time he went to church with his parents. They observed Easter and Christmas, but never at the same church. The whole experience bewildered him. Singing, reading, sometimes watching a bearded man get whipped, then hung by hooks on a wooden cross. They'd strike a real nail with a real hammer, but he could always tell it was a pair of hooks hidden around the actor's wrists.

He found the liturgy discomforting, if only because the experience was too inconsistent to become familiar. Cross hated standing at the front of the congregation pretending to sing when he neither knew how the hymn went nor had the confidence to sing aloud.

Not a skill he'd needed before.

Faced with the self-appointed pressure of his new position, Cross gave the singing portion of each service all the gusto he could. He kept his eyes locked on Osborne as the older man waved his arms about in a strange yet comforting manner. If Cross didn't make eye contact with anyone, he felt assured they didn't notice him.

The congregation sat, and a deacon offered a prayer at the pulpit. On cue with the "Amen," Osborne pointed to the pianist and stood before the choir, his back to the congregation.

As parishioners passed a gold-painted saucer from one end of a pew to another, the silvery strokes of the piano filled the humble sanctuary. The lyrics of the special music failed to enter Cross's ears as he recited his sermon notes in his mind over and over again.

The applause snapped him back to reality, and he took his place behind the pulpit. He positioned his notebook and Bible as he instructed the congregation to open their own Bibles to the book of Philippians. "We're continuing our look at the second chapter today." Cross smiled, confident his opening quip about a mouse and a farmer would be a hit with the agriculture community represented in his church. He lifted his gaze to engage the patient attendees.

The smile dropped.

There, in one of the back rows of the sanctuary, sat Christine Lewis, her eyes smiling at him.

Cross stumbled over his next words, then cleared his throat and gripped the edges of the podium. The skin of his knuckles lost its color, and a bead of sweat formed on his temple. His mind screamed, *Run!*

His legs refused to move. He shifted his eyes to each predetermined exit. He could excuse himself, perhaps feign illness. He struggled with the decision. What was happening? He couldn't will himself off the platform. It didn't make sense. Not him. He never froze.

Something held him there.

Cross averted his gaze back to the notebook. "Excuse me. I guess the choir presentation moved me so much I thought it might be better to just end the morning right now." A smart misdirect. The awkward aura in the room dissipated as the comment elicited a wave of relieved laughter and a shout of "Amen," tempting Cross to follow through with the threat.

Knowing better, he read from his notes, but kept his eyes low. He felt Christine's gaze on him, so he found two or three familiar faces near the front of the room to focus on while he spoke. His hands were locked on the pulpit. He pressed forward into his sermon.

An agonizing twenty-five minutes. That was how much time had passed. Wasn't it?

His notes ended, and he could read no more. He prayed, made eye contact with Christine again, then broke his stare and stepped to the front of the altar.

Osborne beat him there and put a hand on Cross's shoulder. "John, you OK?"

Cross nodded. "I'm fine. Just a little ill, that's all. I'm sure it's nothing."

Osborne smiled and squeezed the shoulder. "OK, well next week don't go so short. Everyone might like it too much."

Cross dipped his head and leaned close. "Wait. How long was I up there?"

"I'd be surprised if you made it over fifteen minutes."

Cross drew a breath. "I'm sorry. I'm sure I'll be fine next week." Lying to Osborne did make him ill. In the next twenty-four hours, he'd neither occupy the state of Virginia nor be identified as John Cross, that much was sure.

He went through the motions of greeting the regulars. He forgot names, showed little interest in their lives, and dismissed small talk. Mrs. Templeton checked his forehead for a fever and promised a delivery of homemade chicken noddle soup.

Lori followed in Mrs. Templeton's footsteps. "That was—"

"Bad?" Cross interrupted.

"I was going to say short. Not that I'm complaining. Gives me more time for my afternoon activities. You know, knitting, cooking, gardening. All the things us old ladies like to do."

His anxiety over Christine subsided, and he smiled for the first time since he'd started his sermon. "You don't know how to knit, you hate gardening, and as good of a cook as you are, you'd prefer sitting in front of the TV with an oven pizza."

"Exactly. I demand a sermon no shorter than thirty minutes. You better bring up that average next week."

"You can count on it." Maybe he would have to stay.

Lori's eyes softened, and she felt his cheek with the palm of her hand. "If you ever need to talk, you know where to find me."

Cross grabbed her hand with his and squeezed. "Thank you. You don't know what that means to me."

Her face beamed, and she returned the squeeze. "We old ladies always need someone to mama." She turned and left Cross standing alone at the altar. A handful of others made their way out of the sanctuary, until the room was empty.

Except for Christine.

She waited near the door in the back, her hands tucked into the pockets of her well-fitted jeans. The light of the stained glass surrounded her in a stunning glow, her blond hair sitting comfortably against her shoulders, a brown leather jacket complementing her figure.

They stood motionless for a moment. Neither spoke, eyes locked.

Cross took a deep breath and asked, "How did you find me?"

Christine laughed. "That's it?" She walked toward him. "No, 'Hi, Christine' or 'Good to see you'?"

Cross hid his hands in the pockets of his suit pants. "I think the way it works is, we're never supposed to see each other again."

Christine stopped just short of the front row of pews. "Well, that doesn't sound like fun," she said with a smile and a wink. "Besides, you never gave me a chance."

"For what?"

Christine took a step closer, her eyes piercing his, her skin flushed. "Thank you. You saved my life."

"You don't have to thank me."

"Yes, actually, I do."

Cross couldn't think. The pews, stained glass, pulpit, all faded as they entered a dream he hadn't prepared for. He wanted this moment, but it meant everything was going to change.

Again.

Still locked in her gaze, he swallowed the lump in his throat and smiled. "I'm glad you're OK."

"Fully recovered. I'm even back at work. I've been doing a lot of interviews this week, in fact."

"I've seen them."

"Oh, you have?" She bent her nose and smirked, a glint dancing off her eyes.

"All of them."

Christine's lips parted, but no words slipped through. Her eyes softened, and the smirk turned into a broad smile capped by flushed cheeks.

Cross rocked back and forth on his heels. "So you're here now. And you got to thank me. Now what?"

She emitted a bewitching laugh. "Now I've got questions. A lot of questions." Her hands came out of the pockets and gestured around the church.

Reality pulled Cross's heels flat against the floor. He straightened, and his white dress shirt tightened against his chest. "Miss Lewis—"

"Oh, now it's Miss Lewis?"

"This is serious. I don't know what you thought would happen, but you've put me in a very compromising position."

"What are you talking about?"

"What happened, it . . ." Her eyes stunned him. His confidence wavered.

Christine crossed her arms, and her neck stiffened. Despite an effort to frown, her complexion remained warm and inviting.

"It's not something I talk about. With anyone. And I'd like to keep it that way." He wanted nothing more than to tell her everything. "It's not safe for you to be here."

"Safe?" The frown deepened. Her eyes narrowed and sliced through his defenses. "What you did in Amman to rescue me was incredible. I get the whole secrecy thing, but all I want to do is talk. Just the two of us. I'm not here to sell you out."

Cross's heart leapt inside his chest cavity. Could he trust her? He wanted to trust her. What if he told her everything? Would she go public with his story?

He trusted her, but paused a bit longer to sell hesitation.

"OK, but it's a long story. And I'm going to need some coffee."

Christine realized she hadn't stopped smiling the entire trip out of Mechanicsville to Richmond. John explained there would be less chance of a church member interrupting them if they went somewhere discreet. Fine by her. It meant more time getting to know him.

During the drive, he peppered her with questions about her recovery and her time spent with family. Christine wanted to interrupt with questions of her own, but let him carry the conversation so he would feel safe divulging all his secrets later.

John guided his humble sedan into a spot in the sparse parking garage. Exiting the vehicle, he led her out of the garage and around a corner to a quaint cobblestoned cul-de-sac lined by tall buildings on all its sides.

They approached a white building labeled with a large sign reading SHOCKOE ESPRESSO & ROASTERY. John grabbed the handle and held the glass door open for her to walk through. A gentleman. She couldn't remember the last time she'd been around one of those.

The scent of fresh roasted coffee beans saturated the interior. Everything from the floor, to the ceiling, to the walls, to the furniture seemed to be fashioned from old wood and brick. A handful of young college students sat engrossed in laptop computers, and one or two older men rubbed their hands in newspaper ink.

John picked a table near the back, and he excused himself to the counter. Christine settled into the chair, made of wood of course, and examined a painting by a local artist, hung on the wall. Still life of fruit. Not bad.

John returned with two paper cups in hand. "Mocha latte." He slid hers onto the table.

"And yours?" Christine asked as she let the cup warm her palms.

"Black coffee."

Christine stuck her tongue out and wrinkled her nose. "Are you trying to punish yourself?"

John only laughed, took a small sip, and smacked his lips. "All right, reporter, fire away."

She took a sip from her own cup and waved her hand. "Look, this isn't an off-the-record, on-the-record sort of thing. I truly am grateful for you saving my life, and I would never want to do anything to compromise you or those you love. I have this problem where I have to know everything about something I'm interested in."

"So you're interested in me?"

The temperature in her cheeks rose. "Well, who wouldn't be after your heroics in Jordan?" She took another drink from her cup, intentionally lifting it higher to shield the blush on her face.

"I wouldn't say heroics. In fact, that wasn't how we'd planned it."

Christine set the cup back on the table. "See," she said. "That's what I'm curious about. Who's the 'we'? The army denied any knowledge of your existence or role in the operation."

"Well, of course they did. That's usually how these things go when you've got an operative undercover in the field. Covert ops are never divulged to the public until after enough time has passed. Ever hear of Tony Mendez?"

"Yeah, the Canadian Caper."

John smirked and saluted her with his coffee cup. "Good job. Most people only know the story by the name Argo."

Christine grinned. "I saw the movie, but I wanted to research the real event. Ended up writing an essay on it for graduate school."

His eyes locked on to hers, and she felt as if she'd won another piece of his admiration. She pulled her hands away from the latte, hoping to regulate the rising temperature in the room.

"Hollywood tends to mix up their facts. For one, CIA personnel are always referred to as agents and not officers, the correct term. With the Canadian Caper, it was two officers and not one like the movie portrays." John paused to sip on the coffee. "Anyway, the operation was executed in 1980, but we didn't make the details public until 1997. I guess that means you've got until, oh, 2033 to write your story."

John Cross would have to work harder than that to corner her. She grunted and took a long swig of the latte. "Well, sounds like I've got my first answer." She smirked and narrowed her eyes.

"Excuse me?"

"You work for the CIA." She leaned back in her chair to wait for him to pick his jaw up off the table. "You said 'we.' Mendez was Central Intelligence."

"I could've meant anything."

"Come on. Who else in the intelligence community is going to send an undercover operative on a rescue mission in the Middle East?"

John's grin failed to distract the flash of embarrassment in his face. "I hear the State Department's got some guys."

His hands rested on the table. Christine slid hers closer and grabbed his in a soft embrace. "You can trust me. I'm not going to write this story now or in 2033. I don't care. I just want to get to know the man who gave me a second chance at life."

John sat still, his head bowed as he stared at her hands over his. His fingers pulsed in concert with her own. Then he straightened, drew his hands back, grabbed the cup of coffee, and looked up at her with a confident gaze. "I'm all yours." The pigment in his cheeks darkened a shade. "I mean, ask away."

Christine straightened in her chair. "What's your real name?"

"I told you my name. It's John. John Cross."

"Really? It's not a cover name?"

"Nope. Boring, I know. And yes, I work for Central Intelligence." Christine smiled.

"Well, I should say I *worked* for Central Intelligence. I don't anymore."

Christine shifted closer to the table in her seat. "What? Why?"

"I joined the army when I was eighteen. I had no family, really. I was in foster homes most of my teenage years, so I just worked hard at being the best soldier I could be. Turns out, I could be one of the best. I would volunteer for tours, take spots from guys who had wives or kids. I don't think I really cared if I ever came back to the States. It didn't take long for the brass at Langley to notice."

"Foster kid who wanted to live on the battlefield sounds like a star recruit."

"Exactly. And they pay really well."

"Let me guess." Christine grinned. "They fitted you for a tuxedo and a five-thousand-dollar watch."

"More like Kevlar and cargo pants. The CIA was interested in fearless orphans, sure, but I piqued their interest for a different reason."

"Which was?"

John drew a deep breath. "I earned expert marksmanship badges in just about every handheld weapon they let me fire. I'm especially good with a rifle."

Christine's imagination replayed the single impossible shot he'd made on the highway in Amman just a couple of short weeks ago. "You are good," she said, then blushed again. Why did she find the conversation so awkward and enchanting at the same time?

"Trust me when I say I've gotten a little rusty in my time off."

"You haven't gotten to that part yet."

John snuck a chug of his coffee. "Right. So they liked what they saw and wanted me to be part of a special unit."

His shoulders drooped, and a faint trace of moisture outlined his eyes. Was he getting emotional? That wouldn't do. Christine's own emotions would crack if he wore his out in the open. She held her breath and waited for him to continue.

"I . . . they, um. I was asked to take on some . . . jobs. Jobs that were hard for others."

"What kind of jobs?" Why did she just ask that question? Did she want him to start sobbing? She could only imagine what kind of jobs the CIA was involved in that no one ever knew about. But her journalistic instincts wouldn't let her leave the question unasked.

John blinked a few times, then stood up. "I think for this next part, I'm gonna need some more coffee. And you?"

"Thank you." She handed him her empty cup.

He turned and marched toward the smiling barista at the counter.

Christine stared at the back of his head. Too bad she couldn't peer inside and see what he was hiding. While the goateed man refilled their cups, John leaned against the countertop and drew deep breaths. She drew her own, then read the spines of a collection of books resting on a shelf built into the window frame across the room. Anything to distract her mind from lingering on him.

He returned with fresh brew. "Sorry," he started. "This is the first time I've ever told someone this."

Well, if he didn't cry, she might still have to. She found a chip in the tabletop to pick with her fingernail and considered guzzling her coffee to wash the lump in her throat down. It wouldn't work anyway.

"The CIA recruited me to do wet work."

She shot him a puzzled expression and hoped for a definition.

He averted his eyes. "Targeted killings."

The admission shook Christine, and her grip on the coffee cup loosened. She squeezed her fingers together before it could fall out of her hand. "You . . . you were an assassin?"

John continued to avoid eye contact and cleared his throat. "Most of my ops were selective assassinations, yes."

She stared at him. Nausea crawled up her throat. Her heart rate accelerated to a furious pace, but something else weighed it down. Invisible knots formed in her lungs and prevented their normal function.

He was a murderer. But it was just his job. It was for national security purposes. He wasn't a murderer, just following orders.

Wait. Christine caught herself. Was she trying to justify his actions? He seemed so perfect.

John leaned across the table and caught her gaze in his. "It was wrong, Christine. I know that now. But I didn't then. I followed orders. And I was good at it. It was the first time in my life I felt appreciated, needed, even loved. I know it sounds weird. I found my identity working for the CIA."

"How many?"

"I'm sorry?"

Christine folded her arms across her chest. Expressing outrage would be justified. She could hold him accountable for his actions, help him understand the depth of his past decisions. Then call a cab and never see him again. Or stay. Try to understand his journey. Reconcile who he was with who he had been. She doubted the results. People never truly changed. "How many people did you kill?"

"It wasn't like that. I didn't keep count. We would complete a mission, then file it away and lie about the pain."

She decided to stay.

He leaned back in his chair. "After a while, I just felt numb every time I would be in the field. Like I wasn't a person anymore. Just an asset. Then one day I was tracking a target in Spain and by chance sat through a Catholic Mass at the Seville Cathedral." John laughed through his nose. "I didn't even understand the service. My Spanish is . . . barely conversational." His eyes glassed over, as if focused on the memory. "I was just sitting there, staring at a crucifix. And then . . . I can't explain it, but it just made sense."

"What made sense?"

"I wasn't sure at first. I just knew this man was drawing me to him. All I wanted was to know more about him. The one on the cross. Jesus Christ."

Christine started laughing and put her hand to her mouth, certain she was being rude. "I'm so sorry. This is just . . . I can't believe it. Well, I guess I should. After all, I did just find you in a church preaching a sermon about Jesus."

John laughed with her. "True. It's kind of obvious. I'd heard about the Bible and Jesus from attending church some as a kid, but whether I was too young or what I heard was too convoluted, it just never stuck. I left the church. I found an English Bible in a bookshop, took it back to my safe house, and read it."

"Wait." Christine held up a hand. "What about your target?"

"I let him go. His trail went cold, and the operation failed. Not the first time an op had ever failed, but the first time it was on my shoulders. I got pulled off for a few weeks and was sent to a counselor in case I was having a psychological break. I spent the time consuming the Bible, but I never told anyone. When I went back into the field, it was different. I couldn't take a life anymore without unbearable guilt, no matter the circumstances. I mean, my missions were always justifiable, but I knew it was wrong. I couldn't do it anymore. So I quit."

"Just like that?"

"Just like that."

"When did all this happen?"

"A little over a year ago." He emptied his second cup of coffee.

Christine laid her palms flat against the table. "So how did you end up in Jordan the Saturday before last?"

"I wasn't really doing much after I left. I held a few odd jobs here and there, but I didn't need the money. I never spent anything anyway, so it gathered dust in a savings account. I tried out churches, read books, found some Internet forums to ask questions on. Then one day I get a call. Members of the National Liberation Army in Colombia abducted an American businessman. Assets were on the ground, but I spent some time there and knew it better. My former boss asked me to do him a favor and assist in the exfiltration."

Christine nodded. "So you did."

"Yes. I think I was at a point where I wasn't sure if I could do anything else, and the idea of a rescue mission instead of, well, a wet job, seemed like just the retribution."

"Did you save him? The businessman?"

"Clean grab. The op went off without a hitch, so I took a few more. A handful of rescues, some reconnaissance. You're my sixth."

"Rescue?"

John affirmed with a crooked grin.

"Wow." She fell back into her seat and sighed. "Now I regret promising you I wouldn't tell this story. It would make my career."

He laughed. She liked hearing it.

"In a strange way," he said. "I think I was seeking penance. Maybe if I saved as many people as I had killed, it would make a difference."

Her heart leapt.

CHAPTER ELEVEN

THEY LEFT THE coffee shop as the afternoon waned and the employees swept floors and shut down equipment. The sharp glow of the setting sun obscured the skyline of Richmond in the mirrors of the car as they traveled back to Mechanicsville. Cross dominated the conversation again. He couldn't help it. He wanted to tell her everything.

For the full extent of the half-hour drive, he spoke about Rural Grove. She couldn't stop smiling as he regaled her with the story of the business meeting where he'd been voted on as the new minister. The smile remained as they arrived at the parsonage and exited the car.

He paused after opening the front door and turned to stare at the silhouette of the church against the burning gray sky.

Christine mimicked his posture.

"Sorry," he said. "Habit. I always take a last look before I go inside. It helps ground me. Reminds me why I'm here."

Christine looked away from the church, and he could feel her eyes studying his face. "You really love that church, don't you?"

He grinned and caught her gaze with his own. "You could say that." He waved her inside and followed. Contrary to habit, he flipped the wall switch, and warm incandescent light basked the interior.

"What do you mean?" she asked, though the contents of the living room seemed to captivate her.

"I love the church, but not the building. The church is really the people. Here, I'll show you." Cross headed for the kitchen, Christine on his heels. He flipped another switch, and the track light over the island countertop served as a spotlight for a tall, cylindrical plastic container. A sticky note on the container read in bold black letters, "The only medicine you need—Mrs. T."

Christine read the note aloud, then rubbed her fingers against the lid.

"Go ahead," Cross said with a laugh. "Open it."

She popped the lid open and leaned forward to catch the first whiff of the homemade meal preserved inside. She chuckled. "Chicken noodle. It smells wonderful."

"Delivered while we were gone. Mrs. T.—Templeton, that is—has diagnosed me with some kind of illness and wants to make sure I'm taken care of."

"How sweet."

The sentiment sounded genuine, though Cross felt everything sounded genuine from her lips. He motioned around the empty kitchen with open palms. "It's all I have to offer you for dinner."

Christine stuck her nose in the air and grinned. "Sounds wonderful. You'll have to thank Mrs. T. for me." Her eyes widened. "Please tell me she's married to a Mr. T."

Cross laughed as he opened a cabinet and retrieved a pair of bowls. "You mind if I ask you a question this time?"

"No."

"Have you ever attended church before today?"

"Come on, now. Just because I work in network news doesn't mean I'm a complete heathen."

He snorted and searched a drawer for the ladle. Christine cleared her throat, and he popped up to see her balancing a large spoon on her index finger.

"Mrs. T. knows how to take care of you, all right."

Cross sighed and grabbed the spoon from her hand. He filled both bowls with the soup, though in truth the chunks of chicken and thick noodles outweighed the broth. "You haven't answered my question."

Christine lifted her shoulders and pulled her arms tight against her body. "I used to attend when I was a child. With my parents. They're Methodist."

"But you're not."

"Same story as you. Not all of the army, CIA stuff. The church part. It just never stuck." Christine took a bite from her bowl and closed her eyes. "This has to be the best chicken noodle soup I've ever eaten."

"Not many home-cooked meals growing up?"

Christine waved her spoon in Cross's face. "Hey now, this is my interrogation. Let's get back to you." She dipped the spoon back into her soup. "You said back at the coffee shop that you don't work for the CIA anymore."

"That's kind of a funny story. I quit again. That Saturday, when I got back."

"Why?"

"The other ops I ran as a contract officer were simple, noncombat. The intel we got on your location made it seem like I could walk you out the front door. But we found a party instead."

"I wouldn't have called it a party."

Cross balanced the spoon against his bowl and breathed deeply. "Christine, I wasn't ready for what happened. I don't know how you're going to feel about this, but I don't think either of us would have made it out alive if it had come down to me taking a life."

Christine placed her own spoon on the countertop and pressed her palm against his bicep. "There's some of this I'm still trying to wrap my brain around, but there's one thing I know for sure: whether you felt like you had to or not, you saved my life without killing a single person. That either makes you brilliant or lucky. And I'd take both."

Cross smiled and resumed eating. "Well," he said after a quiet moment. "There was the guy I threw out of the car. He might have broken a bone or two."

They shared a laugh. Her eyes glistened, and he tried to think of something else he could say to keep her smiling.

A thought crossed his mind, and he blurted, "Sleep."

"Excuse me?"

"I'm sorry." Blood rushed to his face. "I meant to ask where you're staying."

"What makes you think I'm staying?"

Cross cleared his throat, though nothing blocked his airways. "I could get you to Richmond International in time for the last flight if we left now and I broke a few traffic laws on the way. And the 66 Northeast Regional left from Main Street Station . . ." Cross paused to check his watch. "Twenty minutes ago. Besides, you don't seem like a train person."

"Sounds like that's your preferred mode of transportation."

"I know how to get places when I need to. Old habit. And I definitely prefer the sky."

Christine's spoon clanked against her empty bowl. "You're right. I'm staying the night. I've already booked a room at the Hilton near the airport. I was hoping it would be a long interview."

Cross picked up her bowl and placed it on top of his in the sink. He turned back to find her stepping out of the kitchen and into the living room.

"I've noticed something," she called out to him. "About you."

"What's that?" Cross slipped the lid back onto the soup container and placed it in the refrigerator next to the milk. He walked into the living room to find Christine standing in the middle studying his armchair.

She faced him as he entered the room. "This is one of the emptiest houses I've ever seen someone living in."

"I don't have a lot of time to shop for decorative souvenirs."

"No, that's not it."

His comfort with her presence wavered.

She stepped closer to him, her eyes narrowed and her lips pursed. She spoke softer. "I think you still feel guilty about what you've done. The rescue missions. The church. You withhold from yourself and try to give everything you can to others."

Cross's pulse quickened, and a bead of sweat slid down the inside of his arm. Should he be embarrassed? Angry? Indecipherable emotions mixed together. His mind fogged over. What was he doing?

"You're paying for your past. You take no pleasure in food, in con-
venience . . ." She took another step closer to him. Her hair smelled
sweet. ". . . in others."

Run.

Cross's mind snapped back into focus, and he took a step back.

Christine's lips turned down.

"I'm sorry," he said. "But I'm going to have to drive you to your
hotel now."

Cross dropped Christine off at her hotel and agreed to meet her for
breakfast the next morning. She broke the news that she would be
catching a midmorning flight back to New York City. The panic
from her appearance in church that morning subsided. His heart
rate and breathing pattern returned to normal. He fully expected to
be continuing his sermons on the book of Philippians the following
Sunday.

"See you later, exfiltrator," she said with a smile as she exited the car.

He chuckled, remembering the corny line inserted into the Canadian Caper team's final approval the night before flying into Iran to
rescue six American diplomats.

With a polite wave goodbye, Christine disappeared through the front
entrance of the hotel. He waited a long moment, thinking she might
return, and then he decided it would be the worst thing she could do.
He put the old sedan into gear and pulled out onto the roadway, noting the glow of the low-fuel light staring at him from underneath the
steering wheel.

He recalled the handful of relationships he'd had before his conversion to Christianity, though the women only served as playful distrac-
tions more than serious pursuits. Since that day in Seville, the furthest
thing from his mind was a relationship with a woman.

But a year spent practicing asceticism resulted in an abundance of
pent-up desire. Cross said a prayer of thanks for the spiritual inter-

vention that had ended the evening and allowed him to demonstrate respect toward Christine and the pastoral office he now held.

Maybe he was a changed man after all.

He replayed the night in his mind. The emotion, the desire he felt in the coffee shop. He rewound further to the moment he saw her in the church. He wanted to see her, talk to her, tell her everything. But he also saw the consequences. He thought about the congregation. He thought about Al. He could hear Guin's voice in his ear: "You can't hide forever."

He couldn't hide forever. He knew it. So why fight? Christine wasn't going to tell anyone. Cross even considered letting her run with the story of what really happened in Amman. She didn't have to mention the part about his new life as a minister, of course. She could just tell everyone about the heroics of the spy who brought her back from the edge of death. The story would be a sensation.

Her career would be made. They could continue to talk. Maybe he would visit her in New York. She was unique, funny, beautiful. He would visit. Stay for a few days. They could . . .

Stop it.

What was happening? Did he really think he could have some new secret life with Christine in New York? Cross gritted his teeth and swallowed the coarse language fighting its way to his lips. He was losing his grip.

Cross's breathing accelerated, and his grip on the steering wheel tightened. Flashes of his old life reminded him of failed missions. The cause could always be traced to someone else's meddling. In his later years with the CIA, he preferred going alone. Isolation was safe.

Safe.

No. It wasn't right. The plan, his plan, lay crumbled at his feet. He wasn't supposed to make contact. She shouldn't be here. Assured she wouldn't tell his story, the only scenario left was to cut his connection to her. It had been a nice evening, and that was all. He would go back to his new lie.

Life. New life.

He slammed his hand against the dash, warm blood coursing through his veins. He pressed his teeth harder together and held back a verbal tirade. Desire hadn't been the only thing he had buried a year ago. He'd left an angry streak back with his old job at the CIA, and while there was always a flare-up every so often, his attitude was certainly more balanced.

Balance. The key to moving in the right direction. His life had been balanced just so until that beautiful blonde walked through the door. *Lord, help.*

His spirit calmed, and the murkiness dissolved. There was only one thing to do. He had to say goodbye to Christine.

Cross focused on the road in time to catch a glimpse of a billboard for the next exit, advertising several gas station selections. He pointed the car toward the ramp and caught a green light at the intersection. Less than a mile down the road, he found a gas station with a reasonable price.

Four of the six pumps were open, and Cross chose the one closest to the exit. He paid with a bank card and propped his arm against the hood of his car as it guzzled fuel from the hose.

He didn't want to say goodbye, but he had to. She was too intoxicating. Cross's mind sprung to life, and he played out all the possible scenarios for the next morning. He would pick her up and take her to breakfast somewhere bland, like a chain restaurant specializing in breakfast foods. The conversation would be directed toward her, nothing too personal. Work related. The breakfast would last until she needed to depart for the airport. He'd say goodbye. She'd thank him again.

Then he would be fr—

A second look. Christine, breakfast, the church, all wayward thoughts were banished into the darkest corners of his brain as hardwired instinct consumed him. All motion around him froze, and he accounted for every detail at every angle.

At the adjacent pump, a younger bearded man gave a third specific glance in Cross's direction, then nodded.

The dusty red SUV pulled into the lot. Cross had noticed it pass by on the highway sixty seconds earlier.

Two other men, both unshaven, pretended to have a conversation near a dark sedan at the opposite end.

The inside of the adjoining market was lit but devoid of life.

Cross replaced the nozzle of the gas hose in its proper home. In the computerized screen of the pump, he caught the reflection of a knife aimed at the square of his back.

CHAPTER TWELVE

CROSS SPUN AND grabbed the bearded man's wrist, the knife a half inch away from tearing a hole in his suit jacket. He used his attacker's charging momentum and sent the man's fist into the plastic screen cover of the pump. The panel cracked. Blood oozed through the fractures in the plastic.

The bearded man groaned, then attempted to pull his hand free from Cross's grasp. Cross punched into the man's nose with his opposite fist. The man tore his knife hand free and swung the blade at Cross's ear.

Cross dodged. Blood dripped from the man's nostril, and his face contorted. He shrieked and swung again. Cross parried with his left arm and kicked the man's abdomen. The man doubled over, sucking in air.

Rushing footfalls sounded from behind. Cross vaulted the hood of his sedan. His feet barely touched asphalt when another scruffy man with olive skin tackled him from behind into the car. A sharp slice of pain cut through his pinned left shoulder blade. He pulled his right arm free and threw his elbow backward.

Thick bone connected with soft tissue and elicited a shout of distress. The man's embrace relaxed. Cross planted his right foot and ducked his head. He twisted his attacker off his back and slammed him into the driver's-side window. The tough glass held, and the man bounced off. He fell to the pavement.

A third assailant ran for him from behind the sedan. The man with the knife shook away the stars and charged. Cross needed space. He darted across the lot to another set of gas pumps. Movement entered his peripheral vision. Two more men exited the red SUV. Twenty yards to his right. And closing in fast.

Cross veered to his left around the back of knife man's vehicle. A hand caught the neck of his jacket. He pivoted and twisted the jacket in a knot, freeing his arms.

The man paused with the empty jacket in his hands, his mouth agape. This one appeared older, his skin wrinkled. Too many days under a hot sun. The shape of his nose suggested West Asia pedigree. His mouth closed into a growl. He threw the jacket to the ground and charged.

Cross turned into the space between the car and the pump. A hose running into the vehicle blocked his path. He grabbed a squeegee in one hand and the nozzle at the end of the hose in the other. Squeezing the lever tight, he pointed the nozzle in the attacker's direction.

Gasoline spewed. Cross used the squeegee to partially restrict the flow, turning the hose and spout into a makeshift water cannon. His pursuer lifted his hands to block the spray. The man slipped on the greasy pavement. His arm hit the ground with an audible crack.

Cross sensed someone behind him. He dropped the hose and ducked around the dispenser. A knife pierced the plastic sign advertising two-for-one hot dogs where Cross had been standing. Close call.

Three more men descended on him. A bony fist collided with Cross's eye and sent him reeling backward. He swung the squeegee in front of him to buy a half second for the stars to disappear.

A second blade glinted in the stark light overhead. He blocked the strike with the squeegee, but it left him exposed, and another fist connected with the small of his back.

The three didn't let up. He blocked where he needed to and took blows where he could ignore the sting. Escaping a knife-sized hole in his body became his primary focus.

Where's the gun? An attack of this type usually involved firearms. Did they want him alive?

One of them dropped his guard. Cross hooked the man's leg with the squeegee and tugged. The man rotated in midair and crashed into one of his allies. Entangled in each other, they fell to the asphalt.

The man with the knife lunged, but Cross outmatched his speed. A blow with the squeegee sent the dagger sailing. Cross finished the man with a quick strike to the nose.

His first attacker, the one with the bloody nose, arrived with his own knife in hand.

Cross twirled the squeegee like a baton and grinned. "I've got all night."

Behind his opponent, the passenger-side door to the red SUV opened. A hulking monster in a leather jacket stepped from the car, a Colt CM901 assault rifle propped against his hip.

The squeegee dropped from Cross's hand and slid across the pavement. He sprinted as fast as he could in the opposite direction, a line of trees just across an empty grassy lot his only chance at escape.

He stole a quick look over his shoulder. The monster raised the gun and aligned it with Cross's head. The thick fumes of the fuel spill warped the man's silhouette in a grotesque fashion. Cross cut a path left, confident the marksman would lead his target.

The loud crack of gunfire cued the sonic boom of a gasoline explosion. Force lifted Cross's body from the ground and tossed him forward. He slammed against the dirt and rolled to a stop. Pain throbbed from his shoulder to his feet.

Ringing filled his ears.

His head pounded.

Heat crawled across his clothes.

Cross forced his body a few more rolls across the grass to extinguish the flames. No longer on fire, he rested on his stomach and marveled at his good fortune. He'd never expected the blast of the weapon to actually ignite the fumes. It wasn't impossible, but close to it.

Less good fortune, more divine providence the likely reason.

He pushed up on an elbow and looked back at the station. A wall of fire stood in place of the pump. The car beside it was a heap of burning twisted metal. Several of the men lay sprawled against the asphalt.

There was no sign of the man with the rifle.

CHAPTER THIRTEEN

SITTING UP ON his knees, Cross felt a pinch at his left shoulder blade. He winced and rubbed his fingers over the area. A finger slipped through a hole in his dress shirt, and he recognized the familiar mixture of blood and exposed muscle.

That monster had actually shot him.

A graze, not unlike a handful of other wounds Cross had sustained in the field. He took a deep breath and closed his eyes. Through the crackle of the burning gas pump, he made out the faint sound of a police siren.

His eyes snapped open. He couldn't be here when the police arrived. There would be too many questions. He pushed himself up and surveyed the wreckage.

The hulking man who had fired at Cross sprinted straight for him, the rifle left behind somewhere. Black ash covered the man's face, arms, and clothes. The whites of his eyes reflected the glow of the fire and intensified the snarl cutting across his visage.

"You've got to be kidding me," Cross muttered under his breath. He turned and ran for the trees. The sizzle of the blaze spreading through the filling station grew faint. The wail of emergency vehicles overpowered all other sounds.

He crossed the border of the tree line and picked up speed. The ringing in his ears subsided. Cross focused on the trail ahead until even the sirens were a whisper. One wrong step and he would lose his footing to a rut in the ground or an exposed root.

The crunch of underbrush.

Controlled breathing.

Another set of footfalls.

Cross parsed the ambient noise in his ear and pinpointed the sound of his pursuer. Each step through the forest louder than the last. The monster was gaining.

Another sonic boom shifted his concentration. Did another pump fail? Was the entire station leveled?

No, not an explosion.

A train.

Cross strained his eyes to see through the trees and spotted the telltale break the railway left in the landscape. A faint glow speared the darkness across the track, and a second roar of the train's horn shook the surrounding tree trunks.

The air swirled as Cross approached the track. The locomotive came bearing down. The power of its bulk pressed against the vegetation on either side. Trees, bushes, even blades of grass hid their faces from its terrible path.

Cross emerged from the forest as the engine flew by on a northbound heading. Each freight car passed in a blur, and though the weight of its cargo meant the train couldn't be traveling more than thirty-five to forty miles per hour, it resembled a rocket skimming the surface of the earth, looking for a target to eliminate.

Cross ran as fast as he could alongside the track. The motion of the train slowed by half, though his odds had not improved by much.

He suspected the man chasing him was out of the trees and ready to follow, but chose not to steal a glance behind to confirm and risk losing speed. Instead, Cross maintained focus on each successive freight car as it passed.

By fortune the train slowed, perhaps in reaction to an intersection with a road ahead. Or was it divine intervention again? Either way, he took the chance. As a boxcar passed, he jumped and grabbed the rungs of a ladder fastened against its side.

His legs swung inches above the stream of gravel flowing beneath the carriage. He hoisted himself to the next rung and wrapped a foot around one of the ladder's side rails. Squeezing his body against the side of the freight car, he paused for a respite. He took a deep breath, then looked back down the length of the train and spotted the other man leaping for a ladder three boxcars down.

The man slipped off the first rung but caught the second. His feet bounced against the ground. Gravel threatened to wrench him free and claim his body. With inhuman strength, he heaved himself to the top of the ladder one handed.

Cross groaned. Couldn't it ever be easy? He bounded up his own ladder and onto the roof of the freight car. He stood and looked behind him as wind pummeled his back. The man stood on top of his boxcar and glared. Cross detected a clenched jaw and indignation in the man's eyes in spite of the dark distance between them.

Cross studied as much of his opponent as the brief moment allowed. He was big, unnaturally so, and wearing dark stained cargo pants with the leather jacket. Tiny pricks of hair yearning to grow long again obscured the shine you might expect from the man's bald head. Hard muscle bulged beneath his jacket arms, though a knife or small hand-gun could still be hidden in any number of discreet areas.

The train whizzed across a bridge, and the landscape opened to display all eight lanes of Interstate 295 bathed in a blue shade of moonlight. The train slowed to a crawl, traffic froze, and the moon doubled in size as Cross evaluated the possible escape scenarios.

Or battle.

Darkness swallowed them as swaths of tree leaves and branches blocked the moon. Cross ran and took a flying leap from the rear of the freight car. The man jumped as well and landed in step on the opposite carriage. Neither diverted their gaze as they ran full speed toward each other.

Cross was convinced he could take the man in a fair fight, his speed an adequate match to the man's size. But he had a personal opinion that Mao Zedong was wrong.

A shrewd defense was the best defense.

The distance to the gap in the two boxcars closed at a rapid pace. The other man lowered his head, likely in preparation to gain first strike in a flying leap. Cross mirrored the move to sell his intent.

The man's boot slapped against the edge of the carriage and pushed away. He sailed into the air, the force of his jump intensified by the forward momentum of the train, and stretched out his arms like giant cat claws. A fierce war cry escaped his mouth.

Cross let his own feet slip out from under him and fell on his back against the roof of the train car. His momentum carried him off the edge, and he slipped between the two boxcars and landed on the coupling. He looked up and witnessed the man's feet disappear from view as he surely tumbled across the roof empty handed and stunned.

Cross shifted his weight, pushed off the coupling, and grabbed the edge of the opposite car. With brute force, he launched his body up and over the edge. He rolled to stop on his hands and knees and looked back at the car he had just vacated.

Already on his feet and fueled by rage, the other man charged again. Cross took off across the roof and scanned the carriages ahead for any sign of his next move. The train carried only goods and was devoid of human activity. Bulk commodities were his only allies.

He jumped to another boxcar and kept running. In the moonlight, he glimpsed a bulkhead flatcar with a load of downed tree trunks. Treacherous footing would mean a loss in pace.

But it could also mean an advantage.

Cross glanced over his shoulder to spy the man leaping onto the same boxcar. The window of opportunity was tight. Increasing his speed, Cross jumped from the boxcar to the top of the log stack.

His foot slipped on the volatile surface area. He crashed against the trunk and pinned his bad shoulder under his own weight. He swallowed a cry of pain and forced his eyes to remain wide open.

Jumping to his feet, he picked his way across the top of the wood with the care of a high-wire artist and brainstormed another plan. Two thick straps bound the logs to the flatcar. Two metal bars at either end of the car provided an additional layer of security. An idea formed. The strap would be easy.

The metal bar not as much.

Two steps from the end of the stack of logs, his foot slipped again, this time by design. Cross twisted his body against the trunks and grabbed hold of the taut strap. He rode the strap to the bottom of the flatcar. His shoes planted firm against the metal flooring.

He found the ratchet at the base of the strap and released the mechanism. The rocking of the train shifted the logs toward him a scant inch as the opposite strap held firm and the metal brace performed its solitary function.

Cross glanced back to judge his timing and saw a bend in the track ahead as well as the man leaping from the boxcar to the top of the logs. Time was running out. Grabbing the metal bar, Cross swung himself around and searched for the release lever.

The man kept his balance against the trunks as he ran.

Cross found the lever and kicked it as hard as he could. Nothing.

The man was halfway there. The bend in the track closed in.

Cross kicked again, harder, but the lever refused to budge.

The man was on top of him now, the boxcar ahead taking the turn.

Cross brought the full force of his weight down on the lever. It broke free. The metal bar fell away just as the flatcar rounded the bend. It tilted, and the free end of the logs rolled off the edge of the car.

Cross leapt to the bulkhead and out of the path of the crashing tree trunks. He looked up to see the man flailing as the logs disappeared beneath his feet. A trunk slipped off the flatcar and impaled the soil.

The force of the moving train against the solid earth ripped the log in two. Splinters rained around them, and the remaining logs tumbled about in a chaotic attempt to find rest.

Cross heard the man cry out and saw him slip between two logs, his torso pinned by the weight pressing against him. Cross had gained his advantage.

A tank car was next in the freight line. Cross jumped across and scaled a ladder to the top. He turned back to survey the damage.

The logs couldn't settle, and to his disappointment they shifted again, freeing the man. Propelled by sheer adrenaline, the man leapt across the moving tree trunks and headed straight for the tank car.

Cross took off again. Who was this guy? No man had that kind of stamina. His hunter must be a government experiment turned super solider. Cross realized a shrewd defense against the man was futile. Which left him only one other option.

As he jumped from the tank car to the next boxcar, Cross slowed his pace. He looked back and took measure of the distance between them. He needed to ensure the timing of the confrontation if he had any chance of taking the man by surprise.

A hopper was next. He jumped to it and slowed again. A last glance gave him the information he needed, and he shortened his stride once more before his leap to the proceeding car.

The thud of boots alerted him to the man's proximity. Halfway across the car, he dug his heels and rotated his body. With his head lowered, Cross tackled the man around the waist. They crashed against the metal roof. The man bellowed in pain as Cross pressed his weight down on top of him.

The man thrashed against Cross's embrace. Slick blood smeared across his abdomen, an injury from the logs no doubt, made holding him still difficult. Cross shifted his weight to one side. The man rotated his body to try to break free. Digging a knee into the man's back, Cross shifted an arm up and around his neck.

He stood and pulled the man to his knees. He braced his chokehold with his other arm and pressed his bicep into the man's throat. The man dug his fingernails into Cross's arm, his mouth open in an inaudible gasp for air. Four more seconds and the man would be lying unconscious on the roof of the boxcar.

Three.

Two.

The man grabbed Cross's bad shoulder and pinched down. Cross cried out, and his chokehold relaxed. His opponent pushed off the roof of the train car and used his back to lift Cross into the air.

Cross flew over the man and landed hard on his stomach against the metal, sliding at a high rate to the edge of the boxcar. He clawed at the tin in a frantic attempt to halt his momentum, but the boxcar refused to help.

The roof disappeared beneath him as he plummeted toward darkness.

CHAPTER FOURTEEN

CROSS STARED WITH open eyes as the ground welcomed his death with open arms. So this was how he'd go out. Useless, his hands spread before him. They'd offer no salvation.

Tentacles wrapped around his ankle, his freefall jerked to a stop, and his body collided with the boxcar. He grabbed for anything that would help him back on. He saw the handle to the door of the boxcar within reach and thrust his hand toward it. Too late. The handle slipped away as he was pulled back onto the car's roof.

Cross twisted onto his back and saw the big man holding his foot. A fog fell over his brain as he failed to comprehend the reason for his deliverance. The big man still looked ready to rip Cross's limbs clean from his body.

With his other hand, the man grabbed Cross by his shirt collar and pulled his torso close. Releasing Cross's foot, the man balled his fist and punched Cross in the jaw.

Cross took two more blows to the face before he could react. The man's fist hurtled toward him for a fourth time, but this time Cross caught it against his open palm. He twisted, and the man cried out as a ligament in his elbow snapped.

The man lifted Cross from the roof and threw him across its length. Cross rolled to his feet and met the man charging him again. Fists and knees exchanged blows; neither fighter wavered.

Cross aimed his most aggressive strikes at the man's lower stomach underneath his weakened elbow. He found a wide opening and shoved his kneecap into the spot. The man grunted in pain and fell backward.

Cross jumped on the man, pinned his good arm with a foot, and punched him across his nose. The man's body relaxed, but he managed to remain conscious.

"Who are you?" Cross shouted above the rushing wind.

The man babbled broken sentences in a different language, but Cross couldn't pick out a recognizable word.

"Slow down," he said. "I can't understand you." The language sounded familiar, and though he could recognize major dialects, this particular one remained foreign. "Why did you save me? Who sent you?" The questions proved pointless as the man spouted more intelligible words.

Suddenly, a word stood out among the others. He'd heard it before. What did the man say? Kalin? Caleen? It sounded Haitian, possibly Romanian. No, the man had Western Asia features. Cross focused his mind on the region, marking off country after country until . . .

"Kadin." That was the word. A Turkish word. It meant . . .

Rage filled his heart, the beast buried long ago reaching forth from its emotional grave. His eyebrows tightened and nostrils flared. Cross clenched the leather jacket in his fists and pulled the man closer as his lips parted and he bared his teeth.

"What do you want with her?" Cross demanded.

"Kadin." *The woman*. The man continued with a furious string of unfamiliar words followed by another Cross recognized all too well: "ölecek."

Die.

The anger seized Cross by the throat, and he yelled, "No!" The temptation to heave the man from the roof and throw him from the train consumed him. Something hard impacted his chest. All the air escaped his lungs.

The man's body tensed underneath him, and a leg slipped between them. A quick shove sent Cross sprawling. Still on his back, Cross looked up expecting to see the sole of a boot aimed at his nose.

Instead, the man stood near the edge of the boxcar, an arm wrapped gingerly around his waist. The blood from his earlier injury spread in a wider circumference, and the moonlight highlighted the sudden pallor of his skin. His chest struggled to expand with each heavy draw of breath.

The man's head turned and stared ahead. Cross followed his gaze and saw a short break in the trees, the gap spanned by a bridge.

The man looked back at Cross and emitted a sputter of laughter. "You may have won this time," he said in English, "but I know where *she* is. See you soon." He spun and jumped from the train as it passed over the bridge.

Cross stood and ran to the edge of the boxcar in time to see the man treading water in a shallow river below the bridge before more trees obscured his view.

Exhaustion overwhelmed Cross, and he dropped to his knees before falling backward, prostrate against the roof of the boxcar. He watched the countless stars set in motion at the beginning of time.

His heavy eyelids slid shut as the last ounce of adrenaline drained, and he slipped out of consciousness.

CHAPTER FIFTEEN

A SUDDEN JOLT woke Cross from his slumber. He opened his eyes and noticed the stars were invisible in the warm glow of artificial light filling the sky. The boxcar beneath him no longer rocked to and fro.

In the stillness, he heard a distant voice. Then another. Now some footsteps against gravel. Cross strained his ears to perceive the words, expecting to hear Turkish, convinced his assailants had tracked him.

Not Turkish. English. The crass kind. The words reminded him of his own pre-conversion vocabulary. In his new life, he preferred abstaining from such language as much as possible.

The conversation grew in strength.

"I get the bar failure, but the strap?"

"I don't know, Jerry. Some clown probably didn't bother securing the ratchet, and it just worked itself loose."

The train had reached its destination while he was unconscious. Cross slowly edged his body away from the side where the conversation was taking place. He felt along the roof of the boxcar until his fingers touched air.

Gripping the edge of the car, Cross slid his legs over the side and hung against the cold metal. The rumble of an approaching truck disguised the exchange on the opposite side of the train. Cross waited until the truck passed behind the train, then released his hold on the boxcar and dropped to the gravel.

The car blocked his view into the train yard on his left. Two more tracks lay on the right, followed by a service road and a line of trees. Cross sprinted across the two open tracks and the service road. He hit the forest and pressed his body against a wide tree trunk. He stole a glance around the tree but saw no alarm raised. He drew a few deep breaths, then rotated his wrist until he could read his watch by the moonlight.

One o'clock. Four hours since he fell asleep.

Cross kicked the tree and shook his head. Without knowing the speed of the train, other stops, or how long it had sat in the yard, there would be no way he could measure the distance he had just traveled.

Wherever the train had taken him, finding a way to get back to Christine was all that mattered. The thought of her in danger propelled him onward. Cross picked his way through the trees until they parted, and he found himself on a narrow street.

He moved down the sidewalk away from the train yard. A reflective sign on the opposite side of the road read BASHFORD LANE.

Bashford Lane. He knew that street. It'd been years ago, but he could recall a meal shared with a bespectacled yoga instructor. She was a redhead. They had dined on baked moussaka and baklava. That was it, a Greek restaurant. Vaso's Kitchen.

His heart skipped a beat, and Cross broke into a full run down the sidewalk. Within seconds he reached the intersection of Bashford Lane and George Washington Memorial Parkway.

Cross knew exactly where he was. Alexandria, Virginia, 7.3 miles due south of the heart of the nation's capital.

A couple of taxis drove by, but Cross chose to punish his repentant spirit with the chilly two-and-a-half-hour walk into Arlington. As he walked alongside the parkway, he pictured the face of the man from the train. His stomach knotted.

His rage on the train was unexpected and uncharacteristic of his life the past year and a half. The truth bore down on him like the freight train. All the pride of living in relative peace since his conversion was his downfall that night. He hadn't really changed. Only buried what was destined to be eternally true about his heart.

He was a killer.

He would've murdered the man. He was convinced of that. And it soured him. In less than fourteen hours, Cross's quiet, penitent existence had been upturned. Probably deserved.

New questions arose. The men were after Christine. They had to be. His tracks were too clean. It couldn't be a coincidence they'd arrived on the same day. They'd followed her. But why?

Could they be connected to the men who'd held her in Jordan? It was the most likely scenario. But that didn't add up. Christine was a journalist, not a high-profile politician. Why come all the way back to the States to get revenge on a botched media stunt? The Alliance of Islamic Military was reckless, not senseless.

They wanted her, the one fact he knew without a doubt. He replayed the man's words over and over again in his mind, trading the rising anger for a resolve to answer the compounding questions. Why would they want Christine?

Entry into the country was not impossible for terrorists, though it required a wealth of resources funneled from sympathetic officials. With the right help, Cross could determine the origin of the hit squad and perhaps even the identities of each individual. Of course, that meant making a phone call.

The phone call he didn't want to make.

Simpson would relish the return of the prodigal son, especially a son on his knees begging for the full force of Central Intelligence by his side. But it was the only play he had. Unless . . .

Simpson didn't have to know. Cross didn't need the entirety of CIA resources. A single person could access the databases needed to spot a sudden influx of cash into known terrorist markets. And no flags would be triggered. It would be a routine search.

The only caveat was if she would agree to be discreet.

Sometime after 3:00 a.m., the obnoxious tone of her smartphone rudely snatched a deep sleep from Guin Sullivan. In truth, early morning emergency phone calls were the norm. This particular early morning, however, the voice at the other end of the call proved to not be that of her superior.

"Guin, it's John."

A dream? The throbbing in her head said otherwise. Why would John be calling her? The beating of her heart matched the rhythm in her head, and she sat up in her bed. His departure from the building weeks before convinced her he was to be nothing more than a pleasant memory. But he called. Not something she'd expected.

"I need you to do something, and I need you to keep it quiet."

Disoriented, she interjected with more emotion than was becoming of her, "Cross, what's wrong. Are you OK?"

"I'm fine. Meet me at 1111 Lee Highway, Arlington. Unit number two thousand eight. Bring a computer."

A soft beep echoed in her ear, and the call ended just as her mind cleared. She threw back the duvet and sped up her already quick routine. The car she hired arrived just as she shut the front door to her town home and finished pulling on her jacket.

She checked her watch after being dropped off at a beautiful thirty-story tower called the Waterview. A half hour since he'd called. He'd be grateful for her prompt response.

She entered the elevator and tapped her foot as it rose to the top floor. The elevator doors glided apart, and her suspicions were confirmed. This level of the Waterview was home to luxury penthouse apartments.

The doors slid apart. She stepped from the elevator and, confident the hallway was quiet, slipped her Glock 26 from the shoulder holster under her jacket and held it tight against her chest. She cradled her laptop in her other arm and held it over the handgun.

Turning a corner, she came to the door for unit 2008 at the end of the hallway. She stood still at the door as her finger casually disengaged the safety on the Glock.

No need to knock. He would let her in.

The door opened wide, and John stood on the other side, arms down, fatal target areas on his body exposed. His gray suit pants and white dress shirt reeked as bad as they looked. His face bore a handful of puffy black-and-blue bruises. That explained the damp dish towel in his hand. She noticed a blood stain surrounding a hole in the fabric on the right shoulder of his shirt.

She gave him a wide-eyed once-over. "You look like—"

"You should see the other guy." He looked at the laptop in her hand, then back at her eyes and flashed a grin. "Would you like to come in or just shoot me in the doorway?"

Guin drew the Glock from its hiding place and pointed it at his forehead. "You tell me, Officer Cross. I get a phone call from someone who isn't supposed to be calling, asking me to meet said retiree at a clandestine location and bring sensitive CIA equipment. I'm going to guess you don't need help setting up a router for your home wireless network."

John kept his hands down and eyes level, signaling cooperation. "Guin, you know me. This isn't a setup."

"Anybody can be turned, Cross."

John sighed and brought the dish towel to his bruised eye. He turned and walked into the penthouse.

"John, I'm serious. Get back here," Guin called out after him, pouring as much annoyance into her voice as she could.

"I'm not in the mood."

Guin rolled her eyes and dropped the Glock to her side. She crossed the threshold to the penthouse and kicked the door shut behind her. Though of a modest size, the interior was an open floor plan with floor-to-ceiling windows on two sides.

The eyesore of a partially constructed tower dissected the dark horizon and dashed the promise of a breathtaking view of the dormant capital lying just across the Potomac River. She nodded toward it.

"Looks like the new INR construction's going to lower your resale value."

John gazed out the window. "Beats me how they even convinced Congress to let them build on Roosevelt Island."

"Eh, that island is a big waste of space," Guin said as she studied every detail of the penthouse, sparse as it was. The only furniture was a thick, plush couch in the center of expensive hardwood. To her left lay the kitchen. Track lighting over an island counter offered the only illumination apart from the glow of the city beyond the windows. John stood at the sink, water flowing from the faucet into a glass cup in his free hand.

"You can put the gun away. We're alone." He shut off the water and raised the cup to his lips.

Guin acquiesced and scoffed. "Not one for modern conveniences like a chair, are we?"

John laughed. "I never really use this place anymore, but it's bought and paid for, so I'm not in a hurry to get rid of it. I consider it a safe house for emergency purposes. Like tonight."

She examined his battered body again and nodded at his shoulder. "Yeah, about that . . ."

John took another gulp of the water. "Just a scratch. Seriously, you should see the other guys."

"Guys?" Guin stepped up to the island countertop and set down her laptop. She walked up to him and forced him to turn his back to her.

"Yeah," he explained while she removed his shirt. "Five or six of—" He winced as his arm rotated out of the sleeve. "Them," he finished as Guin tossed the shirt into the sink. "They jumped me at a gas station."

"That's what that smell is."

Cross grabbed his undershirt with both hands and lifted it. With a delicate motion, he pulled his injured shoulder out and let the shirt stay wrapped around his neck and opposite arm.

The life of a rural pastor apparently did nothing to hinder his physical fitness. Guin fought the urge to study his well-maintained core. She took the damp dish towel and dabbed the blood and dirt away from the wound. If it was painful, Cross didn't let on. A fresh clot had formed over the "scratch," as he'd put it. "You're lucky he missed," she said.

"I never said I was shot."

Guin snorted. "Oh please, just because I spend most of my time picking up Al's pants from Chinatown doesn't mean I don't know what a firearm injury looks like." She stepped back to view her handiwork. "You got any alcohol around here?"

"It's a little early for that, isn't it?"

Guin didn't bother with a response. Cross opened a red oak cupboard and retrieved an old shoebox. He placed it on the island and opened the lid. Guin shot him an amused glance as she sifted through the eclectic variety of drugstore first-aid paraphernalia.

He shrugged. "I figured a safe house needed supplies."

"Remind me to avoid any of your safe houses if I'm ever in serious trouble." She grabbed a half-empty bottle of rubbing alcohol out of the box, popped the cap, and applied the liquid directly to the wound.

Cross responded with a yelp. "Watch it!"

"Quiet down and let me work. And stop stalling and tell me what's going on."

Cross steadied himself against the counter and let Guin proceed with cleaning out the trench in his muscle. "Remember Christine Lewis?"

"The reporter?"

"She found me."

Guin's hand jerked in surprise, a finger digging at the exposed muscle. Cross cried out again, this time with genuine feeling, and glared at her.

She glared back. "What do you mean she found you?"

"I'm delivering my sermon yesterday morning in church, I look up, and there she is. I don't know how she found me, but she did."

Guin shook her head and dug her fists into her hips to demonstrate her displeasure. She was mad at Christine for tracking him . . . No, she was mad at Cross for letting the woman . . . Wait. Her mind raced. Why was she mad about it? "You let her find you?" was all she could say, though she understood Cross couldn't possibly have led the woman to him. He was too good for that.

Cross's eyebrows knit together in the center of his forehead. "I thought you would be more surprised about the sermon part."

Guin pressed her lips into a thin line and continued cleaning his shoulder. "Please. You worked for the most networked intelligence agency in the world. We knew you were a pastor at a church before you did."

"Well, now Christine knows. And she showed up asking a lot of questions."

"About what?"

"Me, mostly. My story. How I got there."

Guin's imagination went into overdrive. She pictured Cross and this Christine person sitting at a romantic restaurant, candlelight dancing off their pupils, sharing intimate details about each other. She didn't like the image, so she set an imaginary fire to the dive in her mind.

Cross was still going. "I told her about everything that happened in my life. I spared her details about you or Al, or really anything about the CIA. Just why I got out. Then I took her back to her hotel and went home." He swallowed and averted his eyes, classic deception tells. "I had to get gas on the way, so I pulled into a station. That's when my friends arrived to show me a good time."

"Any identification?"

"They didn't give me much time to ask questions, but I can tell you for sure one of them was a Turk."

"You said five or six of them. How did you even get away and make it all the way up here, for that matter?"

"One of them brought a gun to the knife fight, only he fired it too close to a fuel leak." Cross mimed the explosion with his hands. "My ears are still ringing. I got away, but one of them chased me onto a northbound freight train. I managed to get him to talk, except . . ."

"Except what?"

"They weren't trying to kill me, at least I don't think. He had a chance to let me die, but pulled me back onto the train."

Guin's heart skipped a beat, and she swallowed the urge to respond in concern over his near demise. "What did he say?"

"That he knew where she was.'"

"The journalist? Why would they be after her?"

"Your guess is as good as mine. Nothing I can think of makes sense. Unless there's something she's not telling me."

"Or they're using her to get to you."

Cross pushed down the thought that he may have put Christine in danger. He needed to focus. "Right now, it doesn't matter. What does is making sure they never lay a hand on her."

Guin furrowed her brow. That was why he'd called. So she would help the journalist. For a moment, she considered a taxi ride back to her condo, but decided it would only betray her feelings about the situation. "All right," she said. "This looks pretty good." She tossed the dish towel into the sink on top of his ruined shirt and taped a square of gauze against the wound. "There you go. Good as new."

Cross pulled his T-shirt back on and met her eyes. "Thank you," he said, his face soft and lovely.

Guin only nodded, then broke away from his look and rounded the countertop again. She opened her laptop, and the bright screen greeted her with a blank log-in box. She typed her password in a flurry of memorized keystrokes. While the hard drive purred to life, she looked up at Cross. "So you hopped the next Amtrak to DC just to see little ole me?"

"I passed out on top of a boxcar. Next thing I know, I'm waking up in a train yard in Arlington and it's Monday."

The computer beeped a confirmation, and Guin turned her attention to the screen. Cross moved closer to look over her shoulder. "Here's what I'm thinking," he said. "If this group of guys is a revenge squad from AIM, they must've had help entering the country."

"So we check for any flags on high-volume cash flows in and out of the country."

"I also thought you could run a search on any recent identity theft tied to airline ticket purchases."

Guin made a loud sniffing sound with her nose. "You know, if this is going to take a while, I think you'd better consider a shower. That is, unless you're all out of clean clothes too."

Cross pretended to smell an armpit. "Yeah, I guess you're right." He turned to leave, then paused. "Don't try to get the drop on me with that Glock while I'm in there. I didn't dispose of all my necessities."

Guin smirked as he disappeared into another room.

He wishes.

CHAPTER SIXTEEN

THE ID PINCHED between two fingertips pictured his real face and listed his real physical traits, but George Carson was not his real name. The indigenous life of the Aegean still feasted on the body belonging to the real George Carson. And although the ID was necessary to the task at hand, it saddened him to have acquired it at such high a price.

Yunus Anar did not wish an early death upon Mr. George Carson in much the same way he did not wish an early death on those outside the central conflict, but he understood the complexities required in a mission of such high priority. He coveted no death, but death was one of the tools by which a cause or goal could be achieved.

All peoples used the same tools and devices in the pursuit of goals greater than themselves. Not every person was honest about said tools and devices. Death realized many great causes, great ideas, and great advancements in the human existence.

The fight against cancer would flounder were it not for the fatalities. The civil rights movement in the United States of America benefited from the death of its spokesman. All dictatorships were sustained by the threat of execution.

A greater tool than just mere death, however, was one few were capable of: sacrificial death. Threatening death to achieve a goal was one thing. Willingness to die in the pursuit of the glory of others was something else entirely.

Yunus believed in balance. A life for a life. Nothing more. Not bloodshed just for its sake. One of Yunus's countrymen paid for George Carson's life with his own blood. Any life Yunus would have a hand in taking was a transaction for an imbalance on his side. He had lost friends, partners, lovers, but worst of all . . .

Yunus slapped the ID facedown on the side table and stood up from the uncomfortable chair. Even though the sun slept, plenty of light from the orange glow of New York City streetlamps flooded the window of his hotel room.

He breathed deep and stretched his sore back muscles. The cheap bed in the cheap room offered him little comfort in his recovery from jet lag. He preferred to keep to his internal clock, which meant it was time for his morning routine. Stretches, meditation, prayers. Then a hot shower and a greasy breakfast.

They had arrived two long days ago and would be waiting two more before they would finally be welcomed home with open arms. He didn't need patience for the interval, another activity already planned and in its early stages of execution.

A flood of memories flashed before him. Playing with his nephews in a vain attempt to elicit genuine smiles. Arguing with their mother before finally pledging himself to her demands. The months in preparation, training for what would come next.

He thought over the moment in his mind and, as if triggered by some unseen force of coincidence, his phone rang. It could only be one of his, a report from their advance assignment, conducted while he prepared the final details for their ultimate goal.

He padded to the table, his naked form in full view of the window, and answered the phone. "Hello?" It was the only word he could say that disguised his thick Turkish accent. The response on the other end of the call would determine whether he threw the phone out the window and disappeared from the hotel or carried out his business as planned.

"Yunus." It was Erkan. He did not sound well.

Yunus took his hand off the window latch and paced the thin carpet in front of the lumpy bed. "I pray for good news, my friend," he said in Turkish.

"Your prayers have been unanswered, I'm afraid."

Yunus closed his eyes and meditated on the numbers one through ten, the wellspring of rage quieting in his heart. "Tell me."

"We could not capture the target. He proved to be . . . resourceful."

"Was anyone hurt?"

"Burns and bruises, but we'll live."

"You do not sound alive, Erkan."

"No worse injury than any we took in Kobanî."

Erkan's will to live had been tested to an extreme during a recent siege against the capital of a Syrian governorate. Yunus preferred serving from behind, Erkan several yards in front.

"Praise to God."

"You're not angry, Yunus?"

"Of course, but not a madman. This is only proving to be more difficult a diversion than I estimated. For that, your injuries are on my head."

Erkan was silent on the other end. Yunus expected a debate. The two friends long disagreed on the extent to which violence was necessary to achieve peace. Erkan believed in the power of indiscriminate bloodshed. Yunus often found himself on the other extreme. Reluctant soldier, reluctant leader. Case in point—Erkan demanded they . . .

Yunus pushed past the turmoil brewing in his soul and cleared his throat. "I will be there later this afternoon, and we will coordinate our next approach." He couldn't change his plans now, his train ticket already in hand and the package delivery prescheduled for just after daybreak. "Where is he now?"

"Not sure. We are watching his home, but he did not return after his escape."

Yunus nodded, though Erkan couldn't see it. "Thank you, friend. Rest and heal from your injuries. We will regroup tomorrow."

Erkan offered a farewell, then the line went dead. Yunus grabbed hold of the top of the flip phone and pulled against the hinge. The phone snapped in two. He discarded it on the table and marched to the bathroom to take advantage of his last opportunity at a hot shower.

The hot shower rejuvenated Cross's spirit. Doubts about the man he had become were washed down the drain with the dirt and bark. During a period of self-analysis, as he breathed in the searing steam, he decided his snap decision to take a life on the top of the train hours before hadn't been unwarranted. Christine's life was threatened again. His volatile emotional state predicated the violent urge.

Taking a mental step back, he saw the emotional slope he had tumbled down. A moment of weakness in a day of uncertainty. He didn't like uncertainty, nor the new range of passions he experienced as a result of Christine's intrusion in his life.

His relationships in his past life were never a distraction, but a mere pastime. If it didn't count, he could just leave. And he did. Often. One of the many reasons he'd decided against getting to know Guin on a personal level. She was attractive and funny, and Cross would be lying if he denied imagining a life with her on occasion. But it would only hurt.

Now there was an added wrinkle to his life. A committed relationship he had no intention of leaving and that would have to be compatible with any other he would eventually form. His devotion to Jesus Christ was his priority. And whomever he met along the way would have to have the same priority for their paths to align.

It made the decision with Guin simple and would make the decision with Christine simple. The fact he had yet to broach the subject of faith with either was negligence on his part. He chalked the lack of initiative up to still being green in his new ministry position.

He thought through a variety of scenarios to start the conversation with Guin as he shut off the water and stepped from the fog of the shower into the fog of the bathroom. His clothing options were minimal, though he was thankful to have any. A pair of jeans and a gray polo shirt would suffice.

Maybe he could just come right out and say it. *Guin,* he imagined saying, *What have you heard about this Jesus guy?* Cross shook his head as he stuck a leg into the pair of jeans.

Jesus guy? Really?

He'd have to reconsider the opener. He wanted it to feel natural, not forced. She was doing him a favor, a big one. Especially considering he'd asked her to keep quiet about her research. The last thing he wanted was for her to feel uncomfortable at his attempt to proselytize in return.

Still, Cross couldn't help but remember a wise analogy he once heard. If someone was about to get hit by a bus, would they mind being warned? And the prospect of being separated from God for eternity was certainly grimmer than being hit by a bus.

Guin, if you were going to be hit by a bus, would you want me to tell you? That opening line wasn't any better.

Cross pulled the polo shirt over his head and wiped the mirror clean with the back of his hand. He prodded and poked each swollen spot on his face, souvenirs of his train ride to DC, and considered himself lucky to have escaped with such little to show for it.

The door swung open, startling him. Guin flashed an amused smile. "Sorry to interrupt your primping, but I've got a lead."

Cross followed her from the bathroom, through the empty bedroom, and back out into the open living area. The sky over the capital skyline faded from gray to a lighter shade of gray as the sun made its way toward the break of dawn.

Guin stopped at the open laptop and pointed with her index finger. "I started with possible influxes of monetary resources into Amman, then Jordan in general, but there's been nothing warranting a second look in the last fourteen days. I also checked for any reports of fraudulent identity activity, though to be honest, even if they used fake IDs, it might still take weeks to determine."

Cross folded his arms. "A long shot, I know. Someone might not be aware a stranger used their identity to enter the country illegally."

"Or it could be the identity of someone recently deceased. I know you were thinking AIM, but you mentioned the Turk, and it got me thinking, so I shifted my focus to recent activity in Turkey and Syria. There's been a lot of conflict between the Kurds and Islamists along the border of both countries since 2013."

"Still AIM, just a hit squad out of Syria and not Jordan."

"With an apparent Turk ally or two."

Cross ran his fingers through his damp hair. "I wouldn't be surprised. The Turkish government is corrupt. I remember an op years ago when we were arming Syrian rebels. More than a few Turkish government officials sympathized with the militants."

"I don't know if you heard, but we're watching some rioting in Istanbul over this issue."

"It's like the jihadists have tentacles in a lot of governments and infrastructure these days."

Guin nodded. "If they ever organize under a powerful governing authority, we'll have our hands full."

"You said you had a lead?"

"Right. No red flags until I found a missing persons report out of Greece from last Wednesday."

"Greece?"

"Technically, yes. Local authorities filed the report when an American aboard a Mediterranean cruise line failed to board after a long excursion on Santorini. They haven't located him yet."

"And that's interesting, how?"

A full-color photograph of a balding, pudgy Caucasian man filled the screen. "His name is George Carson. And two days ago he boarded a plane in London bound for New York City."

Christine sat comfortably in the back of the airport shuttle and stared out the window at various blurred lines of color speeding by. She checked her watch and calculated the time that it would take for the shuttle to traverse the short distance between her hotel and the terminal.

It wasn't short enough. She wanted nothing more than to leave the state of Virginia after being stood up by the man she thought she was beginning to know. The promise of a continued conversation over hot pancakes had been traded for a solitary engagement with a granola bar from a vending machine.

In such a short span of time, her desire to find him, thank him, then just learn about him developed into a longing to be with John Cross. To listen to his voice, look into his eyes.

She knew what it was. Exactly what it was. There was a name for it, sort of. The term *Stockholm syndrome* kept repeating in her mind, but she knew that had to do with a hostage and their captors. She was attached to the man who had rescued her.

She decided it was infatuation, not love. The information she'd collected about him was scant. His name and that he used to work for the CIA. That was it.

Oh, and that he was a killer. Well, not anymore. She wondered if it was really a religious conversion or if some chemical reaction in his brain resulted in the formation of a kind of conscience. Feigning religious conviction would be one way for him to distance himself from a job he had no passion for anymore.

Was that it? Had he been lying? Christine shook her head. It would take a sociopath of the highest order to go from a long record of successful assassinations to lying about his religious beliefs in order to retreat from the scrutiny of the intelligence community and seduce a group of innocent church attendees.

The thought of his lies to the kind people of Rural Grove made her the angriest. She might have fallen away from church involvement after leaving home, but Christine held no ill feelings toward the Christian community. She even assumed she would return to the church in the twilight of her demanding career.

Was she that stupid? She imagined he'd left the city immediately after dropping her off the night before. Never to be seen again. Not by the good people of Rural Grove. Not her. John Cross would cease to exist, and she'd never be able to prove he ever did. She'd return to NABC empty handed.

She wasn't a liar. She never intended to share his side of the story, not without his permission of course. She planned to bring it up during breakfast and give him as much time as he needed to be comfortable with the idea. They could have worked together on an anonymous statement to corroborate her updated version of the events.

Maybe she should run with the story anyway. Though, there was the danger of being branded a fraud. Journalism was a toxic brand at the moment. High-profile anchors and columnists fabricating news stories wouldn't help restore any former glory.

Christine kicked the empty seat in front of her as the shuttle slid into the Richmond International Airport departure lane. She hated Cross, Jacobs, the military, but most of all herself.

The shuttle driver braked at the airport entrance, left his seat, and pulled her small duffel off the storage shelf near the front. She met him at the door and let him help her down the steps to the sidewalk.

"Enjoy your flight, ma'am," he said with a smile.

"Thank you." She wanted to muster a smile in return, to no avail. She slung the duffel over her shoulder, dug her hands into her jean pockets, and with her head hanging low walked toward the sliding double doors.

The two panes of glass parted in the middle. She stepped across the threshold and nearly collided with a man standing just inside. "Excuse me," she said as she lifted her head. Her eyes widened and her mouth fell open as John Cross stared back her with his tempting coffee-colored eyes.

"Christine, I can't let you get on that plane."

CHAPTER SEVENTEEN

CHRISTINE SLAPPED HIM as hard as she could, then saw the dark-red bruising under his eye and over the bridge of his nose, as well as the split on his bottom lip. She covered her mouth with her hand and gasped. "I'm so sorry," she said breathlessly. "What happened?" She stepped closer to examine his injuries.

"I'm fine," John replied, his demeanor stern. "You can't go back to New York. Not right now."

"Wait. I'm confused." Christine's concern melted away, revealing indignation accrued over the long morning. "You break your promise to meet for breakfast, don't bother calling to explain, then show up right when I'm about to leave and ask me to stay? What do you think I'm going to say, hotshot? You think I'm going to swoon and let you regale me with stories of your glory days in the CIA? Well, if that's the case, then, buddy, I've got news for you—"

John held up both hands and waved off her tirade. "OK, stop. I know, and I'm sorry to leave you hanging. But I'm telling you not to get on that plane. Your life depends on staying here with me."

Christine laughed. John didn't. She ended her laughter in an awkward sputter. "You're serious."

"I'll explain everything. But right now, we have to leave." John grabbed her by the arm and led her back out the double doors to the terminal roadway.

"Hey," she protested, pulling her arm from his grasp. "I can walk on my own." She flashed him her coldest stare, but he didn't seem to notice. Instead, he led the way at a brisk pace across the road and into the neighboring parking garage.

He retrieved a set of keys from the pocket of a pair of tailored-fit jeans. Christine examined the way his muscles pulled the gray polo shirt tight against his back. Her concentration broke when he lifted his hand and pressed the electronic fob between his fingers.

A silver luxury sedan two parking spaces away answered his call with two successive honks. John walked up to the driver's-side door and bent to slide in. Christine stood numb in her tracks, her face scrunched together at her nose.

"What is this?" she asked.

"My car. Get in."

His commanding voice sent an exhilarating chill over her skin. Christine forced her feet to move. She tossed her duffel over the headrest onto the rear floorboard and slipped into the passenger seat.

A reverent silence overtook her as Christine settled into the vehicle. She stroked the warm red leather of her seat, glided fingers across the smooth fine-grain wood inlay, and breathed in the perfume of extravagance. A display rising out of the center of the dash offered detailed information about the car, global positioning, even the news.

She didn't know whether to kiss him or curse him. She opted just to talk. "OK. Tell me what's going on, starting with the bruises and ending with why you're driving this outrageous car."

"I was attacked by a group of men last night. I think they're here for you."

Christine decided to curse this time. "What do you mean, they're here for me?"

"The only detail I got from the attack last night was that he knew where you were. I'm a ghost, but you're all over the news. I don't know why, but it seems like they came here to find and kill you. So an old CIA friend did some digging, and we believe they'll be waiting for you in New York."

Christine's head spun out of control, her emotions swinging like a pendulum. "I don't understand. Why . . . why are they coming after me?" Tears welled in her eyes, nausea spreading through her chest and into her throat.

John grabbed her hand and pulled her close. They made eye contact, and he whispered, "I won't let them get to you."

A single tear left a wet streak down her cheek, and the nausea eased. The prospect of falling back into her captors' hands almost brought her spirit to its knees, but something about John assured the hope of escape. It wasn't infatuation this time. She could read an inner strength in his eyes.

He kept a firm grip on her hand and asked, "Can you think of any reason why they wouldn't want you alive? Did you see someone you recognized? A political figure maybe? Overhear plans of an attack?"

Christine attemped to recall memories from her imprisonment, but it all blurred into a dark blob filled with despair and pain. She shook her head and averted her gaze. "What do we do?"

"It's OK. They might think you saw something you shouldn't have, even if you didn't comprehend it at the time." Or it might be all his fault. He let go of her hand and pressed the ignition button near the steering wheel. "My friend is tracking down a lead. We sit tight for now and pray these guys are identified soon so the right people can step in and take care of the situation." He gripped the gearshift. A loud ringing erupted from the back pocket of his jeans. John looked up, his eyes wide, and a grin spread across his face. "See, probably good news already."

He dug the phone out of his pocket and brought the receiver up to his ear. "Hello? Yes, this is he." The grin faded.

"John, what's wrong?"

He didn't answer, but rubbed his temple and hung his head while listening to the one-sided conversation. "Yes, I understand. I'll be right there." He hung up the phone and sighed.

"Well?" Christine prodded.

"We have to go to the hospital."

"What happened?"

"One of the members of my church fell and sustained some injuries. She's being treated at VCU Medical Center."

Any consideration of danger escaped her mind. "Yes, of course. Let's go."

John shifted the car into reverse and backed out of the parking spot.

In the nine miles between the airport and the medical center of Virginia Commonwealth University, Cross described in detail the attempt on his life the night before. He left out more than a few details about his rendezvous with Guin. They were all business, but maybe Christine wouldn't see it that way.

Christine snorted a skeptical laugh. "You were in Washington this morning? How did you even get here before I was able to board?"

He smiled. "Fortunately, I drove against traffic flow. And this is a nice car."

"Speaking of this car," she interjected. Her hand patted the clean leather of the seat and she raised a questioning eyebrow.

"A relic from my previous life. I kept it and an apartment in Washington for emergency purposes. I like keeping my options open."

Christine's eyes opened wide. "Your other car. The police will know you were at the gas station last night."

"It's OK," he assured her. "The car was clean, just like this one. I don't know if I'll ever be able to own something in my own name. Again, out of habit."

Cross maneuvered the vehicle off the freeway and into the heart of Richmond. Construction forced them in a circle before they could enter the parking garage adjoining the hospital.

They left the car parked on a lower level and rode an elevator to the eighth floor. Cross paused at the reception desk in the atrium and handed his parking ticket to the smiling woman seated on the opposite side. "Clergy," he announced.

She stamped the ticket and handed it back to him. "Have a nice day."

Cross pocketed the ticket and noticed Christine smirking at him. "I know," he said with a sheepish grin. "It still sounds weird to me."

A flight of escalators and a long hallway led them by a well-stocked pharmacy to a set of elevators waiting to escort them to the Critical Care Unit on the ninth floor. They rode in silence, though alone in the car.

The elevator doors opened, and they awkwardly excused themselves around a family waiting to board. Just beyond a small waiting room, wide doors stood guard over the CCU. Cross punched a call button attached to the wall, and after a pause, a voice on the other end asked, "Yes, can I help you?"

"I'm here to see Lori Johnson. I'm her pastor."

"Come on back." A buzzing sound released the magnetic seal on the entrance, and the double doors swung open on their own. Cross took the lead to room 106. He stepped through the curtain, with Christine on his heels.

Lori sat upright in the hospital bed, her arm in a sling and a deep-red bruise running from her ear to the base of her neck. "Oh Lord," she exclaimed, noticing Cross but not acknowledging Christine. "Now I know it's bad if they're bringing the minister in." She tried to use her better arm to push herself upright in the bed, but seemed to only sink farther into the mattress.

Cross walked to the foot of the bed and placed a caring hand on her socked foot peeking out from underneath the bedsheet. "I'm here to keep you from giving the hospital staff any grief. Gary told me you got into a fight with a set of stairs."

Lori squinted as she examined Cross's face. "Speak for yourself, kid."

"Oh." Cross held up a hand to half mask the bruising, half remind himself he still bore the marks of his encounter at the gas station. "This. Yeah, I . . . uh . . ."

"He had his own fight with another man." Christine appeared suddenly next to Cross, and his mouth fell open as she exposed his double life.

127

"I'm sorry," Lori responded with a dubious expression. "Who are you?"

"Christine." She offered her hand to Lori, who mechanically shook it and gazed piercingly into her face. Christine continued, "Mr. Cross here is my guardian angel." She offered a weak laugh and rolled her eyes. "Abusive boyfriend. It's my fault, really, for having stuck with him so long. If John hadn't stood up to him, I think he would've beat me right there in the Publix parking lot."

Cross swore he heard hints of a phony southern accent in her voice.

Lori narrowed her eyes and stuck out her bottom lip in disapproval. "John Cross, did you hit back?"

Cross stopped searching the room for potential escape routes and threw his hands in the air. "Lori, I promise you I acted in self-defense." He stole a glance at Christine to think reprimanding thoughts at her.

Lori exhaled loudly through her mouth and drew the attention back in her direction. "You know what the Bible says: 'Offer your other cheek to the one who strikes you.' Of course, it doesn't say anything about what you do after that." A wicked smile spread from cheek to cheek, and she winked at Christine.

Christine wrapped both arms around Cross's arm and beamed. "To show him my gratitude, I've offered John lunch. Of course, then he got the call about your fall, and, well, here we are."

Cross clenched his fist, and his bicep hardened. Christine got the message and slipped her hands from his arm, chuckling nervously again and glancing about the room. He didn't want to lie to Lori, although technically he hadn't said anything false. It was self-defense, and it was on account of Christine. So it was the truth. Sort of.

The twisted logic did nothing to soothe the unpleasantness of his predicament.

"Nice to meet you, Christine," Lori said. "Although I would have preferred it be under better circumstances."

"It's fine. You look great." Christine stepped around the hospital bed and leaned against the short rail propped up against its side. "How did it happen?"

"Oh, when you get to be my age, sometimes you forget how stairs work. To be honest, I don't even remember what caused it—just the fear of lying at the bottom without a way to get myself up."

Cross didn't move from his perch at her feet. He nodded toward the sling. "Have they given you the damage report?"

"They said I'm lucky." Lori smiled at Christine and raised her voice an extra octave. "I keep telling them the Lord looked out for me."

Christine laughed. It sounded genuine, and Cross liked hearing it. Lori specialized in tearing down relational walls. Another hour in the hospital room and Christine might ditch him to have lunch with the spunky old woman.

"I have two breaks in my arm, one above the elbow and one below. I'm blessed there wasn't any major damage to the joint. The good Lord knows I've already had too many of those replaced."

Cross checked his watch. He opened his mouth with the intention of wrapping up the conversation, when Lori spoke.

"So, Christine, tell me a little bit about yourself, darling. Do you go to church?"

He regretted bringing Christine along.

"My parents raised me in the Methodist church, but I have to be honest, ma'am. I'm not a consistent attender."

"We'll just have to fix that, now won't we? Do you have a job?"

"Yes, I'm a reporter."

"Oh, how nice. Newspaper or TV?"

Cross's phone rang and interrupted the banter. "I'm sorry," he said as he pulled it from his pocket. One look at the incoming number and he knew he needed to answer. He held up his index finger. "I'm really sorry. I have to take this."

"You go," Lori replied, her good hand waving him from the room. "This is girl time anyway."

Cross exited the room and walked down the hall out of earshot. He flipped open the phone and held it to his ear. "Hey, Guin," he said in a hushed tone. "What do you have?"

"Oh, I've got something for you," came the aggressive response from a voice all too familiar. "How about a nice long vacation near the Indian Ocean? I hear there are some terrific black sites in Diego Garcia."

"She told you, didn't she, Al?"

Cross heard a thump and imagined Simpson throwing a heavy object across his desk. "Come on, John. Don't tell me you didn't think she would. That would just confirm you can't play this game anymore, not to mention hurt my feelings."

Yes, Cross suspected Guin would tell her superior about their meeting. But that didn't mean he couldn't hope she would be discreet about it. Even now, with Simpson huffing angrily into the phone, Cross breathed a sigh of relief, glad she did. He didn't have a strong case to involve anyone from Langley. A stolen ID and an assault charge ranked low in priority when it came to national security. If his old boss demonstrated any concern over Cross's situation, perhaps protocol would be broken and they could achieve a resolution.

"I thought Guin would tell you," he replied. "It's her job. And now I'm just some guy. A guy targeted by thugs who have crossed our borders and are running loose in our cities."

"Cut this 'our' bull—"

Cross dropped the phone from his ear to mute the oath, then brought it back up as he stepped farther away from Lori's room.

Simpson continued to yell. ". . . long ago when you quit on us. I gave you a second chance, and you threw that back in my face. Do you know how hard I've worked to even let you live in relative peace? No one else thought you would stay quiet."

"I know. I know," Cross interrupted. "I wouldn't have called her if I thought it was nothing."

Silence. A calculated pause, if he knew Simpson at all. The man's reputation of playing his most aggressive cards up front before offering his consent preceded him. True to form, he snorted and said, "Lucky for you, you're right. It's not nothing."

Cross smiled. Not that he had any doubts.

"This George Carson thing smells pretty rotten. I mean really rotten. Especially after they fished the guy's body out of the Aegean Sea wearing a garrote wire like a necktie."

Stolen ID. Assault. Now murder. His case for help grew stronger. "Any other hits on the ID?"

"Two more. A hotel room in Queens booked last Saturday night, then a pair of train tickets yesterday morning."

"Train tickets?"

"Yeah." The sound of rustling papers created faux static on the line. "Here we go. Two train tickets for a departure this morning, Penn Station to Richmond Main Street."

Cross turned suddenly and locked his eyes on the entrance to Lori's room. They were coming for Christine. And he had put her right where they could reach her. "What time is the train scheduled to arrive?"

"Thirteen hundred and two hours."

Cross glanced at his watch.

"That's thirty minutes from now, John."

"Yeah, that's no good, Al."

"What do you mean?"

"I'm in a hospital nine hundred yards from the station."

"I thought Guin patched you up?"

Was there anything Guin hadn't told him? Cross paused to assess all the possible scenarios and decide on his next course of action.

Simpson must have telepathically witnessed Cross's brain kick into gear. That or the two just knew each other well enough to catch non-verbal cues. Simpson's raspy voice disturbed Cross's train of thought. "Listen, son, don't think about engaging this guy on your own. He's clearly already got backup in the area."

"Have you gotten a visual on our fake George Carson?"

"No," replied a voice unlike Simpson's. Guin's voice sounded like an angel in comparison. "He's been too aware of surveillance cameras for us to get a clean look at his face."

"Sullivan," Simpson hissed. "Didn't I say something about being seen and not heard?"

"The Carson ID is done," Guin continued, ignoring him. "The trail will end if he gets off that train."

"What about the girl, Cross?" Simpson badgered him. A stall tactic if Cross ever heard one.

"They'd never think to look for her right under their noses. They're going to wait for me to resurface and then use me to get to her. Unless I lead them to you first."

"Hold on, cowboy. I've only had the patience to track down this thing from the stolen ID angle. Even if you could attract their attention, I can't pull any officers right now to bail you out if things go south."

Another muffled noise distracted Simpson from the conversation. It sounded like an argument. All Cross heard his former superior say was, "I don't care."

Cross checked his watch again: 12:34. *Twenty-eight more minutes.* "Al," he said. "I don't have all day. Either I bait these guys and lead them to your cage, or I'll identify the primary so I'll at least have something to bribe you with."

"I'm going to give you a piece of advice," Simpson replied.

Cross imagined him waving his finger into the speakerphone.

"Put that girl on the next plane to New York, and let the bureau put a security detail on her. Wash your hands of this. Step away."

Twelve thirty-five. *Twenty-seven more minutes.* Cross kept his eyes focused on the curtain to room 106. Simpson was right. Cross was no stranger to detachment. He could let someone else figure out this mess. He'd already decided he couldn't be around Christine anyway. With the identity thief en route, New York might have just become the safer city for her to be in.

But walking away from someone in need was the old John Cross. Not now. He would see this to the end. And with this one that meant figuring out who was leading the charge in the effort to kill Christine Lewis.

"Sorry, Al. I can't do that."

"John." Guin's voice sounded clear, comforting even. "Be careful."

Cross smiled, and a part of him wished she could see it. "I will.

And thank you." He ended the call before either one of them could say more, and he took his fourth look at what felt like a ticking time bomb on his wrist.

Twelve thirty-seven. *Twenty-five more minutes.*

He wouldn't have much time to reconnoiter the station. He pictured the layout in his mind, a familiar image given previous examination as a possible exit strategy should he find himself the target of an enemy agent trying to prove his worth. Or apparently even the target of his own country anxious to ensure he didn't talk.

He kept a brisk pace back to Lori's room and stepped through the curtain as the two women shared a laugh over some unknown anecdote from Lori's week. He guessed chaos at the hair salon.

Christine's smile dissipated, and she stood from a chair when he entered. "Is everything OK?"

"Yes," he replied, a wide grin hiding the truth. "I just seem to be in high demand today. I'm afraid I'm going to have to step out for a little bit."

Lori lifted her chin and flared her nostrils, her eyes squinting in suspicion. Her signature look. "You don't think you're taking away my new friend Christine right when I was just getting to know her, now are you?"

"Actually, I hoped you wouldn't mind if Christine kept you company while I was away."

Christine shot him a frustrated glance. "John, I don't know if Lori . . ."

Lori patted Christine's hand. "Nonsense. It'll be fine. We don't need him anyway—I don't care how handsome he is. I tell you what. We'll call up the kitchen and have them bring us the finest microwaved turkey they can unwrap. I promise I'll be just as fun of a lunch date as the reverend over there."

Christine's smile returned, and her eyes sparkled as she squeezed Lori's good hand. The old woman's spell worked on everyone. "I don't doubt it," Christine said. She looked back at Cross and added, "If that's what you want."

He projected as much confidence in his eyes as he could and replied, "It won't take long. I promise." Cross wondered if she could read through his partial deception.

If she could, she didn't show it. Instead, Christine turned back to Lori and smiled. "Well, I for one would love to hear more about Kathleen and her Doberman."

Lori smirked at Cross. "She's all mine, Johnny. Go about your business."

Cross leaned over the bed and gave Lori a hug around her neck. "Save me some of that microwave turkey, and you can fill me in on the Doberman when I get back."

Lori squeezed Cross's shoulder with her unbound hand and kissed him on the side of his head. He bit down on his tongue to keep from crying out as the bullet wound burned in her grip.

She picked up her story right where she left off before he crossed the threshold. Her voice trailed off as he marched down the hallway and out of the Critical Care Unit. He caught an elevator primed for descent, divine providence on his side. He stepped inside the compartment and brought his wrist up to his chest as the doors slid shut.

Twelve forty. *Twenty-two more minutes.*

CHAPTER EIGHTEEN

THE PASSENGER TRAIN rocked back and forth as it barreled around a curve enclosed by tall, verdant trees on either side. Yunus spent the entire ride from New York City staring out the window, soaking in the exquisite landscape. The colors of his childhood home were more barren in nature. And given his truncated future, Yunus found enjoyment in even the tiniest measure of beauty in creation.

He didn't take his eyes off the sights just beyond the pane of glass. The train made each of its scheduled stops, and other passengers came and went. At times a stranger would choose the empty seat beside him only to vacate it at a later stop. Not once did he acknowledge their presence.

His companion rode the train on a different car, and Yunus wasn't even sure which one. They ignored each other at Penn Station, and his friend intended to exit the train six stops prior to Yunus's final destination. They would meet again in less than forty-eight hours, assuming all went according to plan. Still, Yunus left specific instructions. Should there be any delay on his part, he was confident in the ability of his compatriots to succeed at their primary mission without him.

At times he often wondered if they really even needed him. He contributed a strategic mind to the group, seemingly the primary reason for his assumption of leadership, and could certainly handle himself in combat. He even failed to trust their mission would have its intended effect. Accepting the offer served as a mere vehicle to his greater purpose. He yearned to make restitution and free Fem and the boys of their pain.

"Next stop, Ashland," shouted the mechanical voice overheard.

The train slowed, then came to a full stop beside a sheltered platform. Faces and bodies of new passengers filled Yunus's field of view, and he at last turned his head from the window to keep from contemplating the latent beauty of humanity.

Yes, humanity was dirty. But that was never the intended design. Yunus remembered his own children, when alive, as examples of how humanity could be beautiful. But with all men, corruption seized control, with the vilest of acts conducted in the name of freedom as a result. The world lacked a just hand to guide it. Thus, men like Erkan resorted to base measures of generating balance between what was evil and what was good. Yunus understood it but rarely stomached it.

The grotesque businessman in the adjoining seat stirred from his deep slumber, no longer lulled by the soothing rock of the train's path down its track. An eye opened to examine the cause for the cessation of his dreams, and unimpressed with the selection of additional fares, it shut once more, accompanied by a snort from his nostrils.

"Never knew the train was this popular," he commented, his eyes still staring at the back of their own lids.

Oh, we are to converse now? Tempted to ignore the man, Yunus decided the less conspicuous action was to speak when spoken to. "Yes, it seems many people like to use it." He didn't try hiding his accent. He found most people pretended to ignore his obvious fresh-off-the-boat nature, too nervous about being given a troubling label.

Sure enough, the businessman kept up his end of the dialogue without hesitation. "I've never ridden before. Prefer to fly, but the company decided to save a few bucks by sending us on these for closer trips." The man punctuated his anecdote with swear words and a deep inhale and exhale that threatened to pop the buttons of his large jacket. "How about you, Muhammad? Ever take the train much?"

The man's use of what he surely meant as a slur took Yunus aback. He wasn't offended. On the contrary, he appreciated the man's refusal to be henpecked by a sensitive society. If referring to a stranger by the name of a respected prophet was the worst the man could do, Yunus was guaranteed a blessed and happy life. Real hatred and intolerance looked like the barrel of a gun pressed against your child's temple.

Still, he couldn't let it rest. "My name is Yunus. And yes, I have traveled by train much in my home country of Turkey."

"Turkey!" Both of the man's eyes shot open, and a wide smile spread across his lips. "Antalya is beautiful. Great food. Oh, and sorry about the name. I thought I would take a shot in the dark since it seems pretty popular among folks from that part of the world." The man started laughing. "I once went on a factory tour in Yemen with three different guys, all named Muhammad. I was so confused. I'm sure you could imagine."

Yunus could learn to enjoy this man. Such a shame the conversation came so late into his journey. And yet the man might serve useful before its end. "No apology necessary. It sounds like you travel all over the world."

"Used to. Different company. Now the most exotic place I get to see is Richmond. What part of Turkey are you from?"

"Mardin."

"That's western Turkey, right? Never made it that far inland."

"The capital is a wonderful city to visit, but I would not recommend much of the remaining province."

"I hear you, brother. Can't recommend much of Virginia either."

The doors to the car closed, the last of those boarding now seated, and the train started its slow climb to cruising speed. Yunus turned his face back to the window to watch the green landscape blend together in a painting of blurred motion.

"Oh, I don't know," he replied. "I rather like it here."

Cross retrieved his car from the garage and maneuvered his way through the winding streets to Highway 60. He spotted Main Street

Station two blocks away but took a sharp right on Fifteenth Street and snatched the first available street-side parking spot across from a franchised sports bar.

Out of the car, the bright sun felt warm but not hot. A steady stream of cars ran back and forth along the street, but Cross saw few pedestrians traversing the sidewalks. He pressed his sunglasses into the bridge of his nose and kept his pace brisk on his way back to the intersection of Fifteenth Street and the highway. At the corner, he paused to survey his path to the front of the station.

The wide sidewalk opposite him hosted few places to hide the body of a full-grown man. The towering overpass of Interstate 95 cutting across the sky above the road did concern him. With the sun overhead, the black shadow of the bridge fell like a cloak over the area just in front of Main Street Station, a great assist to anyone wishing to stand unnoticed behind a concrete pier.

A woman, older with tattered clothing, waddled along farther up the opposite sidewalk. An African American man wearing insulated coveralls ran across the street and disappeared into an adjacent parking lot. No bystanders near the station, that he could tell.

He trekked down the sidewalk, keeping note of any movement in and around the entrance to the station. A freight train sat parked on its own bridge running parallel to the interstate overpass, the clearance between the two bridges just enough for a boxcar to squeak by.

Cross passed under the bridges and came to a stop in line with the wide staircase cut between two walls built out of massive concrete blocks. The station's beautiful French Renaissance architecture–inspired brick facade was considered a monument to the city's rich history. The building was sliced into three layers with a white stone foundation at the bottom, an orange brick middle layer, and a tall roof tiled in red clay.

The clock tower attached to its left, the distinguishing feature of the station, read twelve fifty-three hours. If on schedule, the train would arrive in nine minutes. Cross evaluated his limited options.

The general public used the front entrance as their primary way in and out of the station. He could remain outside the building and examine the arriving passengers as they walked into the sunlight.

What about the other exits? The mark could just as easily slip away undetected. He had to be inside for the best vantage point if he wanted to put an eye on each and every passenger. Just one problem: it would be claustrophobic inside. Not much room for a quick escape should the ex–George Carson bring friends.

It was a chance worth taking. Cross waited for a passing sedan, then stepped off the sidewalk and into the street. He trotted to the stairs and climbed them one at a time. No need alerting a possible rooftop sniper, though if there was one, Cross became a confirmed target the minute he stepped into the street.

He walked through a set of double doors into the bare lobby. The guard desk ahead appeared vacant. Amber light from overhead fixtures bounced off the shiny linoleum floor and collided with white engaged columns framing an ascending set of stairs to his right.

Removing his sunglasses, Cross scaled the stairs to the second-floor ballroom, a beautiful open space lined by tall marble columns. Black café tables for two, three, or four patrons sat irregularly throughout the room. To his left, light filtered through high windows placed just above four sets of double doors leading to a balcony overlooking the street below.

Matching doors to his right led to a waiting area adjacent to the ballroom. Voices echoed through the chamber, but he couldn't spot their owners. Deciding to postpone his entry to the concourse, Cross edged his way around the right-hand corner of the staircase and explored a side area off the hall.

On instinct he peeked through a set of window blinds and spotted an approaching group of four men wearing shades, the curly crops of hair bouncing in rhythm with each step toward the station. One wore a compression sleeve wrapped around his right elbow and walked with a hobble, favoring his left leg.

His friend from the train. Cross beat them there.

Thinking quickly, he snapped off the lengthy lift cord from the blinds and slid over to a balcony exit. He waited for the men to cross the street before cracking the door and tying the lift cord to an exterior café table.

He left the balcony door ajar and moved back through the ballroom and into the waiting area. It was divinely crowded, as crowded as the small station could ever hope to be. Cross bummed a copy of the *Richmond Times Dispatch* from an anxious elderly gentleman.

Taking a seat near a single mother of two, Cross opened the paper full to cover his face as the gang of suspects landed at the top of the stairs and worked their way into the concourse, heads swaying in suspicious gazes about the room.

Cross bent a corner of the newspaper at a slight angle, catching a glimpse of the men as they separated and stationed themselves at various means of egress. He couldn't tell if they'd identified him or just acted according to training.

The clock on the tower above the roof signaled the arrival of thirteen hundred hours, and a sharp train whistle answered its call. The 79 Carolinian was two minutes early.

The concourse came alive as passengers gathered bags and bid farewell to loved ones. An exodus to the platform drove a majority of the crowd out of the waiting area. Peering over the newspaper, Cross spotted two of the four men join the celebration of the train's arrival outside.

He dared not search for the other two and compromise his position, so he let the blurry black-and-white text of the newspaper cover three-fourths of his vision while keeping his focus on the exit from the platform. A handful of employees assisted with baggage, families exchanged hugs and kisses, and first-time travelers eyed the silver bullet with trepidation.

Those arriving swapped places with those leaving. College-age students toted backpacks and continued lively conversation started on the train. Mothers assisted toddlers through the large doors. Passenger after passenger disembarked and marched through the waiting area to the stairs.

Through process of elimination, Cross checked off each person as they passed through the open doorway into the ballroom. Mothers and toddlers made unlikely identity thieves. Loud groups served as great cover for someone wanting to be ignored, but Cross suspected his target to be an older man with West Asian features.

A rotund businessman squeezed through the door from the platform and thundered across the concourse, his hand waving in an excited fashion and his voice carrying around the room and back. He said something about a coffee-rubbed hamburger at a nearby restaurant.

Amused, Cross lowered the newspaper a hint more and watched as the man guided a companion toward the staircase. The businessman's enormous width made it difficult to see the recipient of his eatery sales pitch.

The paper dropped another inch, Cross concentrating on the pair. Just as they turned the corner to pass under the entryway, the overweight orator stepped in front and presented Cross with an unobstructed view of the man he instinctively knew to be masquerading as George Carson.

Sun-beaten skin only accentuated the wrinkles of age, and a dark mustache under his flat nose and peaked nostrils hid his upper lip. Unchecked beard growth cupped his chin, and unruly gray hair forced its way from beneath a short bill cap.

The suspect turned his neck as he followed the businessman, and for a moment Cross thought they made eye contact. The man's eyes looked past him though, and an imperceptible nod at an unseen ally confirmed Cross's suspicions.

Visual confirmation of his identity thief. Now he waited for the others to leave.

The two men monitoring the platform followed a group of young women out of the waiting area, and Cross sensed movement from behind his position. The second pair of lookouts entered his peripheral and joined the final wave of passengers and loved ones heading for the exit.

Cross slipped his sunglasses back on and folded the newspaper into a tight cylinder. He stood from his seat and slipped to the rear of the pack. They passed through the doorway and into the ballroom. The mass of bodies accumulating at the top of the stairs slowed their progress, until Cross came to a standstill and waited for his turn to descend.

A door to his immediate left swung open in a sudden burst of movement, catching him off guard. He looked up to lock eyes with one of the men from the welcoming party exiting the bathroom. Recognition sprang into the man's eyes as they opened wide, and his mouth dropped against his squat neck.

"Onu var!" the man shouted.

His partner took his foot off the top step and shot a confused glance behind him.

Cross didn't wait for the pieces to fall into place. He shoved the first man back into the bathroom door and took off for the balcony exit. The second man lunged, but a swipe at his ear with the rolled-up newspaper stunned him long enough for Cross to slip by.

Behind him pedestrians screamed as shouting erupted from farther down the stairwell, and a commotion filled the space. Cross lowered his shoulder and burst through the door and onto the balcony. He snatched the window blind lift cord bundled on the ground and looked back to see all four men charging the door at the same time.

Without hesitation, Cross took a running leap over the rail of the balcony, plummeting toward the concrete steps below.

CHAPTER NINETEEN

CROSS ARCHED AWAY from the balcony, holding the coil snug in his hand. Gravity pulled him downward, and the cord tightened. The café table fought valiantly against his weight but lost the battle and flipped on its side as the cord dragged it toward the railing.

He looked up and saw the legs of the table smash against the rail and hold like a grappling hook. He let go of the coil and loosened his grip on the line, rappelling the length of cord at a harrowing but survivable pace. His palms burned as he slowed himself to a stop twelve inches above the ground, his body swaying between an astonished group of commuters.

He let go of the lift cord and dropped to his feet. The men on the balcony above stared in disbelief over the rail. One mouthed what was most likely an oath and swatted at the other. They disappeared back into the second level of the station.

Cross didn't wait around for them to join him on ground level. He ran down the steps and into the busy street, dodging an irate delivery van by a narrow margin. Just four yards from the intersection of Fifteenth Street, he heard the angry clapping of boots against pavement behind him.

Rounding the corner, Cross dug his hand into his pocket and pressed the automatic ignition on the keyless remote of his car. Just ahead, the echo of the engine roar faded into a soft purr as the car greeted his arrival.

He made it to the car and opened the door. Before he got in, Cross took one look back at the intersection and saw only one pursuer running full speed in his direction. He slipped into the seat, shut the door, put the car into gear, and peeled from the parking spot.

In the rearview mirror, he saw a black van tear across the intersection, brake to stop, and pick up the man before continuing its pursuit down the street.

After a right turn onto Dock Street, Cross banked hard left and the luxury car shot across the median and onto an exit ramp for Hull Street. He swerved to prevent a head-on collision with an SUV, then jerked the wheel again to keep from becoming a permanent fixture of a brick retaining wall.

The car barreled through the short ramp and two lanes of oncoming traffic before slicing between a pickup truck and a coupe into an appropriate lane. Cross laughed and shouted, "Try to follow that!" to no one in particular, beads of sweat dripping from his temples, his heart pumping faster than the engine's pistons.

That was too close. But it worked. The flow of the interchange blocked the black van, buying Cross enough space to lead them away from the city, and Christine, without trouble. As if to celebrate, the annoying electronic ringer on his phone announced an inbound call from his jean pocket.

Cross slipped the phone from his pocket and answered without studying the incoming number. "Hello?" He balanced the phone between his ear and shoulder, then returned his hands to the two and ten position on the wheel.

"Hello, Pastor Cross."

"Who is this?"

"Who is this?" came the confused reply. "It's Barbara Templeton."

Cross's focus shifted from the mirror to the road. His hands tightened around the steering wheel, and he forced his brain to realign to pastoral mode. Harnessing his focus toward being relational with members of the church meant making a mental disconnect with ingrained training. The information flooded his mind and pressed against the backs of his eyeballs. Barbara Templeton. Knitting. Green bean casserole.

"Yes!" he exclaimed. "Mrs. Templeton, of course. Sorry about that. I'm actually in the car and wasn't thinking when I picked up."

"You worried me there, Pastor. After yesterday morning's service, I was convinced you might be suffering from something just awful. A virus, kidney stone, maybe even an aneurysm."

"I think you would have known if I was having an aneurysm, but I appreciate the concern." Cross checked the rearview mirror but couldn't remember what to look for.

"I had an uncle who died of an aneurysm back in 1983. Of course, this was in Jonesborough, Tennessee, when I was closer to your age."

A black van. That was what it was.

Mrs. Templeton continued, "Poor man lost his vision, couldn't stand up, said his head felt like it was going to explode. Very sad. Lord took him though, and now he's singing praises alongside the heavenly hosts."

"I'm sorry to hear." No sign of the van. Maybe his plan hadn't worked.

"Oh, don't mind it much anymore. It was his time for sure. Sweet man when he was alive. Loved to garden. He would grow the biggest crop of . . ."

Cross lost attention in the conversation as he crossed over the James River and left the skyline of Richmond in his wake. He glanced in his mirrors again but still failed to spot the van. He couldn't be the mouse to their cat if he managed to lose them so quickly. He drummed his fingers on the steering wheel and muttered, "Come on . . . come on."

"Excuse me?" replied Mrs. Templeton.

"I'm sorry. I'm in the car and I'm . . ."

"Distracted, I know. You've said that already. You know, it's not safe to be on your phone if you're driving a car."

No kidding, thought Cross, hoping she would volunteer to call back another time.

"You need one of those cars with the speaker in it that connects to your phone. Blue monkey. Or blue tower."

"Bluetooth."

"That's it. What an odd name."

Cross's car passed over Mayo Island, a privately owned landmass mostly home to vagrants, before finishing its journey across the river. In less than a mile, he could turn left and head south on Jefferson Davis Highway, though he questioned his next move given his original plan had ended so abruptly. Perhaps he could circle around and . . .

Mrs. Templeton asked a question he only half heard.

"I'm not sure," Cross responded, not confident in his answer to half a question.

"Well, I certainly think so."

He passed the Venus, an old theater converted to a furniture store, on his left. He considered pulling over, making a U-turn. He couldn't decide, his mind pulled apart by two different worlds.

"Mrs. Templeton," he said, "may I ask why you called?"

At that moment the black van filled his rearview mirror, and Cross launched forward in his seat as it collided with his bumper at forty miles per hour. His seat belt caught him and threw him back against the seat. Somehow the phone remained glued in position.

"Well, I'll tell you," Mrs. Templeton responded, a tinge of irritation in her voice. "I wanted to ask yesterday morning, but of course I don't have to tell you my mind was just distracted by the peculiar way you were acting."

Cross slammed the gas pedal against the floorboard, and the car sprang itself from the clutches of the van's front grill. He sped down the road, the van maintaining a close distance.

"Then I thought I'd call yesterday afternoon, but considered you might be resting and didn't want to disturb you. I dropped by before sundown with homemade soup, my mother's recipe. Did you get it?"

Cross pulled into the intersection of Hull Street and Jefferson Davis Highway at full speed, waiting until the last minute to turn sharp right and burn a black mark into the asphalt, cutting off a minivan in the process. The black van copied his maneuver, though it managed to shave the paint off a corner of the minivan.

Cross controlled his heavy breathing as he replied, "I did get it. It was delicious."

"Just about every one of Mama's recipes is delicious. But I guess anything's delicious if you put enough salt and butter in the mix." Mrs. Templeton chuckled at her own quip.

Both vehicles barreled down the highway at hazardous speeds, other motorists signaling their displeasure with horn blasts. Cross guided the car through one intersection after another, passing in and out of lanes as he avoided impacts.

"Well, I wasn't going to bother you then either, if you'd been home. That's why I'm calling today. Now that you're feeling better, I have your full and undivided attention."

Cross opened his mouth to remind her driving in a car while talking on a phone was not the place for an attentive conversation, but before he could utter a sound, another car pulled into his lane, forcing him to slam on the brakes.

His car skidded across the blacktop. Cross swerved for an open lane, but the black van caught up and cornered him between it and the other vehicle. He dropped the phone into a hand and pressed it into his chest as he braced for impact.

The van turned into him and collided with the front driver's-side corner of the car. Cross turned the wheel to counteract the force, but to no avail. His car complied and slid sideways toward a hatchback in the next lane.

The passenger in the hatchback alerted the driver to the imminent accident. The hatchback braked, and its wheels rotated toward the shoulder of the road. The rear bumper of Cross's vehicle nicked the other car as he passed by.

Cross brought the phone back up to his ear to hear Mrs. Templeton continuing to talk. ". . . ladies at my knitting group on Saturday night. Well, we've been doing that new Kimberly Hartford study. Have you heard about it? Well, of course you've heard of it. That lady is just something else, you know."

The van pulled parallel to Cross two lanes to his left. He noticed a slower vehicle in the van's path. Seizing the opportunity, Cross veered into the middle lane and connected with the side of the van.

With no room to maneuver, the van cut through a break in the median and careened into the oncoming traffic lanes. Vehicles diverted course and slammed into each other, light poles, and traffic signs as the van plowed its way down the street in the opposite direction.

"Well, the study is all about the Bible and the American dream, how it . . . well, let me just read it to you. She does such a fine job of explaining what she wants us to know, I don't know why I would try to do any better."

Cross pulled ahead of the van's position in his own lane. He watched in the driver's-side mirror as the van passed a sedan, then cut back across the median and ripped through a thin sapling.

"'If you're like me, you've often asked yourself if there's more to life.'" Mrs. Templeton read from the back cover of the Bible study. "'Congregations all over the country crave the latest trends and gim-micks to jump-start a revival of faith . . .'"

Cross dropped the phone from his ear and gripped the steering wheel with both hands as he banked around a delivery truck. The GPS on the LED display in the dash alerted him to the Virginia State Route 150 entrance ramp less than a mile ahead—150 led to Interstate 95, which would lead the men even farther away from Christine. If Mrs. Templeton would get off the phone, he might even be able to convince Simpson to send in reinforcements.

He put the phone back to his ear and said, "Mrs. Templeton, I . . ."

She paid him no attention as she continued to read. "'Broken but hon-est,' which I can vouch for, Pastor," she interjected with a chuckle. "'Kim will inspire you to get out of your comfort zone and acknowledge . . .'"

Her words didn't register in his ear as the car passed under three large road signs signaling the entrance to SR 150, the middle lane the choice for northbound Interstate 95. The van gained. Traffic clogged.

"'There's more to Christianity . . .'"

He hit the accelerator and flew past a merging tractor-trailer.

"'. . . than having your way . . .'"

The car skidded onto the entrance ramp nearing seventy miles per hour.

"'. . . and keeping it that way.'"

Both tires on the left side of the car hovered an inch off the ground for a second as Cross hugged the turn and merged onto the highway.

"Here's what it says at the very bottom," Mrs. Templeton concluded. "'Our generation is ready for a powerful movement of God. Don't be left behind.' I know I'm not in this woman's generation, but it has been such a joy going through this book with the ladies."

A quick glance in the rearview mirror confirmed Cross's assumption. The black van struggled to repeat his high-speed entry and fell two cars behind. Road signs advertising SR 150's pending fuse with Interstate 95 hovered over the pavement just ahead of him.

"Mrs. Templeton," Cross interjected as she paused to breathe for the first time since the conversation began. "I'm sorry, but I am kind of occupied at the moment. What's the specific question you want to ask?"

"Well, I'm getting to it. I was giving you context for the conversation we were having Saturday night."

A familiar sound caught Cross by the ear. He crooked his neck to catch sight of flashing blue emergency lights atop gray state trooper vehicles speeding down the highway half a mile behind him. The black van on his tail accelerated around a slowing coupe.

"We were talking about the book. Then wouldn't you know it, Mary started talking about something else she'd read about the Tribulation."

Here it comes. He'd already scheduled online classes about eschatology, the study of the end times, for next semester. He wasn't looking forward to it.

"What with all of the fighting going on in the Middle East, the conflict between the Palestinians and Israel, that Islamic group—I forget their name—beheading journalists on video."

Cross cut off a minivan as he veered onto the entrance ramp for Interstate 95, the black van on his heels. The state troopers narrowed the distance by half.

"She quoted a pastor—I can't remember his name either—about how all of this fits into end times prophecy."

The van and state police chased Cross up and over the long interchange.

"And he insisted everything we're seeing in the news today is fulfillment of Second Timothy chapter three. Well, you know Mary. She just went on and on. And I have to tell you, at first I was skeptical, but the more she talked about it, the more I started to think she might be onto something."

The procession of luxury sedan, black van, and three police vehicles jetted off the ramp onto the highway, other vehicles swerving from their path.

Cross expertly guided the car with one hand while he concentrated on Mrs. Templeton's story. He couldn't comprehend her question in light of the circuitous route she took to arrive at the main problem of her Saturday night study.

"Wait," he said. "I thought this had to do with the Hartford book."

"Well, it does. The book prompted the discussion."

"So the study is about the end times?" Cross banked the car across two lanes, horns blaring behind him.

"Well, no, though with Mary in the room, any study might as well be."

Frustration swelled inside him as Cross fought the urge to hang up on her. "Barb, will you please just ask your question?" He regretted the harsh tone. And the use of her first name. The other end of the call fell silent. He checked his phone to see if she had hung up on him.

Still connected.

"I'm sorry, Pastor Cross," she said as he returned the phone to his ear. "You're right. I'm intruding. Perhaps we can talk another time. Goodbye." The line clicked dead.

Cross threw his phone onto the passenger-side floorboard and clenched his teeth to keep from swearing. He stared straight ahead and twisted his hands around the steering wheel. The old Cross fought to emerge from the depths, and he was tempted to let it happen.

Out of the corner of his eye, he saw a black blur rush toward the passenger-side window. The black van slammed into the side of his car, forcing him onto the shoulder of the highway. Cross rocked back and forth in his seat as the van shoved his car into the concrete barrier dividing the highway.

Somehow, the two vehicles maintained speed as Cross fought against the strain on the steering wheel. The tinted window of the van slid open, and a gloved hand grasping a pistol extended through the opening.

CHAPTER TWENTY

CROSS BROUGHT HIS foot down hard on the brake, and the forward momentum of the sedan ceased. The car slipped from between the van and the barrier just as the driver's index finger mashed on the trigger of the gun. Bullets sliced across the hood of Cross's car and drove deep holes into the concrete. Bits of steel and sparks sprayed across the windshield.

Cross's foot shifted from the brake to the gas, and his car skidded back onto the road directly behind the van. Blue flashing lights lit up his rearview mirror. A state trooper's vehicle bore down from behind, its grill threatening to strike his bumper.

The rear doors to the van opened. Inside stood one of the men from the station cradling a tan-and-black Tavor automatic rifle. He trained the sleek but lethal weapon on Cross, and a rapid burst of flame erupted from the barrel.

Cross ducked behind the dash and jerked the wheel to the right. Gunfire bombarded the windshield for a brief moment as he swerved into the center lane. The popping ceased, and Cross sat upright to witness the gunman inadvertently unleash the fury of his weapon into the hood of the police car.

The gun crippled the engine of the trooper's vehicle, and it rolled to a stop in the lane. Motorists bailed for either side of the road as the other two police cars diverged from their pursuits to evade the same fate as their colleague.

The gunman ceased fire and disappeared into the van. Cross pressed on the gas again, and his car lurched forward in the center lane parallel to the van.

The side door to the van slid open, and the gunman reappeared. Cross held his position to the last second, then pitched hard to the right and arranged a sluggish truck towing a cargo trailer between him and the van.

Bullets pinged off the large metal beams tied down to the trailer but couldn't penetrate the thick metal to find their intended target. Cross pushed the car even harder forward and shot out from beside the tractor a full automobile length ahead of the van.

The gunman's aim bent downward, and his shots shredded the truck's tires. In his mirror, Cross watched the tractor-trailer careen out of control, smoke billowing from its tires. The van barely escaped a collision with the cab as it pivoted sideways across all three lanes.

The truck driver managed to keep the cab upright, but the forward momentum of the trailer caused it to tip over and skid to a stop against the highway. Straps snapped, and several metal beams tumbled off the bed and littered the road.

Cross kept an eye on the rearview mirror to see if the troopers made it around the trailer, but it didn't appear so. Suddenly the tinted windshield of the van filled his view, the gunman leaning out from the open side door. Sharp bursts from the rifle thundered against the back of the car.

His goal of leading them away from Christine took a back seat to Cross's own survival. Both cars glided from one far lane to the other, weaving in and out of the increasing mass of additional motorists. The gunman's aim continued to be widespread, hitting not only Cross but other vehicles in addition to the roadway and traffic signs.

The thought *We need air support* flashed in Cross's mind. He had to call Simpson. With the group of men shredding civilians with an automatic rifle, it didn't make sense for Simpson not to get involved now.

Cross felt his front jean pocket for the phone before remembering he had hurled it onto the floorboard on the other side of the car. He searched for where it landed but couldn't get a good look, the madness of navigating a bustling interstate demanding his near complete attention.

The skyline of Richmond loomed large as he passed back over the James River. He needed a plan, and fast. Preferably a plan that involved assistance from an armed helicopter.

He whipped the car in a wide circle around a grouping of delivery trucks, the gunfire on pause as he kept to the enclosed side of the van. The tilt in the motion of the car dislodged the phone from whatever cranny of the floorboard it had hidden in, and it rolled into the middle of the mat.

Cross let up the pressure on the gas pedal and dove the upper half of his body to the floorboard. He scooped the phone up and returned to his full upright position in time to see the taillights of an SUV glowing bright red.

A quick glance into his side mirror confirmed his worst fear. The black van bore down on him in the center lane, closing the gap he needed to escape an assured fatal wreck with the car in front of him. It cut him off as the SUV veered to its left.

Cross stepped on the accelerator and piloted the car between the SUV and the van, scraping the paint on both vehicles but eluding certain death without further damage.

Phone in hand, Cross keyed the special number to Simpson's direct line and held it to his ear. It rang three times before Simpson picked up.

"I've got a bird en route, and she's hot," he said without so much as a hello. "It'll be on your position in eight minutes if you keep north."

Good old Al Simpson. Frustrating when you didn't want him to be, dependable when you needed him to be.

"Oh good. I'm glad you've heard about all the excitement."

"Police bands couldn't be more thrilled. And we're tracking your car."

So CIA surveillance technicians had "serviced" the car. Simpson must've neglected to share that fact with him.

"I appreciate the help," Cross yelled into the phone as gunfire pecked the roof of his car from behind. "But I'm going to need my hand back."

"Stay alive. And get to high ground."

Cross tossed the phone onto the passenger seat as he banked left, then right to bypass a crawling cement truck. *Stay alive.* For eight minutes. Easy for the old man to say while watching a satellite feed. *High ground.* Simpson wanted him to lead the van to an open, less crowded area.

It would make his attackers better targets.

With the tap of his finger on the heads-up display, the map view of his GPS system widened to show a ten-mile radius. At the top edge of the map, he noticed an interchange between 95 and Interstate 295, a bypass less frequently traveled and a prime area for a Black Hawk hunt.

Something felt strange. Howling wind found ways into the cabin through fresh bullet holes. More pressure on the gas pedal fed the engine, and it bellowed back at him, its appetite satisfied. He cut off a minivan, and its driver let him know how much he didn't appreciate the gesture. That was all. Cross heard only wind, engine, and road rage.

No gunfire.

No crunching of metal.

Oh no. They've given up. They'd grown tired from the chase and had retreated to try to track down Christine. He saw a marker for an upcoming exit ramp and decided to use it to U-turn and make his way back to the hospital.

The loud, deep growl of another more sinister engine blasted against his door window as the black van pulled alongside. It slammed into him and claimed his side mirror as a casualty.

He recoiled and waited for the shower of bullets to rain upon him from the barrel of the Tavor, but the weapon was silent. Instead, the thud of a body landing on the roof of his car echoed from the ceiling to the floorboard.

Cross turned into the attack from the van and pushed it into the farthest lane. He steered around one car after another while trying to maintain speed and spot his new, unwanted passenger.

He heard the man's arms and legs bang against the roof of the sedan. Cross rocked the car in erratic movements to try to throw the man off, but no luck. A thud against the trunk directed his eyes to the rearview mirror. The man's boots planted against the lid. A fist collided with the fractured rear window.

The fist punched clean through the glass. The man pulled back against the crippled section of window and opened a hole large enough to slide his legs through. His chest came next, followed by a face obscured beneath a black ski mask, and finally a pair of jacketed arms.

The man fell into the back seat and aimed a pistol at Cross's head. Cross put his foot on the brake and pressed it full to the floor. The car skidded to a halt as the black van raced by.

Cross's seat belt performed an admirable job of keeping him in place, but the man was less fortunate. The force of the sudden stop propelled his body forward, the pistol in his hand extending past Cross's head as the assailant pulled the trigger. The bullet pierced the front windshield.

Cross grabbed the man's arm, pulled his body across the center console, and slammed him against the dashboard. The man's grip on the handgun loosened, and it fell onto the floorboard.

Car horns blared and brakes squealed as other cars careened out of control around them. Cross released the pressure on the brake and reapplied it in equal force to the gas pedal. The car thundered to life, and it took only four seconds for the 6.3-liter engine to reach sixty miles per hour.

His unwelcome passenger righted himself in the seat and fumbled for the gun. Cross grabbed him by his jacket collar and pulled his back flush against the leather. The man stared ahead with wide eyes as Cross navigated the busy highway with one hand.

He narrowly missed the rear end of a minivan before settling into an open lane with space ahead. Cross breathed a sigh of relief, then glanced over at the man in the passenger seat. He cocked an eyebrow as the hint of a smile stretched the ski mask across the man's face.

It disappeared in an instant, and the man lunged for Cross, both hands descending like animal claws to devour his neck. Cross deflected the attack with his forearm, then chopped with his hand at the man's throat.

He struck sure. The man's claws retracted and grabbed at his own throat as he strained to breathe through his crushed trachea.

His car caught up to the black van, and Cross needed to take the lead as they inched ever closer to the exit for 295 on his GPS display.

Ski-mask man regained his composure. Cross grabbed him once more by the jacket collar and shoved his face into the dashboard. He repeated the move twice more, then let the man slump against the passenger door, unconscious, blood seeping from both nostrils.

A shiny green sign hanging overhead declared the exit for 295 a quarter mile away. Cross gunned the engine, desperate to beat the van to the ramp and lead it up and out into the open.

Four hundred and forty yards.

He came up behind the van and accelerated even more. The car responded with ease, its speed still well below the capability of the engine.

Three hundred and fifty-two yards.

His attacker in the passenger seat stirred.

Two hundred and sixty-four yards.

The car roared past the van.

One hundred and seventy-six yards.

Cross swung the car full to the right as it shot up the entrance ramp. He braked to keep the car from flipping on the corner and to bait the van into following him, but it was too late. He lost control of the car, and it skidded off the merge lane and onto 295 on its own.

As Cross predicted, no other vehicles greeted them save a tanker already past the entrance ramp and disappearing down the road. He coaxed the steering wheel to ease the car out of its drift and into a straight course down the highway.

The van peeled into the lane behind him, but struggling to catch up, thanks to his luxury sedan's powerful engine. Cross looked out over the trees lining the interstate, hoping to see the hovering black form of a helicopter ready to end the pursuit.

He saw only stars as a blow to his ear disoriented him. Another hand wrapped around his own and yanked down on the steering wheel.

The car pivoted across two lanes of the highway, threatening to flip, but gravity forced the tires to stick like glue. He came to a stop in the middle of the highway, the driver's side facing oncoming traffic.

Cross's vision merged from double back to single as he looked up out his window and watched the black van aim itself like a missile right at him. It closed the gap within seconds as it picked up speed. He waited for his life to play out like a documentary on a movie screen, all the memories, feelings, regrets, and decisions presented as a prologue to his death.

But the only flash he saw belonged to the detonation of a seventy-millimeter Hydra 70 rocket against the pavement just under the left side of the van. The explosion lifted the van from the earth and tossed it like a piece of trash into the embankment of trees along the shoulder of the highway.

Cross sat still and listened to the beat of the Black Hawk rotors envelop the area around him. He breathed heavy, his heart racing.

A cold steel barrel pressed against the back of his head. The wheezing from ski-mask man's narrow throat grew audible over the helicopter blades. He rasped in Cross's ear, "I should kill you myself."

"Drop the weapon!" came the reply from just outside the passenger-side door. "Drop it now!"

The pressure from the barrel disappeared, and Cross turned to see the man holding it over his head, his finger free from the trigger. The passenger door opened, and a soldier clad in tactical gear whisked the man away.

Cross's own door opened, and another similarly dressed soldier greeted him. "Mr. Cross, I need you to come with me, sir. I have orders to deliver you to the Farm."

Great. The Farm.

The one place he prayed he would never see again.

CHAPTER TWENTY-ONE

CHRISTINE STRUGGLED TO understand what happened. An hour passed after John left, and in that short amount of time she grew attached to the old woman nursing a broken arm in a hospital bed. Lori Johnson was the sweetest, wisest woman Christine had ever met. She wanted to learn as much as she could from this woman's life.

They swapped stories of childhood, first loves, and neglected dreams. Christine told Lori things she had yet to confide in her mother about, and her transparency scared her.

She finished laughing about Lori's habitual pranking of her younger brother as the older woman paused her yarns to chew some crushed ice between her teeth. "Lori," Christine said, her lips affixed in a perpetual grin. "You have wonderful stories. Now I understand why John likes you so much."

"Speaking of John," Lori replied after swallowing the ice chips. "I'd like to know why he likes you so much."

Christine averted her eyes and felt the warm flush of her skin spread from her cheeks to her arms. "How do you know he likes me?"

"Oh, I read him like a book when he walked through the door. You too."

Christine hesitated and her smile shrunk. She didn't want to talk about John. Why wasn't he here yet?

Lori adjusted the sling on her arm. "Tell me again how you met? John saw your boyfriend attacking you and fought him off?"

"Well, that's not quite . . ." What was she doing? Christine wanted to lie but found it an impossible task. Something about the woman told Christine it would be fruitless, as though Lori would be able to identify a falsehood from a truth. "I mean . . ." she stammered.

Lori cleared her throat. "It's all right, Christine," she said. "You can tell me. I already know all about John."

Christine started. How much did Lori know? Was it a bluff? Her head spun as she thought of a response.

"Honey, trust me. I'm not as old and ignorant as you might think, and that man isn't as closed and careful as he likes to pretend." Lori's hand rested over Christine's and rubbed her knuckles. "Showing up out of the blue, no real reason to be living in Mechanicsville. Able to get by without a steady job. The most well-built man I've ever seen. Could remember the smallest details. But I see the pain he's running from in his eyes. He'd disappear for days on end. Early on he had fits of anger."

Christine's heart felt like it was swimming laps.

Lori leaned in closer. "I'm also a news junkie, Ms. Lewis."

The charade collapsed, and Christine felt a weight lift from her shoulders. "I'm sorry, Lori. I . . . I was just trying to protect John."

"Like he's protecting you now."

Christine nodded.

"Well, I don't have anywhere to be, and since there's no point in you lying to me anymore, why don't you tell me what happened?"

"John saved me in Jordan. By himself." The truth ripped shackles from her spirit. The room brightened.

"That's not what you said in your interview."

"The government denies John's involvement. Lori, I wasn't going to betray him."

Lori smiled. "I believe you."

"You don't even know me," Christine interjected. She averted her gaze in embarrassment at her compulsive impoliteness.

"We may have just met," Lori replied. "But I've lived long enough to get to know someone very well in a short period of time. Besides, I can tell you trust him just by the look in your eyes."

"Well then." Christine looked back at Lori, the older woman's demeanor soft and inviting, and couldn't help but smile. "What else can you tell about me?"

Lori lifted her chin and narrowed her eyes to study Christine's face. "You're a very driven woman, so young and yet so far in your career. But I would think there's uncertainty about your future. It's as if you're pursuing a goal someone else told you was out there but you've never really seen for yourself."

Christine surprised herself with a swallow louder than she intended. She cleared her throat, but it did nothing to the lump forming inside. Words, images, emotions all flooded her mind. An outside force opened her mouth, and the content of her mind found its way to her tongue.

"Everything changed in Jordan. I believed I would die there. And nothing I had done since I left for college mattered. None of it. Years wasted in pursuit of what everyone else thought was success. But in all that time I missed it. Something. I still don't know what it is."

"It's *true* purpose, Christine. Knowing that what you're doing means more than just passing the time until you die."

The familiar sensation of puffy tear ducts attracted Christine's hand to her eye. Lori's words drew her inner turmoil to the surface. "Do you think that's why I came here to find John? Did I think he could give me purpose?"

Lori laughed. "Oh goodness, how am I to know something like that?"

Christine pulled her hand away and wrinkled her nose in mock resentment. "You're the one who said you knew what I was thinking."

"Dear, the questions you're asking yourself are ones everybody has asked themselves at one time or another. We're born asking why. God did that for a reason. It's the first clue in this big mystery game."

Something prodded Christine's heart. She felt it as clear as the sun beating against the hospital window, but she couldn't determine its source. Though afraid to discover what it was, she found herself compelled to press into the conversation. She took another try at swallowing the lump and asked, "It's Jesus, isn't it? John left the CIA because of Jesus. And now he believes what he does matters."

"You are a good reporter. And yes, he believes, as do I, that the answer to all our questions can be found in the person of Jesus Christ."

"I've read the Bible. Some. I don't remember finding many answers."

"There's reading the Bible, then there's *reading* the Bible. If you're looking for answers to questions like 'What job should I have?' or 'Can I get a tattoo?' you won't find them. What you will find is better than answers. It's a story. A story about *the* answer, not answers."

Christine recalled the stories she'd heard in Sunday school as a child, but what an old boat filled with animals had to do with a battle between a little boy and a giant was lost on her. "You're going to have to give me the summary," she admitted.

"God made human beings to live out a grand purpose on earth, but we rejected his plan in favor of our own. That's what sin is, the rejection of God and the criminal pursuit of our own pleasure and glory. But there's always a penalty for crime. And we face a penalty for ours: eternal death." Lori grabbed Christine's hand again. "God loves you, Christine. He loves you because he created you. And he never wanted you to face that penalty. So he spent thousands of years on a plan. A plan to become a man named Jesus and die on a cross for your sins. But it didn't end there. Three days later he rose from the grave, and he promises to do the same thing for those who believe in him."

Christine couldn't think of a single time from her childhood where she heard a summary of the Jesus story quite like Lori's. Earlier questions evacuated her mind in favor of brand new ones. Was it true? What about other stories in the Bible that seemed so farfetched? What if it *was* true? What then?

"Excuse me," said a masculine voice from the door.

Christine and Lori both jumped at the unexpected interruption. A curly-haired man wearing a knee-length white coat and a stethoscope slung over his shoulder stood inside the room, holding the curtain back with one hand. He shifted his stare from Christine to the bed and asked, "Lori Johnson?"

"Yes, that's me," Lori stammered. "I'm sorry to be so flustered. We were talking, and I didn't see you come in." She offered a nervous chuckle.

"It's quite all right," the man said, smiling wide. "My name's Dr. Bradshaw. I'm one of the resident orthopedic surgeons. How are you feeling?"

"I'm doing OK. They're giving me some good medication." Lori nudged Christine with her elbow and winked.

Bradshaw pointed at Christine and asked, "Would you be Ms. Johnson's daughter?"

Before Christine could reply, Lori interjected, "I'm sorry, young man, but do I look old enough to have a daughter?"

"I . . . uh . . ." The physician backpedaled, his face reddening.

Lori tried to fold her arms, but the cast impeded her. She sat straighter and gripped Christine's hand in her own. "I was a teenage mother."

That is *some good medication*, Christine thought.

Bradshaw coughed and rubbed a finger under his nose. "Well, we've been studying your injury and trying to decide how we want to proceed with treatment. As you've been told, there were two breaks, and even though the joint did not suffer any damage, we're still concerned about ensuring full mobility once it heals, your age being a factor."

Lori huffed and rolled her eyes. Christine disguised her involuntary smile with a pair of fingers.

"If it's all right with you, Miss Johnson, I'd like to discuss your options with your daughter, and then you can decide how you want to proceed after you've, uh, rested."

Christine wanted to object but could tell Lori was having fun.

"I suppose Christine can handle the bad news for me." Lori grinned. "Go ahead, dear."

Bradshaw held open the curtain, and Christine obliged, rising out of the chair and heading into the hallway. The nurses' station appeared vacant, and she detected the familiar sound of a heart monitor several rooms away.

"This way." Bradshaw stood still, his open palm directing her down the hall.

Christine nodded and walked ahead. With each step, she felt less at ease. The air was stale, cold. Lori's antics amused her, but now she questioned the exchange in her mind. Why did the doctor insist on speaking only to her? And why in another location?

Fingers wrapped tightly around her bicep and squeezed.

"Hey, watch it," she protested.

Bradshaw forced her farther down the hallway. She opened her mouth to cry out for help, but he shoved her through a door and into an empty stairwell before she could utter a sound.

Bradshaw moved down the stairs, pulling her forcibly alongside him. She grabbed the rail with her other hand to steady her descent. She fought to control her breathing and calm the trepidation in her heart.

"Who are you? Let go of me!" she demanded.

Bradshaw, if that was even his real name, responded with a tighter grip and a quicker pace. At each landing, as they rounded the corner to the next flight of stairs, Christine held her breath and waited for John to burst through a door.

He wouldn't. She sensed it.

Kidnapped all over again. Most likely by men of the same persuasion as her captors in Jordan. Which meant a repeat of her previous ordeal. Memories of her imprisonment overwhelmed her. She felt the bruises, smelled the musty room, tasted the blood from a cut lip.

No. Not this time.

She didn't need John to rescue her. He wouldn't always be there. He couldn't always be there. She had to fight for herself. Her lungs filled with oxygen. Blood coursed through her muscles. She kept pace with Bradshaw, pulling him forward instead of the other way around.

They stepped onto another landing and rounded the corner. Bradshaw lifted his foot to step down. Christine locked her grip on the railing and thrust her foot across his exposed ankle.

He cried out as he tripped over her leg. He released her arm and tumbled down the stairwell, spreading his hands out to break his fall. After a couple of somersaults, Bradshaw collapsed in a heap at the exit to the seventh floor.

Run!

The command from her mind broke through the fog of surprised relief. Christine swiveled and ran back up the stairs. She could hear Bradshaw saying something behind her, but she couldn't tell if she misheard him or if he spoke a different language altogether.

She spotted the door to the ninth floor. She could run back to Lori's room, where she would be safe. Or would she? Christine hesitated, then passed by the door and ascended the next set of steps. She couldn't involve Lori. And someone else might be waiting. If they wanted her, they would have to work for it.

She picked up her speed as she passed the tenth-floor exit. Another flight, another landing, and she found eleventh. A metal bar blocked her path farther up, a sign latched to it reading NO ENTRY. Christine recalled the buttons in the elevator. Eleven was it. The final stop.

There was nowhere else to go. With no other option available, Christine lowered her shoulder and threw her body into the release bar. The door swung open, and she followed it through into the hallway only to collide with a man on the other side.

Rough, dark hands pressed against her and pushed her out of the hallway and back into the stairwell. She looked up, eyes wide, into the face of a man she didn't recognize. His mustache was darker than his skin, his eyes invisible beneath the shadow of a short bill cap.

"Sorry, Ms. Lewis," he said in a thick accent.

A glint caught Christine's eye, and she spotted the shiny black weapon held at his side. "No . . ." she said as he raised his hand.

What?

She fixated on the thin, rectangular shape of the barrel of the gun. A faint blue glow sliced the darkness inside.

The man pulled the trigger. An electric pop announced the expulsion of a black disc from the barrel.

The disc struck Christine in the chest. Blue electricity snaked its way across her skin, her muscles froze, and she collapsed to the floor. Her eyelids refused to shut, and she watched in terror as the man stepped toward her.

Christine clenched her jaw, her mind screaming signals at every immobile appendage to no avail. Just when she thought her body was going to tear itself apart, the disc released its death grip. Every muscle relaxed, her head slumped, and her eyelids drooped.

Darkness filled her mind and swept her away to unconsciousness.

CHAPTER TWENTY-TWO

CROSS PERCHED ON the edge of the fuselage, his feet dangling out of the open cabin door as the Black Hawk skimmed the tree line toward Williamsburg. A second Black Hawk followed in close proximity, his friends from the van guarded by a Ranger unit inside. Black plumes of cloud covered the distant horizon, a few near imperceptible flashes of lightning promising the arrival of a thunderstorm.

The two specially designed stealth aircraft flew at a whisper, at least the kind of whisper a tactical transport helicopter might utter. Cross shifted his weight backward as he felt the Black Hawk maneuver right. He was tethered to the interior, but he preferred not to spend the rest of the ride dangling against the chassis of the metal beast.

The Rangers in his bird offered no additional information when he questioned them. With the attack squad in custody, he only cared about confirming Christine's safety, but he knew as soon as they landed in the Farm, the vultures would descend.

The Farm.

Memories from his training days at Camp Perry—the Farm, a more affectionate name bestowed on the place by recruits—distracted him from his present apprehensions. Almost all other officers inducted by Central Intelligence in the secluded base detested the Farm. The mock interrogations, subjection to torture techniques, and intentional contamination of meals were all designed to harden an officer into a machine of the state.

Where others bemoaned the treatment, in his youth Cross embraced it. On his first day of many in the uncomfortable conditions, he resolved that whether he died or survived, he favored either outcome over the meaningless existence he'd left behind.

No fear in death. That attitude made him a successful covert operative, and surprisingly, successful in ministry as well. A key difference being he now knew where he would go upon that death.

Just ahead of the Black Hawk, Cross saw the reflective surface of the York River. The copter slowed and descended in a precarious angle. For a second, Cross considered lifting his feet into the helicopter to keep from catching the top branch of a deciduous.

The forest canopy bent backward in a wide arc in obedience to the powerful thrust of the rotors. Right when it seemed they would break apart, the landscape parted into a flat dirt strip. Both helicopters hovered in the space above the strip, and landing gear released. Within seconds, wheels touched earth and the muffled drone of the engines quieted even more.

A Ranger behind him released the strap from around his abdomen. Cross slid off the fuselage and walked toward the two familiar faces at the edge of the runway.

Simpson extended a hand as Cross approached. "Looks like you took a few scratches but kept all the essentials," he said with a smile.

Cross shook the open hand and offered his own grin in return. "I've had worse odds."

Guin only nodded in his direction before pretending to be preoccupied with a tablet in her hand. Simpson pivoted on a heel and marched back to a waiting military jeep. Cross and Guin fell in step behind him.

"Good to see you too," Cross whispered.

Guin didn't look up from the tablet. "They could have killed you," she replied.

"But they didn't."

"This time." She didn't sound amused.

Cross kept silent as he joined her in the back of the jeep. A stoic soldier drove them to a nondescript brick building capped by a green tin roof. They stepped out of the vehicle and made their way inside.

The Farm was intentionally sterile. Gray hallways led to gray doors behind which were gray rooms holding the barest of gray furniture. It wasn't a question of affording luxury, rather squelching an appetite for comfort and leisure.

Guin took the lead, and they followed her into one of the bare rooms at the end of the hall. A single light hung loose over a metal table hosting only two chairs. Simpson grabbed the back of one chair and slid it free from underneath the tabletop. He motioned to Cross and added a gentle, "Please, have a seat."

Cross obliged. Guin kept her nose in the tablet by a corner in the room while Simpson took the seat across the table.

"So this is what it feels like on the other side of an interrogation," Cross said with a chuckle.

Simpson offered no jovial retorts. He picked a few strands of lint from his suit jacket and sighed. "We've got a bit of a mess on our hands, John."

"Yeah, sorry about that. I know how much of a pain the Virginia Department of Transportation can be. I just hope we didn't tear up too much of the interstate."

"That's not what I'm talking about."

Cross straightened in his chair. Simpson's eye twitched too noticeably. He was stiff. Guin didn't speak. The air thickened with tension.

Something was wrong.

"Can you explain to me what you were doing at Main Street Station?" Simpson's eyes glistened like ice as he stared Cross down.

"You know what I was doing there. Trying to put eyes on our identity thief from Greece."

"That lead ran cold."

"Excuse me?"

Guin finally spoke. "A young Greek thug with fake credentials was picked up in DC an hour ago. It was an illegal joyride. He's even confessed to robbing and murdering George Carson."

"No, that's a red herring. I spotted our guy in Richmond. His men are the ones you've taken into custody."

Simpson waved Cross's objections aside with his hand. "The men involved in the freeway altercation have been identified as a private security group out of DC. They claim you threatened a man at the station, a businessman they were hired to protect, and resisted arrest. They attempted to assist law enforcement in your capture, not something they really had the right to do but an understandable response, depending on what exactly occurred in the station."

Cross clenched his loose jaw and balled his fists on the tabletop. "You've got to be messing with me."

Guin moved from the corner and leaned across the table, holding the bright tablet up for him to see. "Their documents are valid." Several photos displayed on the screen, all with the seal of a private Washington security firm and a green label with CONFIRMED stamped under each name.

Cross gathered all the anger swelling at his core into his fingertips and dug his nails deep into his palms. Whoever pulled the strings just executed a skillful maneuver. He had nothing to play in return. No evidence to the contrary, and any credit he held against his body of work with the Company was near empty.

He released the tension in his fists and spread his hands out on the table. "OK," he said. "I don't know what is going on here, but those men are not the same men that were at the station. I don't know who they are. And all I can offer you is my word."

"Don't think your word isn't worth something," Simpson offered. "But you're right. It's all you've got."

"So what happens now?"

"We're in a holding pattern until we can sort this thing out."

"What about Christine? Please tell me you're sending someone to pick her up."

"They should have her in hand any minute."

Cross's heart slowed its pace. The consolation of the nightmare unfolding before him in the cramped, bleak room was Christine's security. "Do me a favor," he said. "Can you let me know when they confirm?"

Simpson stood and tapped the desk with his fingertips. "You bet." With that, both he and Guin left the room.

Cross knew what would happen next. Evidence would be gathered. Stories recorded. Then a timeline pieced together. He was confident nothing could be substantiated. Even if the questionable security force brought a trumped-up charge against him, the proof would be threadbare at best and dismissed in a reasonable amount of time.

It was going to be fine. This was better. The Farm was secure, and with the CIA bringing Christine in, no attempt on her life could be made. Even the tiny room that was now his temporary holding cell seemed like a posh suite in comparison to any number of holes he'd occupied in the field.

His brain processed the new information, and he found himself beguiled by the fake–George Carson ruse. The men from the train station perpetrated the gas station attack. But the black van involved in the chase revealed a new group of suspects. Was it a purposeful diversion to get to Christine? Or backup after the original attempt to detain Cross failed?

What was George Carson doing now? As yet, Cross assumed he was the critical link to Christine's location. She'd left nothing of a trail, outside of him, in the area. Without him there was nowhere to start. Even tracking her to the hotel would lead to a dead end at the airport. Contrary to the reality portrayed on television, facial recognition software was still in its infancy. It would take them a lot of money and connections to find and track his car from the airport to the hospital.

A new batch of unanswerable questions entered his mind: What was the true identity of the man impersonating George Carson? What, if any, organized criminal group was he associated with? How deep did his resources run when it came to locating Christine? Cross had thought the answers would come easy after leading the black van straight into the arms of American intelligence.

Instead, he only faced another brick wall of uncertainty. Cross hated uncertainty. It only prompted his imagination to start building scenarios. And when his imagination got involved, absurd conclusions became too easy to jump on.

His problem wasn't absurd conclusions. It was that those absurd conclusions often turned out to be accurate.

The one thing Cross could count on with any scenario was the more absurd, the more likely to be true. It wasn't just one man who stole an identity and successfully made it onto American soil—it was an entire group of extremists. And entire groups with criminal backgrounds didn't make it through security checkpoints that easy.

Half a dozen men with likely ties to terrorism walked around Virginia's capital in broad daylight. Cash must've filled a lot of loose pockets between when they'd left their country of origin and now.

The most obvious answer to his questions seemed the most absurd: the men weren't there for Christine. They were there for Cross. He closed his eyes and shook his head, hoping it'd shake loose a new theory. It couldn't be him. He didn't exist. He never had. How would they have—

Cross opened his eyes and took a deep breath. Whatever the reason, he knew there was more beneath the surface surrounding Christine and the mystery man from Main Street Station. An answer that included a rat hiding somewhere within the United States' domestic security net.

He detected the barest vibrations of movement in the hallway. When the door did not open, he stood from the chair and pressed against it, straining his ear to pick up any useful sound. The metal door was thick, but not thick enough, thanks to the age of the Farm. He could just make out a pair of voices arguing at a raised volume.

". . . finished sweeping the floors and still nothing," Guin said.

Simpson cursed. "Well, we can't tell him."

"What other choice do you have? He'd know if it was a lie."

"You tell me, Officer Sullivan. I make up a story about new protocols forcing us to process the extraction at a different location, or I inform the volatile, religious fanatic inside this room that we lost his new girlfriend?"

Cross balled his fist and swung at the door. He pulled the punch at the last second and gritted his teeth to keep from yelling. If he shouted through the locked door, it would only confirm Simpson's assessment of his explosive behavior.

The voices faded from his ear as a new set of questions presented themselves to his bewildered mind. How did they found her? No one knew he'd visited the hospital except Gary. And there was no way Gary knew Christine was involved. That could only mean . . .

Oh no.

There *were* others who knew Christine was at the hospital. And at that very moment, they stood on the opposite side of the door. There was always the outside possibility a random dirty officer or analyst brought into the mix had betrayed Christine's location. But the more absurd conclusion . . .

Cross pressed against the door again and picked the conversation back up.

"What do you care, Officer Sullivan?" Simpson pressed, his temper flaring.

"I don't care," Guin replied, trying to prove her indifference with an eye roll. "I'm just saying, this is a more complicated situation than Cross wanting to date the woman."

Simpson grumbled under his breath. "Fine. The story to former officer Cross is that the *journalist*, not his girlfriend, was suspicious of our men and made an attempt to evade the extraction. We took forceful measures, and ultimately we're taking her straight to Langley, where she'll rendezvous with him once we finish up here."

"Sounds fine as long as you can sell it."

"Oh, I'm not going to be the salesman on this one."

Guin leveled her eyes at her boss. "You're joking. I can't possibly—"

Simpson waved her off with a finger. "That's an order. His guard will be down with you."

Guin pursed her lips. He gave the order, which meant her options equaled a grand total of one. She pulled the keycard from her waist and passed it by the computerized lock against the doorframe. A beep and a green light assured her the door could now be opened.

She grabbed the door handle and glared at Simpson. "Consider my protest formal."

"Already did."

He was right though. Cross and his former superior had been close in days past. Simpson would not have been a convincing liar. She, on the other hand, possessed a handful of disarming characteristics to aid in convincing men of just about anything she wanted to. She'd told herself she would always use her powers for good.

She even believed her own lies on occasion.

Guin stepped through the threshold and closed the door behind her. Cross was still seated at the table. She took the other seat and placed her tablet facedown on her lap. "John, I have some unfortunate news."

Cross's eyes widened, and he leaned forward. "Is it about Christine?"

"She's OK. It was just a little hard to convince her we're the good guys. Girl's got some spunk."

He laughed. "Tell me about it. One of her many endearing qualities."

She winced, then covered her hint of jealousy with a chuckle of her own. "Two of our officers have sore kneecaps, but they'll live. Unfortunately, we had to use a moderate amount of force to get her to comply, and because of some new protocols . . ."

"Let me guess," Cross interrupted. "They can't bring her here."

Guin nodded. "She's on a Black Hawk headed to Langley as we speak."

"Red tape, am I right?"

Alarms sounded in Guin's brain, and she nearly pressed her hands against her ears, as if that would keep him from hearing them. He was reacting well to the "news."

Too well.

"John, I'm telling you the truth. Christine is going to be fine."

Cross leaned back in his chair, his eyes soft and a pleasant smile adorning his lips. "I believe you, Guin."

She thought he didn't, but then she couldn't read him. She could always read him. "Good." She stood to leave.

"Hey," he said, prompting her to pause. "Do you think I could have a soda while I wait?"

"Of course," she replied. "Anything to keep you comfortable."

She stole one more look at him as she shut the door to the room. He stared back, smiling, his eyes glistening, his physique shaped perfectly by the dusty polo shirt. Without a word, his demeanor communicated his trust in her, his contentment at the situation, and his willingness to cooperate however they needed him to in order to reach a satisfying resolution.

All of it lies.

An officer entered the room carrying a small red can of dark cola. The black suit and tie he wore seemed like it was regularly laundered with a hydraulic press. He stood six foot one or two by the look of him, and based on how he carried himself, Cross guessed they shared a similar range of numbers on a bathroom scale. The thin, coiled plastic wire tucked behind his ear disappeared down the back of his shirt. His free hand hung poised over the service weapon attached to his hip.

Cross didn't move from his chair. "Well, that was fast. You guys aren't very good at the whole sweatbox thing." He grinned and held out a hand for the soda.

The officer didn't acknowledge the attempts at humor. Silently, he stretched the can toward Cross from across the table. Cross let his fingers collapse against the can with a careless attitude. The other man's grip released, and the can slipped from his palm, crashed against the table, and rolled off to the floor.

"Oops," Cross said. "My fault." He held up both hands as the officer rocked backward and his gun hand twitched. "Easy, cowboy. I'll get it."

Cross took his time shifting in his chair, then kneeling against the table and ducking his torso under it to retrieve the can. Keeping the table as a shield between him and the officer, he shook the soda for good measure.

He sat up and regained the officer's watchful eye. With a thumb positioned against the tab of the can, he opened his free hand and asked, "Did you bring me the aspirin I asked for?"

The officer's neck muscles relaxed, and he reached for his jacket pocket. Cross maintained eye contact, as did the officer, and held his limbs and fingers frozen in place. The officer didn't know it, but he was playing the old schoolyard game of chicken. Instead of bicycles, like he did in elementary school, Cross played this game with his eyes.

He'd won every time in school.

The man's pupils shifted ever so slightly to his pocket as he slipped his fingers into it for the aspirin. Cross flicked the tab of the soda can with his thumb and pressed a finger against the pressurized stream of liquid as it exploded forth.

The cola gushed against the officer's nose and splashed into his eyes. He pulled his handgun from the holster and wiped at his eyes with his other hand. Cross kicked the table into the man's midsection. The officer doubled over. Grabbing him by the jacket collar, Cross pulled him forward over the table and threw him into a heap on the floor.

The man let go of the handgun, and it slid to a stop against a wall behind him. He scrambled for it on his hands and knees, but right as his fingers grazed against the grip, Cross lifted him up from behind and slammed him into the wall.

Cross relaxed his hold on the man to give him a false opening. True to his training, the officer swung an elbow in reverse. Cross ducked and let the man spin onto his back. The officer pushed himself off the wall and prepared for a counterstrike.

He threw his punch quick and hard, a sure hit against any other match, but Cross parried effectively and sent his own punch into the man's nasal cavity with enough force to fracture bone. The officer's head rocked backward and collided with the wall. His eyes crossed, his knees buckled, and he fell to the floor as consciousness slipped away.

Cross slowed his breathing and froze his muscles. He watched the door for the reinforcements descending on him to avenge their fallen comrade, but the room remained silent.

Satisfied with no additional visitors, Cross dragged the officer's body flat against the floor and patted it down. He pulled the officer's security card from a pocket and studied the man's identification.

"Sorry about this, Officer Hardy. But I'm going to need your clothes."

CHAPTER TWENTY-THREE

CROSS EXITED THE building with relative ease thanks to the generous donation of Officer Hardy's black suit and security card. Vacant hallways and unlocked doors greeted him. He spotted a handful of soldiers patrolling the grounds of the Farm, but Cross prided himself in his convincing dramatic portrayal of a Company man sent on a purposeful errand. He kept his distance to minimize visibility of the dull blood and soda stains on the jacket.

The charade worked to a degree, but Cross knew an impasse waited around a corner. His escape from the building might as well have been an afternoon stroll through a park, but the real challenge was leaving the grounds. The CIA took great pains to ensure the Farm was impenetrable from the outside, and even greater pains to make it difficult for its occupants to escape their tortuous training from the inside.

Difficult, but not impossible.

During his tenure at the Farm, Cross and his fellow new recruits heard legends of three different escape routes to the outside world. He wondered if the CIA handlers overseeing the compound left a few deliberate holes to further test a recruit's acumen at circumventing imprisonment.

Cross himself never bothered looking for the mythical tunnels, or whatever new method each escape story proposed. Not for fear of capture and subsequent cruelty, but mere lack of interest.

As he marched across an open field, keeping an eye on a squad of soldiers to his left, he wished he had. He tried recalling any story that seemed valid, any memory that would give him an edge in his escape. He couldn't just walk out the front gate.

He needed a vehicle.

Soldiers on his left stood between him and several SUVs. A tree line on his right hid thick walls capped by barbed wire. Another grouping of buildings ahead formed a concrete fortification against the bank of the York River.

The menacing blackness of the approaching storm stretched low above him, thin arms of clouds reaching forward to the horizon. A rumble of thunder in the distance was answered by the sharp wail of an alarm crying out from behind Cross.

Officer Hardy must be awake.

The riverside buildings would have to do. Cross maintained his pace, though he imagined his back was seconds from becoming a sniper's target practice.

I hope they aim for the knees.

The yelling from behind overtook the noise from the alarm. He kept his eyes glued to the nearest door. Twenty yards and closing. Tires tearing through dirt joined the cacophony of sirens and shouts.

Cross froze within an arm's length of the door handle and paused to glance back at the facility. Across the field, a half-naked Officer Hardy stood huffing and puffing. Simpson and Guin flanked him on either side. Soldiers and SUVs spread out in all directions.

Guin surveyed the compound, and Cross kept his eyes trained until they met hers. He expected a flash of anger, but instead her eyebrows drooped. Hardy spotted him at the same moment and shouted as he pointed toward Cross's position. Soldiers and SUVs spun in their tracks and rushed the building.

Cross grabbed for the door handle, but it pulled away from him as the door opened on its own. An older man in overalls started backward as he cried, "Hey, what's going on?"

Cross shook his head and frowned. Pulling Hardy's handgun from his waistband, Cross forced the older man into the building and shut the door behind them. "Don't do anything stupid and you won't get hurt," he said. "I'm only looking for a way out."

"Good luck, pal," said the old man, more annoyed now than surprised. "This is Camp Perry. You can't get out unless they let you out."

Cross glanced around the open warehouse structure and considered his options. Several enclosed docks floated in water covering half the floor. A mechanized door made up the entire wall of the building, trapped river water lapping at its base in a futile effort to be released back into the river channel. Rigid-hulled inflatable boats used by military police rocked in silence at the docks, three in total.

"This'll do," Cross said and motioned to the wide garage door with an elbow. "I'm gonna need you to open that door, friend."

The old man complied in a calm, somewhat affable manner. With the flip of a heavy switch, gears cranked and forced rusty chains to lift the door up out of the water. Cross kept the handgun trained on the old man as he stepped into one of the inflatable boats and turned the key dangling in the ignition.

Backing the boat away from the dock, Cross grinned at the old man before tossing him the handgun. With his mouth agape and forehead wrinkled in the center, the old man caught the gun and pointed it Cross's direction. "What kind of a fool are you?" he bellowed.

Without waiting for a reply, the old man squeezed the trigger. The gun clicked, but not a single bullet fired. His expression turned sour as he turned the handle over his grip and glared at the empty magazine well.

As the boat puttered under the door, Cross winked back at the man and replied, "The worst kind." He spun the wheel, and the boat groaned in protest as it twisted in the shallow water.

From behind him, Cross heard the door explode, then combat boots smacking against the concrete slab. He jammed the accelerator forward, and the boat lurched. As it sliced through the water and out into the open, Cross looked over his shoulder to see a squad of military police taking aim.

Lightning cracked overhead as fingers depressed triggers and a hailstorm of bullets smashed into the stern. Cross squatted to avoid the gunfire, though the MPs aimed aft in an effort to disable the craft.

The distance between the boat and the covered dock expanded at a rapid rate until he was too far down the river for the rifles to be effective. The shooting stopped, punctuated by yet another web of lightning snaking its way from one storm cloud to another.

Granted a reprieve from danger, Cross stood and gained his bearings. Camp Perry sat on the west bank of the York River, his back to the south. If he kept his nose pointed ahead, it'd take him north toward the river's mouth and the Atlantic Ocean. Cross cycled through the stored map system in his mind and accessed what he knew about the area.

A cold chill iced the blood in his veins. Sure, he'd survived the frying pan. But pushing speeds of over sixty-five knots per hour meant it was less than ten minutes to the fire awaiting him near Yorktown. The navy, coast guard, Virginia Marine Police, you name it, shared access to the sea right there. Simpson could make a single phone call and have all three barricading Cross from the open waters.

Let him. Cross's plan didn't require him to flee that far from Richmond. From Christine. He planned to get a safe distance from Camp Perry, find an obscure riverbank, and ditch the boat.

Cross relaxed his shoulders and leaned against the wheel of the boat to catch his breath. As an exemplary officer, he'd never experienced life on the opposite side of authority. He could recognize the sensation of experiencing beauty or the anxiety of executing a precisely planned mission. This, however, was a new feeling to him. The very organization that had assigned him targets was now targeting him.

His heart beat so fast he could feel the thump in his toes. The wind whipped against his hair, beating him lower and lower beneath the ineffective glass windshield.

It lashed at him from the left, then the right, then swirled in all directions. His toes thumped harder. He slapped a palm against his chest to try to still the beating.

His heart tapped back at him in a regular rhythm. The clouds obscuring the glare of the late-afternoon sun morphed into wicked shapes. Disoriented, he froze his grip on the steering wheel to keep from veering off course.

A clap startled him, and he turned as a burst of light spread its web-like fingers through the clouds.

He gasped.

Against the gray sky rose two black amorphous shapes held aloft by knives slicing long, thin circles above. Cross stared at the noiseless monstrosities, their reality foreign to him. They grew larger and larger, howling in his ear.

No, the wind. The wind howled in his ear. The sun disappeared beneath a storm cloud, the sky turned black, and Cross's stupefaction came crashing around him as the two shapes came into focus and he recognized the distinct outline of stealth Black Hawk helicopters.

They descended as they inched closer to him, the noise of their rotators finally distinguishable above the thunderstorm. Both Black Hawks ignited blinding lights spotting the inflatable boat in a shiny white circle of illumination. Cross struggled to maintain eye contact with each copter's position without going blind.

"Attention, civilian. Cease operation of your water vehicle immediately," echoed the loudspeaker down the channel. "If you do not comply, there will be consequences."

Cross thought he might fire a quick quip back but decided it would be lost within the cyclone of wind descending from above. He gripped the steering wheel and jammed the accelerator as hard forward as it would go, and then some. The boat groaned in protest, then acquiesced and provided a few more knots of speed.

He slipped away from the condemnation of the spotlight before the pilots could react. They increased air speed. Cross drove the boat erratically across the channel, dodging the incessant search of the lights.

The two beams split from following each other, and each Black Hawk swept the surface of the river in an attempt to keep up with Cross's evasive maneuvers. He veered to the left and let one of the lights reflect off the rigid hull of the boat before cutting a sharp right and disappearing into the darkness once more.

He breathed easy. Though the pilot of the lead Hawk mentioned consequences, those did not appear to include the use of force.

The black silhouette of one helicopter buzzed over him at a precariously low altitude. Cross surmised they intended to intimidate him into surrender. The lead Hawk broke off to his left as the other made a similar approach downriver.

He plotted their trajectories in his mind and deduced an impending window of time in which he would be in both their blind spots. He had seconds, and would only get seconds. His brain clear, he trusted his calculation to provide him the chance he needed. If he stayed in open water, it would only be a matter of time before they goaded him into the expected blockade near Yorktown.

A narrow branch of the river disappeared beneath a dark tree line just ahead on the right. Cross let the boat get carried in a natural drift by the storm-charged river system until the nose of the stern pointed at his escape path.

The second Black Hawk passed overhead with the barest hum, and with its underbelly only feet above his head, he jerked the helm. The inflatable boat agreed to his command and sliced waves into the small waterway.

Cross kept the engine gunning as he held the wheel in his firm grip and guided the craft down the passage and around obstacles nature provided. He couldn't be sure if the two pilots witnessed his escape. Without the typical advanced warning of thunderous rotator blades, the Black Hawks could descend upon him and he wouldn't know it until they wanted him to.

He caught sight of a large grouping of trees with thick branches providing a canopy over the water. Aiming the boat for the base of the trees, he braced himself for impact.

The vehicle's hull smashed into exposed branches and lodged itself into the riverbank. Uninterested in the damage done to either boat or tree, Cross vaulted out of the craft and burrowed himself into the underbrush.

He refused to breathe, resolved on transmitting his body's resources into his auditory senses. He listened, searching. Either the light would pierce the trees and give chase, or the pilots would be disoriented and have to conduct a more thorough search.

Seconds, then minutes, passed. In the distance, Cross caught the reflection of a searchlight pass behind the trees against the river's edge. A clean getaway. Butch Cassidy would be proud.

He jumped to his feet and ran farther into the forest with only one objective in focus: find Christine.

CHAPTER TWENTY-FOUR

WHERE WAS SHE?

Her consciousness had returned to its normal state minutes ago, but Christine still struggled to trust her senses. The space wasn't cold, though she felt a tinge of cold on the side of her body pressed against a hard surface. Her brain interpreted the sensation and concluded she was lying on a dark, cold floor.

Her senses sharpened further. Everything was unfamiliar, though *everything* amounted to only a hint of four dark walls surrounding the floor and capped by a dark ceiling. And as far as she could tell, her body was the room's sole furnishing.

She retraced the events leading to her capture and remembered awakening for a brief moment in what she assumed was the back seat of a car. Someone had slipped a warm material over her nose and caused her to return to a peaceful slumber, the memory passing as mere shadow.

Christine wondered when the panic would set in. She recalled its grip around her heart for the initial time period of her capture in Jordan. Was a second kidnapping supposed to be easy? She imagined John in a fight to win her back just outside the room. Perhaps that abated the crippling anxiety she expected.

Or maybe she was resigned to a fate involving abduction, torture, and eventual execution. In Jordan, she'd decided it was her destiny. It may not have come then, but you could only outrun your destiny for so long.

She pushed all the justifications from her mind. None of them would do. Only one thing remained—the reason fear took a back seat to patience and trust: her conversation with Lori. And not the entire conversation. Over and over in her mind, Christine listened to Lori's voice describing the story of the Bible.

Not a story of the Bible. *The* story of the Bible. A summary of the entire work that contained one simple thread. A thread leading to the man named Jesus, a name Christine had heard countless times as a child but never paused to consider.

The logical simplicity of Lori's words surprised her. No one spoke about the Bible the way Lori did, at least no one Christine knew. And it sparked something in her. An undeniable, wonderful spark. Be it simple curiosity or something beyond the natural order of the world, her fixation on Lori's discourse filled her heart with peace despite her circumstances.

Whatever lay beyond the four walls of her prison, she believed in the certainty of her survival. And when she survived, she would return to the hospital and ask Lori to tell her more.

A metal clank alerted her to the suggestion of movement at the facing wall. Feeling in full control of her limbs, she pulled herself into a seated position and dragged her rear across the slick floor until her back contacted the nearest barrier. Thick ridges in the wall prevented her from relaxing against it.

Far on the opposite side, the metal wall inched its way open with anguishing screeches against itself. The bright glow of the sun pierced the air from the top of the room to its bottom. Christine raised a hand to shield her eyes from its burn.

A dark blob appeared within the expanding glow and grew in size as it wobbled toward her. The blob slowly took the form of a man carrying a chair in his right hand. She strained her eyes to try to identify him, but only one distinguishing feature stood out: her abductor wore a stylish hat.

Christine's eyes adjusted to the new environment, and distracted from the man's approach, she studied her makeshift jail. Ridges bore deep vertical lines in all four walls. The lines ran parallel to each other spaced ten or so inches apart. Flat metal sheets covered the ceiling and floor.

A cargo container, just like ones she'd seen on large transport ships crossing the ocean. Recognition of her surroundings calmed her for only a second before the four legs of a metal chair scraped the floor and reminded her of her visitor.

Christine looked up into the black silhouette of the figure taking the seat. The light was still bright to her eyes, and she adjusted her hand to spy identifying features. It looked like a man. Dark skin. Well dressed. She recognized the hat as a classic, short-billed driving cap.

Under alternative circumstances, Christine would've assumed she was about to engage in conversation with a professor of ancient history, or perhaps a connoisseur of classic literature. She supposed either could still be a kidnapper.

"Hello. I hope your rest was not too uncomfortable." His voice tilted into higher ranges than one would expect, his accent unrestrained. It was similar yet different than her captors' accents in Jordan. A seed of confusion sprang within her mind.

"Where am I?" The question, one of many, surprised Christine with the sloppiness with which her voice had delivered it. The numbness in her tongue lingered.

"Don't worry," the man replied. "The adverse effects of the chloroform will wear off soon. As to where you are, I can tell you we are still within the borders of Virginia."

So she wasn't on a ship headed back across the Atlantic to a Middle Eastern destination. Good news.

"What do you want with me?"

"Though I can only offer scant detail, I would like to assure you our motives do not involve harm."

That made the situation already a vast improvement over her last imprisonment. She took her time forming words in her mouth to keep from tripping over letters. "So you don't want to hurt me, and you aren't taking me out of the country. Would it do any good to ask why you've put me in this shipping container?"

"Trust me when I say better accommodations were preferred. It just couldn't be helped. This was, unfortunately, all we had at our disposal. Your stay won't be prolonged. I promise."

"OK, hold on. I don't understand. You're being way too nice for having just electrocuted and abducted me. So even though I already did, I'm going to have to ask what you want with me."

The man chuckled. "I don't want anything from you, Christine Lewis. I want John Cross. And you're going to help me get him."

CHAPTER TWENTY-FIVE

IT DIDN'T TAKE long for Cross to find civilization. And with civilization came the opportunity to procure transportation. He found an inconspicuous sedan and went to work on the window with a thin piece of metal scooped from the roadside. Unlocking the car proved to be less a chore than starting the ignition with the same piece of metal.

When the engine finally turned, Cross put the car in gear and sped away from the scene of his crime. He would drop the car in Richmond at a safe location where it could be recovered and returned to its owner. Even so, stealing the car lashed sharply at his soul.

Where to even start? Cross played various scenarios over in his mind, looking for the right approach to finding Christine. Doubt slithered about in the recesses of his brain. The CIA had near limitless resources. They would pick up Christine's trail quicker than he could on his own. Why hadn't he stayed?

He couldn't bear to be locked up in the room until then, that was why. Impulsive behavior was outside his normal operating mode, but something about the woman made him willing to take on any and all challengers to ensure her safety once again.

Heavy pills of rain smacked the windshield of the car. With a flick of his index finger, Cross activated the wipers. He turned the sedan onto a busy highway and balanced his speed between urgency and legality.

Even though it made navigation difficult, Cross welcomed the stream of traffic flowing both directions on the road. Groups made anonymity easy. The trick would be evading an encounter with local law enforcement. He didn't doubt his face was plastered across laptop screens in every patrol car within a thirty-mile radius.

Cross's ear tingled with the announcement of a faint ringing sound. A ring just like . . . his phone? Cross overlooked taking inventory of his pockets since leaving Camp Perry, and he suddenly remembered the CIA neglected to confiscate his phone. He fished for it in his pocket and received the call and held it to his ear in one swift motion.

"Hey, Al, took you long enough to call," he said, confident Simpson intended to trace the phone to a narrow search radius. He planned to entertain his former employer with enough conversation to tease, but not enough to betray his location. His phone wasn't GPS enabled, though that wouldn't stop them from succeeding. Cross calculated ninety seconds to pinpoint. Long enough for a retort or two.

"Good evening, Mr. Cross," said an unfamiliar voice with a similar Turkish accent as Cross's attacker on the train. "We finally have a chance to speak to one another unencumbered. It is a pleasure."

Cross didn't have to ask for identification. "George Carson, I presume. Or at least that was your name on the train. Who did you murder this time to steal their ID? Let me guess: the overweight guy you walked in with."

"I have no further need for false credentials, I assure you, though I cannot reveal my true identity to you as of yet."

"Where's Christine?"

"You are right to assume I am in possession of Miss Lewis, and I have no intention of bringing her misfortune."

A shuffle occurred over the phone, followed by Christine's voice. "John?"

"Christine! Are you OK?"

The accented-man replied, "Proof of her life, Mr. Cross. And now you will do exactly as I say."

Cross didn't respond. His chest rose up and down in violent fashion with each inhale and exhale. He wrapped his fingers harder around the steering wheel, wrinkling its leather cover. His teeth hurt as they pressed into each other.

"I want you to go to church tonight," the man said.

Church? Cross's mind raced. What was the man doing?

"I will bring Miss Lewis along, and we will discuss my terms of her safe return."

Cross struggled to explain his current situation. Most of the scenarios he formed involved Christine's abductors fleeing the country with their prize. But they hadn't. Which meant she wasn't the prize. A knot formed in his stomach as the dread consumed him.

"I'm twenty minutes away," Cross said.

"Everything has been prepared in advance. Twenty minutes."

Click. The call died along with any chance for Cross to have a rational thought about what he would face next.

Cross drove to the church, languishing in disgust. The pendulum of his emotions swung to the opposite extreme in a wide arc as he pulled into the full parking lot.

Fear mingled with the anger, and his mind clouded. He recognized each and every car in the lot as those of the tiny church congregation. What were they doing there? On a Monday night? During a rainstorm?

The unrelenting downpour seemed eager to intensify and consume the area in a catastrophic flood. Cross stepped out of the car, and the rain soaked through his clothes before he could reach the front door of the church.

He opened the door and entered the empty vestibule. A draft descended from the ceiling, and he shivered. Raising a hand to the opposite shoulder, he rubbed the damp jacket and remembered he'd stolen Officer Hardy's black suit and tie.

Cross considered a quick jog to the house to exchange clothes and search for a weapon, but apprehension beckoned him toward the sanctuary. Before he could think again, Cross found himself standing in the center aisle, water droplets from his suit pants staining the burnt-red carpet a darker shade in an uneven circle at his feet.

Every single member of Rural Grove Baptist Church sat in his or her customary pew. The door creaked shut behind him, cuing each head to turn in unison and stare at him. Barbara Templeton covered her mouth with a hand to refrain from a verbal outburst. Gary Osborne stood at the front of the sanctuary, his jaw hanging as limp as his arms.

Cross contemplated the possibility he had morphed into an alien creature based on the looks he received as he walked down the aisle. No one spoke to him. Only their eyes followed his path.

He kept his head low until he came to a stop in front of Gary. Without any sudden movement, he leaned in and whispered, "Gary, what's going on?"

"I was about to ask you the same thing."

Cross looked up and quizzed Gary with his eyes.

Gary motioned to the silent audience. "I got a call telling me it was an emergency and to get everyone together here tonight. So here we are."

"A call? From who?"

"A woman named Christine. She said she knew you." Gary leaned in and lowered his voice. "She knew Lori was in the hospital, John. So why don't you tell me: What's going on?"

Both doors in the rear of the sanctuary opened suddenly. Cross and Gary turned in unison along with each church member. Several gasps emanated from the pews, and two of the strapping men in the group stood to shield children.

"Christine," Cross said involuntarily when he spotted her standing in the center of the doorway. He wanted to run to her, but automatic weapons in the hands of the group of men encircling her convinced him it wasn't a prudent idea.

From behind her stepped the man from Main Street Station, his lips pressed together and his brow wrinkled in solemn knots. He removed the short bill cap, grabbed Christine by the arm, and led the group down the center aisle. "Good evening, my friends," he said as they walked. "Thank you for joining us on this special occasion."

Behind him marched the giant man from the train. He sneered at the hostages with a gleeful grin.

Anger bubbled from deep within Cross's gut. As the gap between them closed, he stared the leader of the group down. Cross's eyebrows grew heavy and pinched together just above his nose. His ears burned, and he winced at the sensation of pain caused by his own fingernails digging into the palms of each hand as he tightened his balled fists.

Gary said something incomprehensible. The men holding the rifles spread themselves through the congregation, forcing the overprotective fathers to sit. Christine caught Cross's gaze and mouthed the words *I'm OK.*

It didn't matter. None of them would make it out alive.

The leader assisted Christine into the front pew. He held a palm open to the seat beside her and said to Gary, "Please, sit."

Gary consented and sat next to Christine. He whispered something in her ear, and she nodded. Cross darted his eyes back and forth between the leader, his armed compatriots, and the grinning giant of a man stationed to the front of the center aisle.

The leader circled Cross in a slow, methodical manner. "You," he said from behind Cross's ear, "look rather . . . oh, what is the idiom? . . . *worse for wear*, Mr. Cross."

"No more than you're going to be after this." The threat slipped out before Cross could catch it. Was he, an unarmed ex-CIA officer with a vow against killing, seriously going to threaten the men who held the entire church hostage?

The leader chuckled through his nostrils as he rounded Cross's left shoulder and stood facing him. "A bold statement. Not at all unexpected from a bold man such as yourself." He took a few steps backward into the aisle, spread his arms apart, and raised his voice. "Not that these kind, innocent people know anything about that, do they?"

Cross at once understood the purpose of the man's actions. He'd called everyone to this one place and this one time for this one purpose: the unmasking of John Cross. Cross's shoulders sank, and he shot a wavering glance at Christine.

The leader returned to an uncomfortable distance and held a hand to his temple in a faux display of embarrassment. "I'm sorry. Forgive me. I completely forgot to introduce myself. My name is Yunus Anar."

A mission report buried deep in Cross's subconscious opened, and a myriad of images, words, and feelings stormed through his mind. In the midst of the chaos, the awful truth flashed behind his eyes like a giant neon sign. He'd rejected the obvious for too long. Now it forced its way into the open and he couldn't look away. They'd never wanted Christine.

It had always been *him*.

Yunus's eyes widened, and his lips formed a thin, crooked smile. "Good. I thought you might not remember." The Turk turned and took a seat on the front pew across the aisle from Christine and Gary. Raising his voice again, he declared, "And now, Mr. Cross, please catch the rest of your friends up on our shared history. Help them see. Help them understand why they feel threatened in this moment."

The wet suit jacket seemed heavier on his shoulders. Cross attempted to breathe deep, but his lungs refused to cooperate with his practiced calming techniques. He opened his mouth to speak, but Yunus cut him off with a frantic waving of his hands.

"No, no, no. Please, take the place of honor for your speech."

With no other choice, Cross stepped onto the stage and stood behind the cross-shaped wooden pulpit.

Yunus crossed his arms and feet. "And now," he said, "tell them who you really are."

Cross hung his head and closed his eyes. *Lord, help* was all he could muster for a prayer. Though his heart churned at no less of a pace, Cross felt a resolve form in his chest, and he opened his eyes and lifted his chin to the congregation.

"I just want you all to know that everything is going to be OK, and I will be forever grateful for the love you have shown me over the past year. My name *is* John Cross, but I'm not who you think I am. When I first began attending the church, I claimed I lost a government job in Washington due to the recession. That was a lie."

A chorus of gasps rippled through the audience.

"I didn't lose my job. I quit. And while it was technically a government job, I wasn't a paper pusher. I worked for the Central Intelligence Agency as a covert field operative."

Cross didn't have to look in Gary's direction to know the man was seething. He felt the heat emanating from the front pew. More than anything, he wanted to look to Christine for support, but he refrained, worried he would make eye contact with the head deacon and lose his composure.

A raised hand caught Cross's attention. Yunus wiggled a condemning finger at him. "Ah, ah, Mr. Cross. I don't think 'covert field operative' is an appropriate description of the type of work you performed for your country."

Dry fingers of shame wrapped around Cross's throat. He coughed to relax the pressure and continued. "As an operative for the CIA, I was asked to do things that I now regret. Terrible things. All of which I did before I accepted Jesus as my . . ."

A bang echoed through the sanctuary. Cross looked over to see Yunus's balled fist resting in a fresh depression in the wooden seatback of the pew. His eyes flamed, and his chest rose in rapid fashion. "Tell them," he frothed through clenched teeth. "Tell them what you did." Yunus closed his eyes, and his breathing relaxed.

Cross looked back out over the congregation and took a deep breath. "My primary function at the CIA was to find and track hostile targets in order to terminate them for the sake of national security."

Yunus jumped from his seat and onto the stage. He positioned himself behind the pulpit next to Cross, reached behind his back, and produced a knife with a long, partially serrated blade. He propped his wrist against the front edge of the lectern and let the overhead lights glint against the cold steel. "I can see why you were misled," he declared to the captive audience. "Mr. Cross certainly has a way with words." Directing his voice at Cross, he added, "Explain to us in terms we can all understand. Tell us what you did. Confess your sins, John Cross."

No way out. He had to say it. "I was an assassin. I killed people. People who were considered threats to the welfare of our nation and citizens."

No gasps, no sounds, not a breath.

"How many people did you kill?" Yunus's voice dripped in hubris.

"I don't know."

Yunus's fingers squeezed tighter around the handle of the knife. "I'll ask again: How many people did you kill?"

"I didn't keep count. I only followed orders."

"How about a guess? Since it seems these people didn't matter to you, how about you take a guess as to how many missions you completed. How many families you tore apart." Yunus's voice peaked in volume. "How many murders you accomplished by your own hands."

Cross paused as Yunus's choice of the word "murder" worked its way through the crowd. A rise in murmuring drew his gaze to the right middle of the crowd, where a neighboring congregant fanned a faint Mrs. Templeton.

Missions. Cross never bothered with documenting kills, but he could recall a mission total. Not all were targeted assassinations, but it would've certainly been a majority. He subtracted a plausible percentage and recalculated a potential total in his head.

"Seventeen. I think."

Cross felt thankful for the presence of the armed men. Otherwise he was sure the church would have become the scene of an impromptu riot. Horror stories of rage-filled church business meetings he'd read about on the Internet would have paled in comparison to the display of outrage his confession would have elicited under different circumstances.

He raised his eyes and looked at each and every congregant despite the animosity he felt in return. "I'm so sorry."

"Oh, we've only just begun, Mr. Cross. If you don't mind, I would like for you to recount just how you know me and the events that have resulted in our being here together this evening."

Cross lowered his head for a brief moment to fight back the wellspring of emotion trying to force its way out of his tear ducts. He spoke with his head down. "Back in 2014, I was sent on an operation into Turkey to investigate a potential arms deal to Syrian rebels. We tracked the sale to a corrupt government official. My orders were to terminate the official and disrupt the deal."

"His name."

"The man I killed was Ali Anar. Your brother."

Yunus drew a deep breath, and the knife quivered against the pulpit. "Tell them how he died."

"I shot Ali using a high-precision rifle while he was working in his home office late one night."

"While his two sons slept in an adjacent bedroom. And his wife brewed tea in the kitchen. A single gunshot to the back of his head." Yunus lifted the knife and used its tip to demonstrate the path of the bullet. "I'm curious, Mr. Cross. Were you still around to hear Fem's screams when she found her husband slumped over his desk?"

"Your brother was not a good man . . ."

Cross sensed Yunus's fist rising from the pulpit a second before it came rushing toward his temple, but he tensed his muscles and welcomed the punishing blow as penance for his stupidity. The blunt end of the knife's handle connected with his head and sent Cross sprawling across the stage.

He pushed himself off the floor and onto an elbow. Beneath the ringing in his ears, he could hear several cries from the congregation, along with Christine's voice saying, "No!" Cross held up a hand to stay her advance, but noticed Gary grabbing at her elbow. Christine froze in her tracks, her moist eyes pleading for Cross to act.

A stinging sensation brought Cross's fingertips to his eyebrow. He pulled his fingers away to see traces of blood where the knife handle awarded him a fresh gash. His vision remained unsteady, so he left his body prone to the stage floor.

Yunus's voice boomed across the room as he remained at the pulpit and addressed the crowd. "My brother had his faults, just as all of you. Just as I. But neither of our gods gave this man the right to be the judge and jury that demanded my brother's life. John Cross took a life, no matter my brother's guilt. Justice demands a life in return."

Cross's head swirled. Yunus held the upper hand. He could wipe them all out with a simple order to his men. Yet it seemed apparent only one death interested him. An atoning death for his brother's. That was why they wanted Christine. Cross took one of the few people Yunus cared for, and Yunus was about to do the same.

"No, I . . ." he protested, but Yunus cut him off.

"I want to thank each and every one of you for coming out tonight. You see, this moment was just as important as the one that is soon to follow. It is not enough that John Cross die. He must die the man he was the night he shot my brother. John Cross is no longer your friend. He is no longer your leader. He is only a killer. And justice can finally be had." Yunus motioned for his men to stand down. "Please find your way to your vehicles. And do not consider calling the authorities. We will be long gone by the time they arrive, and I can assure you we will know and will ensure you pay for your interference."

The giant man in the center of the aisle scowled and took a step forward, but Yunus halted his advance with the wave of a hand.

The congregation hesitated, unsure of whether or not to trust the words of the madman standing before them. Yunus sighed. "I promise you will not be harmed. Please . . ." He held a raised hand to the door and shouted in a menacing tone, "Go!"

Motivated by his aggressive tone, everyone rose from their pews and filed into the aisle. The armed men held their positions and glared at each person as they exited. The giant man inhaled and exhaled loudly at frequent intervals. Cross brought himself to one knee and watched Gary start to lead Christine to the rear of the sanctuary.

"No," Yunus called out to them. "The girl stays."

Gary paused and looked at Cross, his eyes drooped in somber concern. Cross nodded his approval. Gary assented to Yunus's request, let go of Christine, and walked out the door, the last to leave. The reporter remained still in the middle of the aisle.

Yunus stepped over to Cross and squatted. He slipped an arm, knife in hand, around Cross's shoulder and leaned close to his ear. "You should be happy to know that I only intend on killing you, Mr. Cross. And as an honorable man, I am going to afford you a luxury you did not give my brother. A fighting chance. There will be no firearms. Ms. Lewis and I will be escorting my men to their vehicles and bidding them farewell. I will allot you fifteen minutes to prepare yourself, though it will not matter. I am going to kill you. And I'm going to do it while the woman watches. Know that she will carry that pain with her for the remainder of her life. Just as my brother's wife has."

Yunus stood and left the stage. With a hand on Christine's back, he led her out the door. His men followed suit. Cross watched as the giant man walked last through the door, shooting Cross an evil wink as he closed it behind him. Cross stayed still, silent, crouching on one knee on the wooden stage floor. Alone.

CHAPTER TWENTY-SIX

RAIN FELL IN sheets across the empty parking lot. Thunder and lightning danced about the dark clouds overhead. Christine dreaded the walk to the vehicles without an umbrella.

Yunus led her back to the dark SUVs parked behind the building and shoved her into the back seat of the nearest one. It surprised her that he appeared so trusting. He'd refrained from ordering his men to constrain her after they'd released her from the cargo container. Though she kept an eye open for an opportunity to slip away, the armed men surrounded her at all times.

She heard their muffled voices outside of the car and watched Yunus's silhouette move between each of his comrades. There seemed to be a heated argument with the large one, but then they hugged. A strange decision to make in the middle of a violent rainstorm. After interacting with the final man in the group, their black forms dissolved away. Multiple car doors opened and closed. Engines turned. One by one, the other vehicles departed.

The driver's-side door opened, and Yunus shook beads of water from his shoulders as he slid onto the seat. "What a night, eh?"

Christine forced her jaw to stay shut, though it wanted to drop open at the man's cordial tone. "Small talk? Really?"

Yunus peered at her in the rearview mirror. "Please, Ms. Lewis. By now you must know my quarrel is with John alone. There's no reason we can't be civil."

"Civil? You just held a church congregation at gunpoint. Explain to me how that is civil."

"I regret the anxiety they all felt, please believe me, but a strong statement was necessary. No one was in any real danger. I made sure of it."

"You said it yourself: John's the only one to blame. Why involve everyone else?"

"Could I have executed John in the streets? Or perhaps at home, just as he did my brother? Or even lured him to a desolate place? Yes, of course. But then it wouldn't really be him. The man I killed would not have been the man who murdered my brother. And I will not do that."

"What do you mean?"

"The John Cross these people know was a charlatan. A fraud. To them he was a white knight, while in reality the darkness lies just beneath his skin. I had to strip away the false image before the real John Cross could emerge. That is the man who must pay for his sins."

"Sounds like your brother had his share of sins too."

She might have pushed too hard. Yunus sat still, his eyes averted, his breathing coming and going in a slow, rhythmic pattern. The rain clawed at the roof of the car, desperate to enter and drench them both.

Finally, he said, "My brother had his regrets, as do I. As do you. And death is a certainty, often a necessity. But there is a difference between a life taken in war and a life taken in the name of business."

"Business? Is that what you call the Syrian conflict?"

Yunus reestablished eye contact. "Do you understand what John confessed inside the church? He shot my brother for a deal to provide arms to Syrian rebels. Your own government is about to do the very same thing. Ms. Lewis, that man shot my brother not because of Ali's crimes but because the United States wasn't getting their cut."

Christine opened her mouth to speak but found no words waiting.

"Everyone thinks chaos around the world is about competing ideals." Yunus shook his head. "It's about money. It's always about the money. Who is getting paid, and who will pay the most."

Christine shot a piercing stare back against the mirror. "And who is paying you?"

Yunus smiled. "I know this may sound like a contradiction to my previous claim, but I am not doing this for money. Not this."

"You're right. It doesn't sound true."

"I have not always been proud of what I've done. And I'm sure I will continue to find only regret in life's turns. But this one thing I do for honor, nothing more."

"You think it honors your brother to take another man's life?"

"It must. For there is nothing else."

Christine leaned forward and braced herself against the back of the driver's seat. A sense of urgency sprang from her heart. If only she could plant the right seed, perhaps she could stave off Yunus's thirst for revenge. "What if there's something else?" she asked. "What if there's another way? A way for you to find closure without harming anyone ever again?"

Yunus's silence prompted her to continue.

"You're wrong about John. He may have killed your brother in cold blood for a terrible reason, but that's not him anymore. He knows he was wrong. And he found something that helped him move forward despite the guilt. Forgiveness."

The sound of the rain filled the awkward silence between them.

"I know this is going to sound ridiculous," Christine admitted. "But I think if you stopped and considered forgiving him, it will bring your brother more honor than anything else you could ever do. Killing John won't take away the pain. It won't bring your brother back. All it will do is ensure that you're lost too."

She tried reading Yunus's expression, hoping to find some glimmer of possibility that he would back away from his vengeful quest. He just sat, eyes ahead, lost in the mesmerizing drizzle of rain cascading down the windshield.

Silence better than anything else, Christine let her words hang alone in the space between them and sat back into her seat. Movement caught her eye across the parking lot. She turned and stared out the rain-streaked window. A dark shape stood on the edge of the asphalt between the white brick of the church building and the metal frame of the unfinished expansion.

Christine bent toward the window to get a better view and gasped. John glared at the car with his eyes narrowed in a menacing stare. His hands hung in tight fists by his sides. Though the rain fell hard, the anger emanating from his body seemed as if it would protect him from its drench.

"It appears, Ms. Lewis, that our mutual friend does not agree with your position."

The driver's-side door opened, and Yunus exited the vehicle. Christine shot her hand to the handle of her own door, but before she could pull on it, Yunus stuck his head back into view and said, "Please, I would ask that you remain inside unless you wish to suffer a similar fate."

Her hand froze. Conflicted, she nodded and kept her eyes locked on him as he stepped away from the SUV and shut the driver's-side door behind him. She broke her gaze, slid across the back seat, and pressed her nose against the glass to try to see past the raindrops.

Yunus appeared in her view as he rounded the front of the car. He held his arms open in greeting. She spotted a knife handle protruding from his waistband against his back. He said something inaudible as thunder cracked overhead.

"This ends here, tonight," John shouted back, his words muffled but discernable. "I'm not going to let you hurt anyone, anymore."

Christine's heart thumped in a violent rhythm against her rib cage. She wanted to leap out of the car and plead with him to stand down, to try to speak reason to both of them, but her body refused her commands to move. She sat and stared out the window, her mouth moving in the right way but the words falling in a whispered breath against the glass.

"No, please no . . ."

Rain flowed in a furious cascade against the skeletal steel structure of the unfinished expansion. Lightning leapt from cloud to cloud and illuminated the sheet of unending water, giving it the look of a wall planned for but never finished.

The shell of an abandoned future seemed a fitting environment for the confrontation of his past. Cross ignored the weight of the white dress shirt and dark dress pants pressed against his body by the merciless downpour. He ignored the feeling of his shoes sinking into the softened sod beneath him. Ignored the clap of thunder at unexpected intervals.

There was only one thing worth his attention: Yunus Anar.

"You're right," Yunus shouted over the storm. "It ends here. Not only my suffering, but yours as well." He waved a hand at the church building. "This isn't who you really are. This was nothing but a pathetic attempt to save a soul you lost long ago. Let us both end our pain tonight."

The anger clawed at the seams of his heart. Cross pictured the congregation, their faces drawn in horror at his unmasking. Pictured his own attempts at penance. Then further back. All the sin. All the pain he'd inflicted on others. The deaths.

All the other images faded, leaving only a single face. His first target. The moment his soul died. He couldn't remember her name or why the CIA considered her a threat.

But he did remember her daughter on the playground a few yards away.

It was all a lie. He'd never changed. He never would. This was who he was. Yunus was right.

Yunus is right.

The least he could do was save Christine—the one person who accepted him no matter what. A chill coursed its way through his veins. A dark hue tinged the corners of his vision. He bit down on his teeth and let the monster within loose.

His shoes lifted from the damp earth, and he ran toward his opponent. The gap closed in seconds. His fury amplified with each step, his eyes locked on Yunus's vexing, toothy grin.

Cross lifted a fist. The rain scattered in fear. With a wrathful cry, he swung. For an inexplicable reason, Yunus stood his ground. Cross's knuckles connected with the man's nose, and the blow sent him downward on his knees and elbows.

"Get up!" Cross yelled. "I said get up!"

Yunus wiped at his nose with an arm, leaving a trail of blood along his sleeve. He swiveled his torso and looked up at Cross, blood caking his upper lip. He laughed. "And that, Mr. Cross, was your fighting chance." He offered a shout of his own as his arm flew in an arc over his head, the point of the knife clenched in his fist aimed at Cross's chest.

Cross leapt backward. The knife sliced through his shirt and tie, the tip tearing flesh. Yunus rose from his kneeling position and ran toward Cross. His smile disappeared, a scowl in its place.

Cross parried blow after blow as he backpedaled. Yunus spun the blade on his fingers, then flipped it to his opposite hand. Cross reacted too slow as Yunus sliced the knife down through the rain and nicked Cross's forearm.

Cross grimaced and fought against the instinct to grab at the wound. Yunus advanced and cut downward with the knife once more. Tired of backing down, Cross shifted his tactic and jumped into Yunus's charge. The Turk's forearm slammed against Cross's shoulder.

Cross wrapped his arms around Yunus's waist and heaved him in a circle. As their bodies tumbled out of control, Cross caught sight of something he didn't expect. Too late to stop their momentum, he tightened his embrace.

Yunus screamed as they slipped over the side of the exposed foundation of the unfinished building and fell into nothingness.

Cross's back connected with a scaffolding plank. His diaphragm tightened, and his lungs refused to cooperate. Yunus rolled off him and spat blood from his mouth. Cross cradled his abdomen and took a deep breath to gain composure.

From beside him, Yunus kicked out with his boot, connected with Cross's shoulder, and pushed Cross from the platform. Cross grabbed at the wet structure, but his fingers slipped. Just as he went over the edge, his hand found a grip around the metal frame.

His body lurched to a stop, and Cross hung over the invisible abyss below. Yunus appeared above him, a bright burst of lightning overhead glinting off the exposed knife still in his possession.

The knife swung at his exposed wrist. Cross released his hold on the scaffolding and dropped into a free fall. His descent was short, impeded by his feet landing flat against a neatly stacked pile of cement block.

Cross lost his footing and slipped off the pile. He braced for impact as his body connected with the ground. The mud cushioned his landing, sparing him serious injury.

His lungs decided to work again, and he sucked in large mouthfuls of air. A thump alerted Cross to Yunus towering over him on top of the cement blocks. Yunus vaulted off the pile and plunged the knife in a downward strike with both hands.

Cross rolled to one side, and the knife sank into the wet earth. Yunus pulled it free and swung again. Cross jumped to his feet and met the blow with a knee. His grip released, Yunus growled as he watched the knife sail out of his hand and into the shadows of the framework.

With another swift kick, Cross connected the bottom of his shoe with Yunus's chest and sent the man flying into a load of lumber. Yunus coughed as he righted his body and wiped the mixture of spit and blood from his chin.

Cross tightened his core and brought both of his fists together to cover his face. "Now it's a fair fight," he yelled over the flow of rain spraying them from above.

Yunus smiled, then charged. Cross blocked the incoming attack and lashed out with a left jab. Yunus threw punch after punch, but Cross anticipated every move and countered with crushing blows to the other man's torso.

Punch, block, duck. They beat and beat on each other as the rain fell, the thunder clapped, and the lightning threatened to enter the fray itself.

Confident he held the upper hand, Cross dropped a fist from his chin. He sensed Yunus's swing too late. A set of knuckles impacted his exposed abdomen. Cross grunted and doubled back.

Sharp fists struck against his skull. Dazed, Cross threw both arms over his head to try to stave off the unrelenting fury. He tasted blood. The edges of his vision blackened.

And then it stopped.

His vision returned, and Cross looked up into the black clouds threatening to reach down and pull him into the afterlife. A big raindrop splashed against his nose and washed into his eyes. He blinked, the spell interrupted.

He searched for Yunus as he pulled himself upright against the pile of lumber. The other man fished in the mud a few yards away. He found the object of his search and wiped it clean with the disheveled tail of his shirt.

Lightning flashed overhead, and the knife blade glistened. Yunus turned to face Cross and held it aloft. "I thought about just shooting you," he proclaimed, pointing the knife tip to his temple. "In the head. Like you did to Ali. Then I imagined beating you to death with my hands, or wrapping my fingers around your throat and squeezing until you drew your last breath."

Cross breathed in heavy bursts. His arms and legs hung limp like thick, lifeless tree trunks. Yunus stalked toward him as he tapped the knife against his pant leg.

"But I think this instrument will do fine. Just the right duration of pain before you pass on." Yunus wrapped the fingers of his free hand around Cross's throat, pressed his body against the beams, and aimed the knife at his stomach. "For Ali."

Cross tensed his body and caught Yunus's strike with both hands. Pulling the Turk closer, he kicked out with his shoe and struck Yunus's abdominal aortic plexus.

With a grip on Yunus's knife hand, Cross twisted and pulled against the hilt. The knife slipped free, and Cross grabbed it. Yunus staggered backward cradling his injured abdomen.

Cross charged. A few well-placed punches and kicks drove Yunus into the scaffolding. Yunus wrapped an arm around the frame to keep his body from fainting into the mud.

With a squeeze of the handle, Cross raised the knife and held it high in a triumphant stance.

"Do it," Yunus cried. "Send me to my brother!"

His thoughts exactly. Killing Yunus was the only way to end the terror. He knew it. It was how the world worked. How it had always worked. Nothing ever changed.

Nothing.

"John!"

Christine's voice echoed against the thick metal beams of the unfinished structure, punctuated by the rumble of thunder growing distant. "John, don't do it! This isn't you! Not who you really are."

She was wrong. He had never changed. It was all a . . .

A . . .

He couldn't think it. "A . . ." He tried to utter the word aloud. But it wasn't. His new life had *not* been a futile exercise in meaningless penance. In the midst of the darkness shrouding his heart, Cross heard a whisper.

Truth.

What truth? The truth that before Christ, he was nothing. And since his decision, Cross had discovered true meaning, true purpose. It *was* true. All of it. His wrong, Yunus's wrong, the world's wrong, none of it meant truth couldn't be found. It could. But only in one place. In one person.

The shroud lifted, and Cross lowered the knife. Yunus stared at him, his eyes narrow and his mouth open, yet not speaking. Cross backed away as he spoke. "You're right. About me. I've done many, many terrible things. And I regret every single one of them. I can't tell you why God still rescued me. All I can tell you is, he did."

Cross stared at the knife in his hand. "I wish I could bring your brother back. I can't. But if this is what you need . . ." Cross tossed the knife into the mud at Yunus's feet.

"John, no . . ." Christine called out from above.

Standing firm, his arms by his side, Cross nodded to Yunus. "I wish you could find it in your heart to forgive me. But the least I can do is offer you my life in exchange for your brother's. All I ask in return is that you investigate my claims. Find out for yourself if what I've told you is true."

Yunus stood still, staring at Cross. His eyes narrowed, and his lips parted as he ground his teeth. Suddenly, he moved. Scooping up the knife, he slopped through the mud toward Cross.

Just behind the terrorist, Christine dropped from the edge of the foundation wall and onto the top plank of the scaffolding. She screamed in horror as Yunus raised the knife and targeted Cross's heart.

"No!" she yelled. "Stop!"

Cross stared into Yunus's eyes and said, "I forgive you."

A deep, animalistic roar erupted from Yunus's throat. He held the knife high, but it wavered. An unseen force prevented his arm from unleashing the fatal strike.

He roared again, but the knife held fixed. Yunus's eyes softened, the corners of his lips dropped, and his arm lost its will to sustain the altitude of his hand. His fingers relaxed, and the knife slipped from his grasp to the floor.

Yunus dropped to his knees in the mud, sobbing. He muttered something under his breath as Cross took a step closer and fell to his own knees.

"I've failed you, brother. I've failed you," he slurred, tears clinging to his chapped lips as he spoke.

"It's OK," Cross assured him.

"Why can't I kill you?"

"Because we're the same. We're both killers who don't want to kill."

"I can't forgive you . . . I won't. You killed my brother. You have to pay . . ."

Yunus's words trailed, and he continued to weep. Cross extended a hand in an offer to assist him up. Yunus blinked twice at the hand before raising his own and clutching Cross in a firm grip.

CHAPTER TWENTY-SEVEN

CHRISTINE SHIVERED, LESS from the chill of the wet clothes pressed against her skin and more from the numbness of her heart as she stared at the terrorist sitting on the steps of the small church stage.

Yunus sat still on the middle step, his head hung low. John stood a few feet away from him in the aisle, his breathing still labored from exhaustion. She still couldn't believe John pulled Yunus to his feet and out of the pit only minutes before.

Christine took a closer step in and whispered in John's ear, "Are you sure about this?"

He only nodded in reply. She stepped back and grimaced at the patches of red seeping through the dress shirt John wore. It used to be pressed and white. Now nothing more than a collection of dirty rags draped over his shoulders. He slid closer to Yunus and spoke softly.

"Yunus, I believe God stopped you from killing me for a reason. He's ready to forgive you, and he's ready to help you forgive me."

Yunus looked up into John's eyes. "How could anyone forgive me, let alone God?"

John slid his hand behind the front pew and grabbed a worn Bible from the stiff pocket built into the back. He sat down next to Yunus and for the next ten minutes shared a similar story to what Lori shared with Christine in the hospital.

God's eternal rescue plan. Jesus. A cross. Payment for sin. Words she had heard but never comprehended. Not like this. When Lori spoke before, and John now, it just seemed to make . . .

". . . sense?"

Christine caught John's last word before Yunus answered, "Never before. But now . . . now it seems so plain. As if my eyes are opening to something I have never seen before."

"You know, we like to use that phrase a lot to describe what happens when God's Spirit intervenes, but I can't say I've ever heard anyone actually use it."

Yunus's eyes opened. He'd wanted to kill John, probably her too. What did he see that she couldn't?

Yunus threw his strong hand onto John's bicep, and Christine's heart skipped. She was about to jump to his aid, when the older man spoke.

"Listen to me. There's something you need to know. My being here tonight was no coincidence. It has been manufactured from the beginning."

"Beginning? Beginning of what?" John asked.

"My arrangement with your government."

The oxygen level of the space dipped. John looked back into Christine's eyes, an expression of surprise a mirror of her own.

He turned back as Yunus continued. "My quest for revenge was used as leverage to get my men to commit to a greater mission. Your government received the benefit of deniability while I could find closure for my loss. You were only the bait. The real objective . . ." Yunus paused and glanced at Christine for the first time. "Well, it's worth much more news."

John stood, and the tone of his voiced shifted to command mode. "Who were you working with? Who's the mole?"

"He got us in. Set our team up. Delivered you to us." Yunus shook his head. "There are others, but I only worked with him. I don't know how far up it goes."

"I need a name."

Yunus swallowed. His eyes sank farther beneath his brow. "He worked for your Central Intelligence. I only knew his code name: Alamo."

John breathed an unintelligible word from his mouth, one Christine guessed he would ask forgiveness for later. "Who is it? Do you know him?" she asked.

"That code name belongs to Al Simpson, my boss at the CIA. We were close. I thought I knew him. Obviously, I don't."

"There's more." Yunus stood. "Alamo's primary goal is to reengage your country's focus on terror. He feels both sides have grown complacent. He believes an aggressive act of violence would rouse the apathetic. I didn't want to be involved, but then I was presented with the opportunity to kill you . . ." Yunus paused, his cheeks turned red, and his voice trailed.

"What was your target? What were you going to do?"

"Even though I managed the plan and the team, I was never going to do anything but kill you here tonight. My team is on their way now to complete the mission. I thought I might join them later in the escape to our country, but in all honesty, I think I wanted to die with you."

"Where are they headed? Can you stop them?"

"There's no way to reach them. They're halfway there by now. To Washington."

"There's not much they can accomplish in DC. Security will be tight at all government facilities."

"Not government. My men are headed to Union Station. They're going to set off a chemical bomb in the center of the station at eight o'clock in the morning."

Christine gasped, held a hand to her lips, and said, "Oh my—"

"God?" Yunus interrupted. "Yes, I believe this is a situation that calls for his intervention. I'm deeply sorry. There's nothing I can do."

John waved his palm. "Informing us is enough. Thank you."

Christine turned to him and asked, "What are we going to do?"

"I'm going to have to call it in."

"Is there anyone you can even trust?"

John didn't respond. He glanced back at Yunus and extended an open hand. "I'm going to need your car keys."

Yunus dug the keys from his pocket and handed them over. He nodded to the both of them. "Go. I will be here. There's more I must do." Without another word, he turned and knelt at the altar.

Christine hesitated as John motioned for her to follow him. She eyed him, then motioned back at Yunus. They couldn't just leave him.

John looked back at the man crumpled against the stage, then back at Christine and leaned in close. "He'll be here when the authorities arrive," he said softly.

"Are you sure?"

John replied with an assuring nod, then led Christine down the center aisle toward the exit. "We're going to have to make it to the station before rush hour. You and I are the only ones who can identify any of Yunus's men."

They left the building and splashed through the damp parking lot to the black SUV, the rain on its last breath. They buckled in unison, and John started the car's engine. The clock on the dashboard read 11:42.

As he backed the car out of the space and headed for the main road, Christine asked, "How long is it going to take us to get there?"

"There's no telling if we run into traffic on the interstate. I don't think we'll be late." He drew a breath and looked her in the eyes. "We can't be late."

With one hand on the steering wheel, John pulled a phone from his pocket and flipped it open. He dialed in a number and held the receiver to his ear.

Christine stared at the dark road ahead. It would take them hours to reach Union Station. She didn't care for the feeling of helplessness, so she chose to bury it deep.

"Guin, it's John."

Christine looked back at John while he drove and talked at the same time. She couldn't hear the voice on the other end.

"I know, and I'm going to tell you everything. But right now, I need you to listen. Whatever you do, keep this between us. You've got to trust me."

John paused for an interruption on the other end, the muffled tones of a female voice speaking at a raised volume barely audible.

"But you're going to. Right now you're going to help me stop a terrorist attack in DC."

The voice on the other end went silent.

John continued. "I've got our terrorist in custody. Sort of. It's a long story, but his name is Yunus Anar. I took out his brother a long time ago. He was gunning for me, but his team is headed to Union Station. They're going to detonate a chemical bomb."

The voice returned, the volume lower but the pace quickened.

"No, Guin, you can't take this to anyone. The agency's been compromised. Anar told us everything."

John paused, and his eyes darted from the road to Christine.

"Yes, she's with me."

Christine raised an eyebrow as John backed the phone away from his ear and stared at the screen. "She hung up." With a flick of his wrist, he closed the phone and placed it on the dash.

They drove in silence for half a minute before he spoke up. "Don't worry. She'll call back."

The phone buzzed against the dashboard. John smirked at Christine as he picked it up and answered the call.

"Guin, you've got to believe me. The intel is solid. We—" His eyebrows sank as he listened to the interruption. "It's Al. He paid Anar off with a shot at me. He's gone rouge, Guin. I know it sounds impossible, but it's true. Anar gave him up. And the only reason I think you should believe what I'm telling you is that I've never lied to you before."

Another pause. John listened, then said, "Thank you," and hung up the phone. He shot a glance at Christine. "She's in."

"Great," Christine replied. "A reporter, a CIA officer, and an ex-CIA officer turned evangelist team up to stop a terrorist attack on Union Station. Sounds like a terrible movie."

John snorted. "Yeah, it does." He stared out the windshield for a brief moment, then raised the phone and dialed another number. "Let's see if we can even the odds."

CHAPTER TWENTY-EIGHT

HIS SECOND PHONE call was to a man named Eric Paulson, another officer with the Central Intelligence Agency. John assured Christine they could trust him. Apparently, Eric was Anglican.

The drive to Union Station proved difficult as the first rays of the sun sliced upward through the now clear and brightening sky. Within two hours, traffic clogged as emergency vehicles dealt with an overturned pickup. Time passed, and all they found on the opposite side of the delay was more traffic lined bumper to bumper into the city.

The dashboard clock read 7:19 as they pulled into what was likely the last available spot in the parking garage adjacent to the station. They exited the SUV and walked at a brisk pace in the direction a dull sign labeled ESCALATORS pointed them.

As they neared the end of the row of parked cars, Christine spotted a man and a woman standing near the down escalator watching them approach. Eric Paulson adjusted his black suit jacket to disguise a slight bulge beneath his arm. The woman, who must be Guin, dug both fists into the hips of her navy dress pants, a matching blazer perfectly framing a plain white oxford shirt.

"They don't look suspicious at all," Christine said with a snort.

"Less suspicious than you two grave robbers," Guin responded as Christine and John came to a stop.

Christine looked down at her clothes and realized for the first time how filthy she was. The entire drive to the station, she'd focused on remembering each face of the men who'd held the church hostage. Dry mud streaks ran the length of her body. She imagined her face and hair bore a similar texture.

Guin picked up two bags sitting between her and Eric. "We don't have much time," she noted as she handed them each a large black paper bag. "And you'll draw too much attention if you don't get changed. Over there." With the point of a finger, she directed them to a pair of restrooms.

Christine clutched the bag and sprinted into the bathroom. She chose the largest stall and lifted her shirt over her head before she even locked the door. Dumping the contents of the bag onto the floor, she was relieved to find a fashionable wardrobe of jeans, flannel shirt, and boots. No doubt Guin's handiwork.

She was dressed and out of the stall in sixty seconds. She splashed water on her face and rubbed off as much of the mud as she could with a handful of paper towels. Using her hands, she combed her hair into a manageable shape. Confident she could blend in, Christine dumped the bag of her old clothes into the trash bin and walked out the door.

Eric and Guin paused a discreet conversation between them as she walked up to them. Eric inspected her wardrobe and said, "I hope you liked what I picked out."

"Oh," Christine uttered as she glanced away to hide her surprise. "It fits great. Thank you."

Guin held out her open palm, a silver bracelet on it. "Here. This should make you feel a little more normal."

Christine smiled as she took the bracelet and slipped it over her wrist. The design was simple, but she liked it.

John appeared next to Christine and tossed his own bag into a large trash receptacle near the escalator. He wore the dark jeans and T-shirt well, though Christine spotted a few patches of mud he'd missed on his skin while cleaning up.

Guin handed them both a small tan earbud. "We'll split up and canvas the station in four quadrants. My guess is the bomber will target the concourse."

Eric interjected and gestured to the two civilians. "We don't know what the men look like, so we'll be counting on you two to give us some direction in there."

John nodded in Christine's direction. "She spent the most time with them. Christine and Guin can take the main hall. Eric, you and I will stay on the mezzanine level and check around the shops."

"It's going to be packed in there," Guin said, shaking her head.

John shook his head. "We can't involve anyone else. We don't know who we can trust."

Eric swallowed loud enough for everyone to hear. "I guess now would be the right time to start praying."

Guin motioned for Christine and John to insert the earbuds. Christine pressed the soft foam piece into her right ear canal and noticed something hard at its center.

Guin said, "Check," her voice magnified within Christine's head.

"It's working," Christine responded.

John started toward the escalator. Guin held out a hand to stop him and pressed the butt of a handgun into his belly. He looked into her eyes, a look that lingered too long for Christine, and pushed her hand away.

"Take it," she said with an eye roll. "You can at least take out their knees."

John glanced from Guin to Christine. She gazed into his eyes, yearning to telepathically tell him everything would be OK.

It worked, possible proof of latent superpowers. He grabbed the gun from Guin and stowed it in the waistband of his jeans near the small of his back. The T-shirt fell just long enough to hide the grip.

His eyes darted to each one of them. With a deep breath, he said, "Let's go."

John took the escalator down first, followed by Eric.

Guin held Christine back as a couple boarded next. "Don't worry," Guin whispered into Christine's ear. "I'll be there."

Christine nodded and took her place behind the couple. She suspected Guin waited before descending on the escalator, but didn't dare glance behind to see. Up ahead, she watched John disembark, followed by Eric. They parted in opposite directions, John left, Eric right, and disappeared. The couple exited next and walked straight ahead.

It was Christine's turn. She stepped from the escalator and followed the couple until the sight ahead brought her feet to a halt. The mezzanine level opened in a wide expanse on both sides, the massive ceiling decorated in coffered plaster hexagons. Light poured from overhead windows and added an angelic sheen to the marbled floor.

Christine couldn't remember ever having visited Union Station and regretted the circumstances of her first experience.

"On your right," said a soft voice in her ear. Guin passed by without making eye contact and headed to a nearby spiral staircase leading to the second level. "Follow me down the staircase and straight ahead into the main hall."

Christine paused for a few seconds, then complied. She slid her palm along the polished wooden handrail of the staircase as she descended and decided a future return trip was in order. Maybe even by train.

To visit the station, of course. Not see John. Unless he wanted to—

"Can somebody give me an idea of what I'm looking for?"

The surprise of Eric's voice caused her to almost lose her footing on the last step.

"Christine," John replied. "Give us a quick rundown on what you can remember."

"I only ever saw five of them. I'm not sure if there's more than that." She wondered if she spoke too softly. Wasn't she also supposed to hold her hand on her ear? According to Hollywood maybe, but the reception seemed fine in the bud. "One is short, thin. Eyes set a little apart, and a mustache. Another is average build, with a nose that turns up. Curly dark hair. One's balding, with glasses. They all have darker skin, more olive than tan."

"I remember one of them has a flat face, a lot of stubble on his chin," John added.

"That's right. The only other man I saw is big and ugly. He walked with a limp."

"He's welcome."

"I take it you've met. He's the only one I heard called to by name. Erkan."

Eric grunted. "It'd be nice to put a face with the name."

"Don't worry." John's voice crackled in the earbud. "You'll know him when you see him."

As he spoke, Christine stepped through the entryway to the main hall of the station, a colossal monument to Roman architecture. The high barrel vault overhead mesmerized her. Large white tiles connected by smaller, diamond-patterned brown tiles flowed toward a beautiful round open café in the center of the hall.

Guin's voice snapped Christine back to reality. "I need you to look down, Christine. At faces. Focus."

Christine remembered the task at hand and worked her way through the crowd, scanning faces as she walked.

"I've got something," Eric said in a hushed tone. "Hold on."

Silence. Christine kept searching as she rounded the café. She slowed to peer across the tables for any recognizable features. Nothing. No one familiar. No one suspicious.

"Seventeen minutes," Guin announced, breaking the silence.

Eric's voice followed. "I've got eyes on a possible suspect. Tall, broad shoulders. Carrying a messenger bag. He's walking with a limp. I can't get a vantage on the face."

Christine stopped in her tracks and strained to catch every word as a woman's voice boomed over the public address system. She lifted a hand to cup it around her ear just as she heard Guin.

"Keep your hand down."

Christine dropped her hand to her side. "I'm sorry. I just . . ."

Her words trailed off as she looked up and stared ahead into the face of someone she knew. He stood a few yards ahead of her, dressed in a pair of jeans and a dark jacket, with a ball cap sitting low on his brow. He clutched a small duffel bag in one hand and stared straight at her.

The nostrils of his concave nose flared.

All the breath in Christine's lungs escaped through her mouth carrying the words, "It's him."

The man bared his clenched teeth and took a step toward her. A crack echoed off the marble columns. The man jerked as a dust cloud exploded from his jacket behind his left shoulder. He fell facedown to the ground as screams erupted around them, and the crowd scattered in all directions.

Guin stood behind him, a trail of smoke escaping from the barrel of the gun in her hand. Christine watched her mouth move as her voice sounded clear through the earbud. "Suspect down."

Christine and Guin both ran to the downed man. Guin flipped his body over and checked for a pulse. "Still alive, but I'll bet he loses the use of that arm."

Christine grabbed the duffel and opened it. She pulled a handful of wadded newspaper from inside and looked up at Guin. "Where's the bomb?"

Guin swore and holstered her weapon. "It's a decoy. I repeat—the real bomber is still active."

Armed police officers descended on their position, weapons drawn, and yelled commands.

Guin held up a leather wallet with a badge and ID clipped to the inside. She spoke in a thunderous, commanding voice. "Central Intelligence. I need you to stand down." With her hands in the air, Guin shot a glance at Christine and whispered, "Run."

Without hesitation, Christine jumped to her feet and ran past a startled officer. "Hey!" he shouted as she passed.

She rounded the corner of the café and disappeared from their view as she heard him call instructions into his radio. She shot by frightened pedestrians and caught another officer barreling his way toward her out of the corner of her eye. She waited for him to get close enough before dropping to the ground and skidding across the slick tiled floor.

The police officer tumbled over her and bowled into a group of travelers huddled together for safety. Christine jumped back on her feet and ran out of the main hall and back into the shopping plaza.

"John, where are you?" she exclaimed.

"I'm heading to Eric's position. To your left. End of the hall, then another left. He's heading to the Metro."

Christine ran down the long walkway, dodging from one side to another to avoid a collision with confused patrons filing in and out of the various shops. She didn't bother looking over her shoulder, certain she'd only spy the blur of navy-blue uniforms in pursuit.

She rounded the second left and headed for the down escalator. Pushing her way around passengers, she took a second to glance over a shoulder. No one yet.

"We don't have a lot of time. Permission to engage?" Eric's voice rang louder as the chatter and ambient noise of the underground Metro stop invaded the radio space.

"Negative," John replied. "I'm not there yet."

"Eric, where are you? I'm coming down," Christine said as she bounded off the escalator and ran to the top of the stairs leading to the rail.

"Trying to keep my distance so he doesn't . . ." Eric's voice trailed off. Sounds of muffled excitement followed.

Christine took the stairs two at a time and made it to the bottom of the long stairway only to find the balding, bespectacled man choking the life out of Officer Eric Paulson.

CHAPTER TWENTY-NINE

CROSS SPOTTED CHRISTINE disappearing just under the concrete overhanging as he sprinted down the stairwell leading to the Metro platform. Either she kicked into a gear he hadn't witnessed, or he was slowing with age. Confident he wasn't old enough to be losing it, a half smile creased the corner of his mouth as he thought about her impressive determination.

At the bottom of the steps, it only took an approximate two seconds for him to assess the situation. Christine stood frozen as Paulson grappled with an unknown assailant a handful of yards ahead of her.

Over his earbud, Paulson's voice crackled, "He's getting away!"

Cross watched the connected cars of the Red Line pull to a stop just ahead on the track. A large man carrying a messenger bag glanced over a shoulder and stared back at Cross with eyes of angry recognition. Then he disappeared into the crowd.

Erkan.

Cross broke into a run and grabbed Christine's elbow from behind. No choice in the matter, she fell into equal step beside him.

"What about Eric?" she exclaimed.

"He'll be fine," Cross replied.

As they neared the two fighters, Paulson bent his knees and pushed backward. The bald man lost his footing, giving the CIA officer just enough leverage to flip him upside down over his back. The terrorist landed on his own back with a thud and cried out. Paulson held a tight grip on the man's hand and twisted. Another sharp exclamation rang out.

Paulson looked up as Cross and Christine passed by and shouted, "Go! I've got this!"

They didn't skip a step. Cross heard Christine mutter under her breath, "No kidding."

The doors to the Red Line train stood open as pedestrians filed in and out. No sign of Erkan. "He's got to be on board. Don't hesitate," Cross ordered.

Christine matched his pace. Five yards out, the doors automatically moved to close. They both jumped into the car with not nearly enough room to spare, and fellow passengers greeted them with glances of annoyance.

"That was lucky," Christine said after a deep exhale.

The car bounced as the train started its journey into the heart of downtown DC. Cross picked out the name of the next station from a scrambled public announcement echoing from an overhead speaker.

"Judiciary Square. Union Station must be plan A."

Christine's eyes grew in size. "What's plan B?"

Cross shook his head and strained his eyes to look through the scratched dirty glass of the doors separating the cars. "We've got to get our hands on that bag." He took a step toward the door leading into the next car, then held up a hand. "You'd better stay here, where it's safe."

She raised a scowling eyebrow. "I'm pretty sure none of us are safe if that bomb goes off inside this tunnel. Besides, you're going to need me to grab the bag while you have fun with the jerk carrying it."

Cross smiled. "You sure you don't want to take a crack at him?"

"I just might," she replied as she stepped up to the door.

They passed through the gap and paused just inside the door of the adjacent train car. It was full, and it took time to move through the crowd to the rear, with no sign of Erkan among them.

The train came to a stop with the announcement of passengers to exit to the right.

"What if he gets out?" Christine asked.

"Get into the next car. I'll jump out and see if I can spot him. Your earbud still good?"

Christine nodded. She put a hand on the exit door as he slipped from her side and followed a shaggy college student out of the train.

He worked his way down the platform, taking a couple of glances into the train to track Christine's movements. More people filed into the already crowded stop, making it impossible to catch a glimpse of Erkan before he could slip away.

"This is ridiculous," Christine said over the radio. "How are we going to find him during rush hour?"

Cross tuned out her question, his eyes darting from face to face and his mind recalling as many details about Erkan's appearance as had captured in the few seconds before the man had disappeared near the Red Line. His shaved head uncovered, a jean jacket, and the dark strap of the messenger bag slung over a shoulder. Erkan was tall and broad. If the brute stepped off the train, Cross doubted he would miss it.

An announcement over the PA cued Cross to jump back into the car Christine scouted. She stood facing the door into the next car in line. He took a step toward her when her voice whispered into his ear, "Got him."

The Red Line bounced as it pulled away from the platform and picked up speed into the tunnel. The screech of wheel against metal echoed against brick.

"Sit down," Cross ordered.

She slipped into a red leather seat facing him, her back to the rear wall of the car. "Did he spot you?"

She shook her head. Cross nodded in reply, then grabbed the nearest handlebar to steady the sway of his body in rhythm to the motion of the Metro car. He squinted his eyes to peer through the double-layered glass into the next car. It was a small window, and though he couldn't see the entire car, he spotted the shoulder of a jean jacket sitting near the center.

"What are you going to do?"

Cross thought for a moment before he replied, a variety of scenarios playing out in his mind. "Not sure. He'll see us coming through the door, and we'll lose the element of surprise. We may just wait and see where he gets off."

"He could set the bomb off inside the car."

Not a scenario Cross wanted to imagine. At the right location, Erkan could kill dozens. Not as catastrophic as Union Station, but still devastating.

"I'm praying he's patient."

Christine exhaled a deep breath. "You'll have to teach me how to do that sometime."

Cross smiled at her. "We'll grab coffee."

An elderly woman clinging to the crossbar beside him narrowed her eyes in his direction. He gave her a wink, then locked his eyes on the back of Erkan's head.

"Now approaching Chinatown Station, doors open on the left," announced a bored voice over the loudspeaker. The train braked, and passengers hoping to disembark shifted positions.

"Guin, Eric, do you copy?" Cross pretended to scratch the back of his head and cupped his hand around his ear to block out the irritating squeal of the train tire. "I've got eyes on . . ."

Erkan stood and slipped between a woman toting groceries and a businessman fidgeting near the exit just as the ding of a bell overhead signaled the moment of escape.

"He's on the move," Cross said, half toward his ear and half toward Christine.

She stood and squeezed around a large sweat-covered man. On instinct, Cross offered his hand to her. She grabbed it tight. He ignored her eyes, startled by the intense wave of excitement washing over him. Pushing away his feelings, he focused on a single word.

Mission.

It was all that mattered now. Just as it had so many times before. Only this time he wasn't in the business of taking lives. This time he would save them.

The doors to the platform slid open and cued the mass exodus from the Red Line. Cross lost sight of Erkan for only seconds as they pushed their way through the exit.

"Get ready," Cross whispered. "If he turns toward us, we're blown."

It was a risk, but Cross kept his eyes trained in the direction he expected to find Erkan. They were both a few inches on the tall side. He was certain to be identified. By divine providence, the terrorist turned his back to them on the platform and headed for the nearest escalator to ground level.

"Praise God," Cross breathed. He tightened his grip around Christine's hand, and they filed in line with a few dozen others heading the same direction.

"What's he waiting for? Is this not enough people to kill?"

He hesitated to answer her question. What *was* Erkan waiting for? The longer he walked around town holding a chemical bomb in his hands, the greater chance of failure. Cross opened his mouth to speak, but the words caught in his throat as another voice interrupted his ear cavity with a crackle of static.

"My guess, he'll detonate in the open. Greater spread of the chemical. Oh, and Cross, no coffee for the rest of us?" Guin added a scoff for emphasis.

Cross felt his cheeks warm. *Mission.* Their feet hit the first rising step, and they paused as their bodies were lifted upward. "If you're standing at the top of this escalator with a Stunner, I'll buy everyone a round."

Christine let go of Cross's hand and glanced at him with a quizzical eye. "Stunner?"

"The handy little piece I used in Jordan." He fought back the disappointment of losing her touch.

"Sorry, John," Guin interjected. "You'll have to hold on to your money this time."

"Guin, are you OK?" Christine asked. "Were you arrested?"

"I'm fine. The boys in blue are satisfied with my credentials and helping us try to catch up to you."

"Paulson?" Cross wondered aloud.

"At my side. We're heading for some cruisers now, but with traffic it's going to be difficult to reach Chinatown before the target's in the open."

"How did you—" Christine started to say.

"That loudspeaker on the Metro is the most annoying thing, isn't it? The tracker in your earpiece helps too. John, you're going to have to stick to this guy if we're going to have any chance at getting ahold of that bag. There's a unit nearby. They're going to try to meet you."

Cross swallowed the lump forming in his throat. "Guin—"

"I know," she cut him off. "It's too late. I had to call it in."

Without a second thought, Cross dug a finger into his ear, retrieved the bud from inside, and tossed it away. He motioned to Christine and mouthed, *Take it out.*

She hesitated and questioned him with her eyes, but before he could respond, she repeated his action and tossed her own earbud. "What's going on?" she asked as they stepped off the top of the escalator and moved with the crowd to the Metro exit.

"The agency's involved now, which means Al will be involved, and I don't know how deep this goes. If he's compromised anyone else, we could walk right into an ambush."

"So what you're saying is, no backup."

Cross nodded.

She sighed. "Then it's just the two of us." With a grin, she added, "Like old times."

Cross grinned back, then focused on the back of Erkan's head. The crowds parted like the Red Sea, and they stepped out onto the sun-drenched sidewalk of the corner of H Street Northwest and Seventh. The magnificent Chinese gate known as the Friendship Archway towered over the street directly ahead of them. Dragon designs of gold, blue, and red glistened in the bright light. The embellishment helped the gate stand out against the chaotic bustle of Chinatown.

Erkan stood still at the H Street crosswalk. Cross slipped his hand around Christine's arm and slowed them both to a stop as a crowd mingled, waiting for permission to cross. "Keep your head down," he breathed into her ear.

Christine obliged and hung her chin low. Cross did the same as he turned his body in to hers. "Don't look his direction. Pretend like you're on a phone."

He couldn't help but smile as she mimed tapping on a smartphone. He caught a wisp of a scent from her hair. Beneath the sweat and dirt top layer was a hint of apple.

A row of cars slowed to a stop at the traffic light. "Three seconds."

The signal to go flashed, and the crowd surged. Cross and Christine followed Erkan across the street at a safe distance. Halfway across, he stepped around the next curb and through the open back doors of a black service van.

"John!" Christine exclaimed.

Another man pulled the doors shut behind them as Erkan slid onto a bench seat and cradled the messenger bag on his lap. Just as the door closed shut, he looked back in their direction, made eye contact with Cross, and gave a malevolent grin.

Cross broke into a run. The left turn signal on the van pulsated as it pulled away from the curb and into the flow of traffic heading north on Seventh Street. He skidded to a stop, and Christine appeared beside him. Gritting his teeth, he kicked the curb and said, "We're going to lose him. And the bomb."

CHAPTER THIRTY

"Not if I can help it," Christine responded as she took off from his side down the sidewalk.

"Hey!" she heard John call out from behind. "Where are you going?"

Ignoring him, she slid to a stop next to the driver's side of a black Jeep Wrangler idling in a parking spot. The yuppie male checking his teeth in the mirror of his sun visor let loose a muffled shriek and rose a few inches off the leather seat.

Flashing her best flirtatious eyes, she said, "I need to borrow your car."

"Excuse me?"

John appeared on the passenger side, the barrel of his gun poking just over the door. "Get out," he ordered.

The panicked man unbuckled his seat belt as Christine opened his door. He stumbled out of the seat, and she took his place. John was already buckled. She shut the door and put the Jeep in gear.

"Thanks!" she said to the man with a wave, then pressed her foot down on the accelerator and cut off a delivery truck as she pulled out of the spot and raced to catch up to the black van.

A car horn blared, and John braced himself against the dash. "Looks like you should've done all the driving in Jordan," he shouted over the rushing wind.

She glanced at him long enough to catch the charming grin flashed in her direction.

Christine couldn't help but smile. She felt courageous, ready for a showdown. "You're the marksman," she replied. "Time to show me how good you are at shooting tires."

She pressed her foot toward the floorboard, and the Jeep skidded around a lethargic sedan. She squinted against the sunlight and focused as far down Seventh Street as she could. A flash of metallic black paint appeared as the van changed lanes.

"There," she announced as she poked her index finger out over the steering wheel.

"I see them. Get in the left lane. He's going to take K Street."

Christine obeyed, and sure to John's prediction the black van veered left just as the traffic light on the corner flashed from green to yellow. "Hold on!"

The Jeep shot into the intersection and struck a puff of smoke against the asphalt as she cranked hard left on the wheel. For a moment, the weight of the Jeep leaned precariously to one side, convincing Christine they would flip. Gravity caught them and the car leveled as she accelerated down K Street in pursuit of the now weaponized cargo van.

She didn't look at John for fear of catching a startled reaction, but her heart rate soothed when he quipped, "Like a pro."

More car horns announced the displeasure of other motorists, but the wind whipping through the open top of the Jeep clipped the sound like a pair of scissors against paper. Christine wanted to slow their pace, but the van increased speed, and the gap between them widened.

"They're onto us," John said, confirming her suspicion. "Not a great day for traffic to be manageable."

Fighting against her better judgment, Christine pressed the weight of her foot against the gas pedal, and the needle on the speedometer moved right. She gripped the wheel tighter to quell any fear of a mere slip of her fingers sending them to a head-on collision with certain death.

"He's aiming right."

"That's a one way!"

"They're going to try to lose us."

Christine stifled a scream as she followed the van's lead and turned the wrong way down Ninth Street. More car horns and raised fists welcomed them. The van struck the curb as it banked left. Christine took a wider angle and breathed a sigh of relief as they rejoined K Street heading in the appropriate direction.

"You're doing great," John's voice boomed from the passenger side.

In the previous harrowing seconds, she'd forgotten he sat next to her.

"Get as close as you can, and I'll try to slow them down."

The Jeep's engine groaned as she pushed it harder. The distance closed. John pulled the gun from his waistband, gripped it in both hands, and leaned over the passenger-side door.

Christine let off the gas pedal and jerked down on the steering wheel to skirt ramming an SUV as she sped through a red light. The maneuver pitched John back into his seat.

"Sorry!" she yelled.

Without a retort, he jumped back to his position and leveled the pistol with his elbows pinned against the Jeep's bouncing frame. Christine regained the short distance they'd lost and slid into the lane adjacent to the black van.

The wail of sirens wafted into the cab, and Christine caught sight of red and blue bulbs alternating at a distance in the rearview mirror.

Her eyes darted from the mirror back to John and the van in time to catch movement at the back. "John, look out!"

A flat-faced man cracked the back door open and aimed a submachine gun in their direction. John dropped a hand, grabbed the steering wheel, and pushed downward against her grip.

The Jeep swung toward the van as John unleashed a volley of shots into its bumper. The flat-faced man ducked backward to dodge the spray of bullets as the two vehicles smashed into each other.

John teetered on the edge of the passenger door, the force of the blow threatening to tear him from the seat belt's hold around his waist. Christine whipped the Jeep away from the van, and he fell back into place against the passenger seat.

The bellow of a truck's horn startled her. She looked forward to see the truck's grill bearing down on them. She piloted the Jeep back into the right lane, just missing a kiss with the truck's front bumper.

The van recovered and raced off. Police sirens pierced the air in an unseemly cacophony surrounding their car. John braced himself, his neck bent at an awkward angle as he stared over his shoulder. "The cavalry's here."

Ahead, the van drifted into the right lane. K Street split apart, the middle lanes descending into a tunnel and the outer access roads rising upward.

"John!" Christine kept her eyes straight, not daring to look at him.

"Just follow them, whatever they do."

The van maintained a straight course as the curb rose and blocked off an exit to the outer lanes. Just before a guardrail would guarantee their route, the driver swerved right and bounced over the sidewalk and into the outer lane.

Christine followed suit, and the Jeep scaled the curb as expected. In the rearview mirror, she watched the police cars slow to traverse the obstacle.

"No, no, no!"

She looked back at the van as it turned left into a crossing street against the flow of traffic. A cascade of horn blasts flowed from the line of cars veering out of its path. The van cut right and entered the chaos of the roundabout just ahead of them. One of the police cars broke off to pursue but clipped a bus and slammed into a light pole.

Christine slowed to merge and watched the van escape a collision with a sedan before it disappeared around another corner. "What do we do?"

"You caught them once. Time to do it again."

She stole a glance at John's smart smile. Narrowing her eyes, she pressed on the pedal and guided the Jeep around the bewildered vehicles clogging Washington Circle. She bullied her way through, but it felt like it took too long to reach the van's chosen escape route: Twenty-Third Street, though less a street and more a zoo.

"This is nuts. We're going to lose them."

John's hand touched hers on the wheel, sending her heart into a greater state of commotion than it already was. "It's OK," he replied. "They're in this too. He can only get so far." His hand left hers and the thumping in her chest died down.

Christine relaxed enough to notice the lack of flashing lights and sirens behind them. "What happened to that other cop car?"

"They couldn't keep up."

"John, we've got to do something."

"I am."

Christine pumped the brake as an SUV pulled out from the exit of a George Washington University Medical Center parking garage and merged ahead of them. Red brake lights announced a momentary cease of activity for their lane.

She looked over at him and knit her eyebrows together above her nose. "What?"

He couldn't return her gaze, as he sat facing forward, both eyes shut tight. "I'm praying."

Praying? Now? At a time in the past, Christine might have mocked his judgment. Or perhaps scolded him for such mystic behavior during a crisis. But for a strange reason, it seemed precisely the right exercise at the moment. She believed God was real. She had to. It was the only explanation for what she'd witnessed only hours before.

In Yunus Anar's shoes, the act of a divine being would've been the only way she could have seen fit to forgive John Cross for the murder of her brother. And that was exactly what Yunus did.

God, her mind whispered, *help us.*

A flash of black metal startled her. She couldn't believe it. God answered her prayer. But something about it seemed odd. Her brain fought through the cloud of confusion, and she realized the problem.

It was a black van, sure. But she saw it in the rearview mirror.

"How did they—" Before she could utter another word, the van struck them from behind.

She and John lurched forward in their seats. Christine pressed harder on the brake to keep from ramming the SUV. Plumes of white smoke consumed the screech of crushing metal.

John looked over his shoulder. His upper lip curved in a snarl. "Simpson."

The van pushed harder, and the Jeep lurched forward an inch. Christine pumped the brake, but it wouldn't give her anything more. "They're going to push us right into a three-car pileup if we don't do something!"

But there was nowhere to go. Traffic clogged the lane beside them, and there wasn't enough room for the Jeep to get around the stopped cars ahead.

God, please.

The squeal of tires alerted Christine to the mirror again, and she watched, mouth agape, as a white van marked METROPOLITAN POLICE barreled out of the parking garage exit and T-boned the black van behind them into a dump truck in the next lane.

The cars ahead rolled forward as the jam cleared. Christine hesitated and looked over her shoulder at the wreckage. The smoke cleared enough for her to recognize Guin pushing away from the passenger airbag of the police van and coughing out the window.

"Go!" Guin yelled, her voice thick with pain.

Christine stepped on the pedal, and the Jeep took off.

"She'll be fine," John said, answering the unspoken question.

The traffic ahead thinned, and Christine accelerated the Jeep. The turbulent wind inside the open cab tugged at her hair. "I don't see them." Panic threatened to seize her mind.

They crossed H Street, then swerved around a delivery truck parked at an awkward angle at the entrance to an Episcopal church.

"Up ahead."

Christine strained her eyes, then caught sight of the back of the black van a hundred yards down the road. She increased speed, and the distance closed.

Cars in both lanes slowed as a traffic light at the intersection of Virginia Avenue flashed from green to yellow.

"Hold on!" Christine shouted as she yanked on the steering wheel. They shot around the stopped cars and through the crossway. Half a football field ahead, Erkan's van cut off a taxi as it slid into the right lane.

Movement beside her prompted Christine to avert her eyes for a brief moment. John leaned out of the Jeep pointing his gun at the van. Returning her focus to the road, Christine gripped the steering wheel and mentally willed the car to hold steady.

Gunshots rang over the howling wind. Sparks bounced off the back bumper of the van. A short explosion sounded. Smoke poured from the back left tire, and large slices of rubber tore across the road in the van's wake.

John ducked back into his seat and grimaced.

"What's wrong?"

"I'm slipping. It took me more than one shot."

The van hugged the curb and swerved right at the next intersection. Christine followed close behind. A tall apartment complex sat on the right, and a freeway rose from a tunnel in the ground on the left.

The van careened around other vehicles traveling both directions on the two-lane road, and the skin on Christine's fingers rubbed raw against the steering wheel as she guided the Jeep through the chaos the van left behind.

The oncoming lane disappeared as they entered the entrance ramp for Whitehurst Freeway. A guardrail to the left ended as another entrance lane merged. The van slowed, then cut hard to the left and bounced over a short median. It hopped another curb and tore up a grassy hill before sailing onto another ramp, a trail of rubber crumbs making it easy to follow the van's path.

The Jeep made it easy for Christine to copy the van's stunt. She zoomed up the ascending lane to catch the limping van. Rounding a curve, the modern white block architecture of the John F. Kennedy Memorial Center for the Performing Arts came into full view.

"They're heading out of the city," John noted. "We're about to merge with Interstate 66 and cross the Potomac."

"Do you think they're trying to get to Dulles?" Christine's familiarity with the DC metroplex was limited to its airports.

"Not anymore. They won't make another mile on that tire."

If he was right, the van would stop on the bridge. The bomb could do little harm there. Christine drew a deep breath. *Thank you, God.*

And now she thanked him. What next?

True to John's word, the lane merged with three more as they approached Theodore Roosevelt Memorial Bridge. The van moved as fast as it could on three tires, though still fast enough to elicit angry horn blasts from motorists braking to prevent a collision.

The van slowed even more. "I think they're going to stop," Christine said as its brake lights flashed.

But they didn't. Instead, the van lurched forward and cut across several lanes as it tried once more to lose its tail.

Christine groaned and attempted to accelerate, but a nervous soccer mom in a minivan forced her to brake and switch lanes. The van put a handful of other vehicles between them, somehow generating more velocity than Christine decided it should be capable of.

"Speed up!" John shouted.

"I am," Christine growled back. Erkan's driver had caught her relaxed and used her mistake to his advantage, though she wasn't sure what kind of escape plan they had in mind. Maybe jump off the bridge into the Potomac?

She'd be fine with that.

What she didn't bank on was an exit ramp that suddenly appeared just ahead on the right.

"What?" she said aloud in confusion.

John's hand smacked against the dash. "New development on Roosevelt Island. Look out. He's cutting through!"

The van cut across the bridge again and shot down the exit ramp. Christine lay on her horn as she intimidated a service truck onto the shoulder and rushed down after it. The asphalt disappeared beneath flat pressed dirt, and a dust cloud surrounded the Jeep.

Dodging construction materials and equipment in her path, Christine aimed the Jeep toward the enormous half-finished structure in the middle. Most of it enclosed, the top quarter of the building remained a steel skeleton. Its highest section stood twelve stories tall, with various other annexes taking shape around it. A tall yellow tower crane sat on the bank of the Potomac, guarding the building.

"What in the world is this?" Christine yelled.

"They're running out of space for all the corrupt bureaucrats." John followed his quip with an index finger pointing through the windshield. "There!"

The black van came to a stop in front of the tallest section of the building. Erkan leapt from the back and sprinted to the nearest open doorway. The flat-faced passenger with a submachine gun stepped from the van and lowered the weapon at them.

"Brace yourself!" Christine ordered as she shoved the gas pedal underfoot. The speedometer climbed with a cheerful gait.

The Jeep closed the distance much quicker than she expected, but Christine didn't relent the pressure on the pedal. Flat-face's eyes widened, and instead of firing, he jumped backward through the open back doors of the van.

Christine screamed a carnal cry in the second before the Jeep harpooned the back of the van and drove it straight into the concrete block wall of the new construction.

The sonic crunch of metal filled her ears.

Blurred white obscured her vision.

In a surreal passage of time, Christine's head welcomed the soft cuddle of fabric enveloping her until it stiffened and pushed her violently backward. The Jeep jostled her back and forth before it settled in the dust and let her slump against the headrest.

Brilliant colors and shapes formed a soup in her vision. And what was that? Bees? Convinced she'd entered the space between heaven and earth, Christine ordered her hands to reach out and to experience the touch of this new dimension.

Tan muscular fingers slipped by her outstretched hand and caressed her cheek. The colors and shapes stopped moving, and reality returned.

She saw the smoking wreckage of the van over the deflated airbag of the Jeep's steering wheel.

"Christine," John said over the noise.

She turned to face him, and the buzzing in her ears fell away.

"Are you OK?"

She closed her eyes for a moment, then reopened them to full clarity. "Yes," she said. "You?"

"I'd prefer never to do that again."

"No kidding." Christine remembered the open doorway. "Erkan!"

John unbuckled his safety belt and climbed over the warped passenger door. Christine's door was unhinged, and it pushed free with little effort. They sprinted from the crash to the building.

John paused at the doorway and grabbed Christine by the hand. "I'll go after Erkan. You get these men out of here. If that bomb goes off, we need to minimize the causalities."

Causalities, meaning Erkan and him.

Christine opened her mouth but paused mid-protest as John leaned into her. Just when she thought he would close the gap and kiss her, he stuck his hand behind his back and pulled the handgun from his waistband, his finger ticking the safety at the same time. She touched him on the arm before he could leave and said, "God will forgive you if you shoot him in the head."

John smirked, then turned and ran into the building.

CHAPTER THIRTY-ONE

CROSS FOUND A stairwell and took the steps two at a time. He knew Erkan's only remaining option, if he could predict Simpson as well as he expected. And that meant going up. All the way to the top.

Where the helicopter would meet him.

The Smith & Wesson nine millimeter in his right hand felt less like a foreign object since he'd procured it from Guin. That did little to ease his mind at the thought of dispatching Erkan. Cross hadn't yet created a scenario that didn't require a bullet through some part of the terrorist's body.

He passed the gaping hole of a future window and stole a glance over the edge. Christine waved her arms at a group of builders jogging to the crash site. Concrete infrastructure obscured his view, and Cross turned back to the rising flights of the stairway.

Her driving was an exemplary display of skill, he admitted. If the journalism thing ever got old, he would have to recommend her to a national intelligence job. That, or a stuntwoman in Hollywood.

The crash of debris echoed down the stairwell, followed by shouts of curses.

Cross picked up speed and held the nine millimeter at eye level. Forced to pause at every level to clear hallways, he fought the temptation to wipe the sweat dripping off his brow. Or was it blood? The likelihood of injury from the wreck was high, but the adrenaline coursing through his veins prevented him from being aware of any.

On the eighth-floor landing, a construction worker lay on his back-side, nursing a bruise forming on his temple. He sat up, startled at the sight of Cross's gun.

"Where?" Cross demanded.

The worker pointed up the stairs. "That way."

"Get out of here, now!"

The man didn't hesitate. Cross kept climbing. The howling wind outside took on an unnatural cadence and morphed into the familiar thumping of rotor blades.

On the ninth level, the walls disappeared and blue sky peeked through thick columns supporting the next three floors. The stairwell ended, replaced with a network of ladders running through open gaps in the ceiling.

Cross paused on the last step and scanned the floor. The building ended a short distance to his right, the skyline of DC obscured by the yellow frame of the tower crane hugging the concrete wall. The vast future home of stuffy analysts and brownnosers spread far and wide on his left.

A flash caught his eye, and he saw the messenger bag disappear through a hole in the ceiling to the tenth floor. Cross took off from the stair and scaled the first ladder he found.

He copied Erkan's route through the next level and onto the exposed infrastructure of the eventual twelfth-floor's steel beams. Erkan wrapped an arm around a beam and waved at the helicopter hovering high in the air.

Cross walked tight along the edge of the building, taking care not to peer down. His heart beat too fast to get a clean shot. The helicopter descended, and he spotted a thin wire dangling from a winch attached inside.

Only a few feet from the terrorist, Cross gripped the nine milli-meter and leveled it at the back of Erkan's head. "Hey, buddy," he shouted. "Where you headed?"

Erkan turned and narrowed his eyes. A muffled guttural sound slipped between his clenched teeth. Then he laughed. "John Cross. The preacher. What are you going to do? Shoot me? Like all the others? I thought you didn't do that anymore."

"I'm considering some exceptions."

Erkan spread his hands and walked toward Cross. "Make me your exception then. Pull the trigger and end my life."

Cross ordered his finger to press down on the trigger, but his muscles tensed and disobeyed the command. "Don't come any closer."

"You won't do it. You can't do it." Erkan's eyes flamed, and his hands dropped to his side.

Cross took a deep breath. "You're right. I can't kill you." He shifted the gun's sight from Erkan's head to just over the man's shoulder. "But I can't let you leave." Cross unleashed a barrage of bullets into the sky at the approaching helicopter. Sparks exploded off the cabin, and the copter veered away from its attacker.

Erkan rushed him and collided with Cross. The two men fell together against the steel beam and rolled off. Cross released his grip on the gun and caught the edge of the beam with both hands. His plummet slowed, but his fingers slipped, and he dropped to the cement floor beneath him.

Cross bent his knees just before impact. His feet hit, and he tucked into an ungraceful roll, tumbled over twice, and splayed across the rough surface. Shaking the stars from his eyes, he looked up to see Erkan crawling toward the gun, the messenger bag missing from his shoulder.

The terrorist grabbed the nine millimeter and leapt to his feet before Cross could reach him. "Unlike you," Erkan snarled, "I have a taste for blood."

Cross froze, waiting for the bullet to explode from the barrel and rip through his chest. Erkan's muscles tensed, but before he could pull the trigger, a two-by-four swung in an arc behind him and connected with the back of his head. Erkan launched forward, the gun falling from his limp hand and sliding across the floor, away from both of them.

Christine stood over the man's dazed body, holding the two-by-four in both hands and panting. "Taste any blood now?" She looked up from Erkan and creased her nose at Cross. "Where's the bag?"

Where? The messenger bag was gone from Erkan's shoulder. Cross scanned the floor, then lifted his eyes back up. The bag lay on its side on the beam above them. He pointed to it and exclaimed, "There!"

Erkan stirred, pressed his palms flat on the floor, and pushed himself up. Cross nodded to Christine. "Get the bomb. Go!"

She ran to the nearest ladder.

Cross reached Erkan and swung for his chin as the man stood to his feet. Erkan took the hit like a brick wall, then shoved his own fist into Cross's shoulder. They exchanged more blows until an uppercut threw Cross backward against a workbench piled high with metal tubing.

Erkan took off for the nearest steel column and climbed it like a monkey up a tree. Christine ran toward the bag as he neared the top. Cross righted himself and raced for the ladder.

The beating of helicopter rotors descended on them. The wire dangling from the winch flew past Christine as she took the last few steps to the messenger bag. Cross climbed the ladder and reached the beam as Erkan stormed toward her.

Too late. Erkan beat him to her.

Instead of fighting Erkan for the bag, Christine dropped to a knee, scooped up the bag's strap, and slung it as hard as she could. The bag sailed through the air, and everyone froze in anticipation of the explosion sure to follow its impact with the floor below.

Instead of consuming them in a fiery blaze, the bag struck harmlessly against a stack of concrete-mix bags, slid to the ground, and dropped through a hole in the floor to the lower level.

Cross ran and hurdled Christine as Erkan gaped at the hole. At the same moment, the wire from the helicopter swung back over them. Cross grabbed it in midair before colliding with Erkan's chest. He snagged Erkan's belt with the hook at the end of the wire and pushed as hard as he could. Erkan swung out over the edge of the building, screaming.

Cross helped Christine find her balance on the beam. "Are you OK?"

"Come on!" she said as she grabbed his hand. "We've got to get the bomb!"

Cross tightened his fingers around hers and kept her from running off. "Wait a minute. What's that noise?" The faint sound of an electronic beeping pricked at his eardrum again.

Christine's eyes widened as she became aware of the noise. She lifted her arm, Cross's hand in tow. The silver bracelet around her wrist blinked at them. "My wrist is ringing."

Cross slid a finger over the bracelet, and a screen appeared with the words, "THIRTY SECONDS -G."

"What does that mean—"

Cross didn't let her finish her question. "Run!" Pulling her along, he dashed over the beam toward the opposite end of the building.

At the edge, he let go of Christine's hand and jumped the short distance to the idling yellow tower crane. He turned and caught Christine as she followed his lead.

"What are we doing?" she demanded.

Cross ducked his head into the control booth of the crane and jammed the control stick down. The long arm of the crane swung at a crawl away from the building. He looked back at Christine and pointed up. "Go!"

She hesitated, looked into his eyes, then climbed. Cross followed her up the grid work to the top of the jib. They ran down the length of the jib as it pointed out over the Potomac.

Behind them, Cross heard the sound he didn't want to hear. The sonic boom drew Christine's eyes over her shoulder, and she gasped at what he already knew was coming. "Keep running!"

She slid to a stop at the head and looked back again. Cross grabbed her around the waist and looked over his own shoulder. Sunlight glinted off an F-22 fighter jet as it threaded the sky toward the helicopter hovering above the unfinished building. A missile burst from its bay, and smoke trailed in a straight line toward the copter.

"Point your feet down and hold your arms in!" Pulling her with him, Cross leapt from the head of the jib.

Wind beat at them as they plunged toward the water and hung in the air for eternal seconds. As the Potomac filled Cross's vision, he heard and felt the impact of the missile against the helicopter behind them.

As a flame stretched its fingers for them, their toes sliced through the liquid floor and the river consumed their bodies.

CHAPTER THIRTY-TWO

AL SIMPSON DIDN'T bother flipping on his office light as he walked through the door. He crossed the dark carpet to his desk and unlocked a single drawer. He extracted a small thumb drive, then returned the drawer to its original state.

Before Simpson moved again, Cross slipped from a dark corner and flicked the switch, flooding the office with a warm glow.

Simpson's head jerked up, and he huffed when he recognized Cross. "You look good for a man who just took a hundred-and-twenty-foot dive into the Potomac."

Cross didn't feel good. Every bone in his body protested his refusal to lie down. He pushed the pain signals to a deep well in the back of his mind and took a few steps into the middle of Simpson's office.

"Why, Al?"

Simpson smiled. He pulled the leather chair away from the desk and plopped down onto it. Raising one hand in a sign of surrender, he reached the other into his inside jacket pocket and removed a flask. Unscrewing the top, he took a swig and wiped his chin before responding. "How about a game? I'll answer your questions if you answer mine."

Cross stayed silent.

"Who told you about the strike?"

"Guin slipped a smart bracelet on Christine."

"That b—" Simpson paused before he could insult her, and sniggered. "Clever."

"Now mine. Why?"

"What do you want me to say? I was bored? They offered me money? You of all people should realize by now, John—there's no such thing as good people in the world. We're all sick, stupid ants." He took another sip from the flask. "My job is, it's always been, about maintaining the established order of things. That goes both ways, pal. One side wins, and that puts us all out of business." He balanced the flask on top of a pile of papers on his desk. "And yeah, they paid me. My turn. How did you convince Anar not to kill you?"

"I don't think I really had much to do with it."

Simpson howled. "Let me guess. An angel appeared in the night sky. Announced a peace accord between you two. To be honest, I figured you'd beat him. Idiot wanted to take you on man to man instead of putting a bullet through your skull from behind like I recommended." His grin faded momentarily. "And take that as a compliment."

"I would've said the same thing."

"Anar never had it in him. I suppose he'll offer up some juicy intel to DOJ in exchange for a return trip home."

"You and I both know he'll be paraded around the Beltway as an anti-terror grand prize."

"I'll bet that really ticks you off, doesn't it?"

Cross took a step forward as a smirk formed across his lips. "No, no, no. It's my turn. And I've only got one more question."

"What's that, preacher boy?"

"Was Jordan a setup?"

Another laugh, followed by a vulgarity. "Son, sometimes things just go nuts."

Simpson pulled a gun from underneath the desk, pointed it at Cross's chest, and pulled the trigger multiple times. The gun clacked with each pull, nothing to show for the effort. Simpson tossed it down on the desk and sighed. "I figured you got to it first, but I'm not going to say it didn't make me feel better."

Cross took a few more steps to the desk and reached for the butt of the gun pressed against the small of his back. "Did I ever tell you how

I got the drop on the AIM guys in Jordan? With the help of a handy little gadget the boys in R and D call a Smart Stunner." He pulled the gun from his back and showed it off. "Shoots a small disc that releases an electric charge on impact." Cross stopped at the edge of the desk and pointed the weapon at Simpson. "Want to see how it works?"

Before Simpson answered the question, Cross fired the disc into his former director's chest. The black circular cartridge latched on to his shirt and emitted blue sparks. Simpson's body convulsed. His eyes rolled into the back of his head, and he slumped into the chair, unconscious.

CHAPTER THIRTY-THREE

CHRISTINE BACKED THE rental car out of the parking space and headed for the airport exit. Few cars impeded her way onto the interstate. She hoped it wasn't too late.

She didn't mind the early morning, though in the days since the thwarted attack on Washington, DC, she'd managed to evade a full night's rest. The story of her miraculous rescue from Jordan took last place to the scoop of a planned terrorist attack on the nation's capital combined with corruption in the ranks of the most famous intelligence agency on the planet.

Jacobs had insisted she take the lead and offer a firsthand account on as many stations at as many hours as they could book. She couldn't close her eyes without seeing the footage that always shared the screen with her—Yunus being transferred to a maximum-security prison by the FBI. Every answer she gave at each interview replayed in her mind.

"In the course of my investigation, I became an eyewitness to the identities of the members of the cell."

"Mr. Anar willingly chose to betray his countrymen and reveal their plan to me, a fact I trust the Federal Bureau of Investigation will consider in their treatment of him."

"Authorities needed my assistance during the engagement in order to positively identify the suspects."

"Officers from multiple organizations worked together to ensure the safety of this country's citizens."

"We owe them a great debt."

She left details out, as before, but this time she considered it her duty to protect the identities of Eric and Guin. Memories of her two new friends brought a smile to Christine's face. Eric promised to be in touch, though she didn't think she would ever see him or Guin again. John mentioned that he would recommend Guin for his old boss's job.

A broader smile forced Christine to open her mouth, and a quick, happy breath escaped. She believed his heart ached as much as hers over the days they were apart. There was a connection, and it grew only stronger as time passed.

Separating wasn't their first choice, but Christine knew her obligation to the network meant flying back to New York. And John had other business to take care of back in Mechanicsville.

She still couldn't believe the church had welcomed him back. He'd spent most of his time since the incident meeting with congregants in their homes. And a business meeting was scheduled at the church Thursday or Friday night—she couldn't remember.

Her source for all the details stood tapping a toe on the sidewalk in front of Rural Grove as Christine pulled the rental car to a stop in an open space. Her smile didn't fade as Lori greeted her with as much of a hug as the cast on her arm would allow.

"Oh, Lori, you look wonderful!" Christine said as she pressed in. The faint sound of a choir singing alongside musical accompaniment drifted into the air from the crack between the double wooden doors leading into the church.

"I think they'd have to break all my limbs to get me to stay down for any length of time," Lori said with a laugh. "And you've looked beautiful in every single interview."

Christine wrinkled her nose. "You didn't watch them all."

"What's a gimpy old lady to do all day but binge watch her favorite reporter tell the biggest news story in a decade?"

"Well, I'm glad you're doing better."

"And I'm glad you're here."

"You're going to need to tell me what happened. I didn't think anyone would ever forgive John for what happened."

Lori snorted. "Dear, for the most part, people can be really terrible. But every once in a while, a group of folks will demonstrate what it really means to follow Jesus. And when that happens, it can be powerful enough to change the world. They didn't have to forgive John, even when he came and talked to us all. But they did anyway."

Christine's eyes moistened, and she bit her tongue to keep from breaking into a cry. The demonstration of character on the part of the people of Rural Grove proved to be the final push her spirit needed toward the story Lori had shared in the hospital.

Lori leaned in to look deep into Christine's eyes and beamed. "Are you ready for more?"

Christine nodded and took Lori by the hand. Together, the two women walked through the double doors and into the back of the sanctuary. They took an open spot in a pew near the middle of the room as the choir finished their anthem and exited the loft. Gary Osborne left the stage and hugged John on his way to the podium.

John placed his notebook and Bible on the pulpit and looked up into the crowd, making eye contact with Christine immediately. For a brief second, they both just stared, then he smiled and continued smiling as he gazed into the eyes of every other person awaiting his words.

"This morning I'd like to talk to you about forgiveness. But not any forgiveness. The ultimate forgiveness God offers us in his Son, Jesus Christ. Turn with me in your Bibles . . ."

As John continued with his sermon, Christine's heart overflowed with joy. There was no other place she would rather be. And she knew exactly what she planned to do when he finished.

Fewer than a hundred people would witness the salvation of Christine Lewis, and not one of them was going to stop it.

COMING SOON!

A SHEPHERD SUSPENSE NOVEL • #2

CROSS SHADOW

ANDREW HUFF

Kregel
Publications

CHAPTER ONE

A BRISK WIND prompted Christine Lewis to draw her coat tighter as she exited the headquarters of the National American Broadcasting Channel and joined the herd of New York City natives and tourists mingling in the open-air plaza out front. Pushing past a group of senior citizens organizing a photo op in front of the network gift shop, she picked up her pace and trotted through the 49th Street crosswalk just as time expired on the pedestrian signal.

The plaza access street between 49th and 48th offered a quaint block length of traffic-free asphalt perfect for a pleasant lunchtime stroll, but her meeting with her cameraman, Mike, had run over and she didn't want to be late for her clandestine meeting. If she missed the next B Sixth Avenue Express car arriving in six minutes, she would be.

Even as she marched toward the intersection, she couldn't help but imagine any number of scenarios of how her resignation would impact the network. Most of her coworkers wouldn't care. Her boss, Steven Jacobs, would be furious, but when wasn't he when things didn't go his way?

Janeen and Mike would want to come with her, but Christine didn't expect United News Network to accept terms that included full-time jobs for best friends and amazing cameramen. Still, maybe the door would open. Someday. A pit formed in her stomach as she listened to imaginary Janeen's reaction to the news. Christine pushed the emotional farewell from her mind and searched for a happier face to picture.

John.

But he wasn't alone. She couldn't think about her budding romance with John without also thinking about Lori Johnson, her "second mother." Lori hadn't insisted Christine call her "Mom." Yet. Christine laughed to herself as she imagined the impending demand.

The smile on her face faded as she recalled the last time she'd been able to travel to Virginia to see them. How long had it been? A week? No, longer.

Three.

Christine pulled her hand from her jacket pocket, the phone secure in her grip. As she rounded the corner onto 48th, she swiped the screen open and quickly found John's contact in video chat. It didn't take long for the call to be accepted, and after a quick pause to load, the handsome, gentle face of John Cross appeared.

"Hey," he said with a smile.

"Hi." She returned the smile and allowed herself to enjoy the richness of his hazel eyes and the symmetry of his features. "Your hair's gotten a little longer than you usually have it."

"Yeah, I haven't been able to get to the barber." He ran his fingers through the waves of hair falling behind his ear. "Are you headed there now?"

"Yeah, on 48th, about to the station."

"I'm glad you called. I've been praying all morning."

Christine smiled more broadly. She and John talked often, but never often enough in her opinion. They'd argued many times over whose fault it was. It was mostly hers, though she acknowledged the 24/7 nature of ministry that also pulled John's attention away from their relationship.

"Where are you?" she asked. Hearing about his day always helped make the distance seem shorter.

"St. Francis Hospital. Nick called this morning. Bri's in delivery right now."

"Oh my goodness!" Christine held a hand to her mouth. "That's early. I hope everything is okay."

"So far it looks like the little guy is just eager to come. Nick's with her, I've just been in the waiting room . . . with both sets of parents."

"That sounds . . . fun?"

John lowered his voice and winked. "Let's just say I'll have some great stories for my sermons. How do you feel?"

"Good, I guess. I don't know how I should feel about the most important interview of my life."

"You're going to do great. Why wouldn't the biggest name in cable news want Christine Lewis on their team? They should've offered you anchor eight months ago."

Rounding up, that made the hundredth time for the same compliment. And she doubted him every time he said it. Just because he thought she deserved the opportunity didn't mean anyone else did. They pursued her, sure, but in this business one wrong conversation could spell doom.

The piercing blare of a truck horn caught her attention and Christine looked up to see the driver expressing his disagreement with the poor decision-making of a small sedan. She also noticed a larger than usual mob of pedestrians heading down the steps to the express subway station at 6th Avenue and 48th.

"John, I've got to go. Looks like the platform's going to be busy and I don't want to miss my train."

"Call me after, if you can. Love you."

She hated the hesitation she felt before she replied, "Love you too." The video call ended, and she buried her phone back in her jacket pocket as she stepped into the line of people taking the stairs down.

They'd both used the "l-word" too soon in her opinion, though it came easy in the early weeks of their dating relationship. After the novelty wore off, it was apparent they'd rushed into a handful of the trappings of dating they both normally eschewed. Life-threatening situations tend to do that.

She pushed her thoughts on the subject out of her mind and used one of John's techniques to focus her senses on the chaotic scene in front of her. A date with an ex-CIA officer tended to be anything but boring and predictable. Instead of movies or shopping, they drank coffee in between self-defense and surveillance lessons.

During her morning commutes prior to dating John, Christine never paid attention to her surroundings. But now she saw a detailed map of the station in her mind. Down the stairs, veer left, straight to the turnstiles, a quick left, then right down another flight of stairs to the platform.

With the layout pictured in her brain, she used her eyes and ears to surveil the crowd for possible obstacles. She weaved through the masses with the grace of a ballet dancer, avoiding a large family digging through pockets for fare passes, a small gathering of pedestrians admiring a busker drumming on empty rain barrels, and a lady with blue hair balancing an assortment of handbags in one hand and a cat carrier in the other.

Exactly why she rarely carried a bag anymore. Too much to deal with when trying to move fast.

She made it to the platform just as the B train rolled to a stop. She moved in sync with the rest of the crowd as they boarded, choosing the car farthest from the front.

As she settled into a hard orange plastic seat near the car's center, the train pulled away from the platform. Christine checked her watch.

Right on time.

For the train as well as the crushing anxiety. The past eight months might as well have been eight years in the ever-changing landscape of national news. The attempted detonation of a chemical bomb in Washington, DC, was old news the second a juicier political scandal was exposed. Which overhyped crisis of the moment was it? Christine couldn't recall.

Probably an "imminent threat to our democracy." She imagined esteemed NABC anchor Daniel Meyers saying those exact words to open his nightly news program, though in her opinion it was more tabloid than news. Funny how experiencing a real imminent threat makes political posturing feel partisan and petty.

And her boss and work at NABC only made things worse, which was why she was headed to a meeting with the United News Network producers.

Christine drew slow, deep breaths and focused her mind on the car's passengers. If she didn't occupy her ride with mental exercises, she'd only think of the many ways she was certain to bomb the interview. She scanned the crowded car to pick out interesting subjects.

Across from her sat a young adult female, Asian features, dressed in chic leggings and boots, her head buried in her phone.

An African American male, slightly younger, with long hair and baggy clothes, braced himself upright against a stanchion connecting the floor to the ceiling. Even though his eyes were closed, he grinned from ear to ear as he subtly air-drummed to whatever was piped into his bulky but fashionable headphones.

She scanned the remaining passengers, noting small details until her eyes settled on a young adult male at the front end of the car. A drop of sweat left a shiny trail of moisture down the side of his face. He licked his lips more than once and kept his eyes focused on the floor.

Christine sat straighter and studied him further. His complexion was dark, but more from a tan than ethnicity, his frayed hair retreated from his forehead, and he wore a large faded-blue jacket. His left knee trembled, and he kept trying to bury his hands farther than they could go into the jacket's pockets.

The jacket. His thin neck looked silly protruding from it. He appeared to be more of a medium build in contrast to the likely extra-large size of the jacket. His abdomen, though, filled it out.

He fit a profile, she just didn't remember which one. And yet it nagged at her. She knew she'd heard those characteristics in connection to something before. She focused on everything John taught her. Nothing. She dug further, before John, before the kidnapping. But not much before. During her time as a foreign correspondent. Time she spent with . . .

The explosive ordinance disposal unit stationed in Afghanistan.

Christine forced back an audible gasp. She took more deep breaths to ease the increased fluttering in her chest. Her planned route to the UNN building faded into the dark recesses of her mind as she considered her startling new reality.

A suicide bomber rode the 11:54 B Sixth Avenue Express heading deep into New York City.